SURVIVOR
THE BENNY TURNER STORY

BENNY TURNER

WITH BILL DAHL

Published, organized and edited by Sallie A. Bengtson
© Nola Blue, Inc. 2017
Second Edition
ISBN: 978-1-54390-128-3 (print)
ISBN: 978-1-54390-129-0 (ebook)

FOREWORD

The music we call blues emanates from the African American people of the south, who worked in oppression as slaves and sharecroppers on the plantations. While there isn't a person alive who hasn't experienced "the blues" in some fashion, the blues which define the genre results from a lifestyle most would find very difficult to imagine, let alone endure. This was the lifestyle Benny Turner was born into; the heritage from his immediate ancestors. Although slavery was officially abolished during the Civil War, his paternal grandmother would tell you that it just went underground, speaking from her experience with a life of servitude. His mother and father both picked cotton and worked in the fields, their souls indebted to the proverbial company store. The American History I learned in school is the family history Benny lived and breathed.

Benny's mother, Ella Mae King, was born in 1918. Raised in rural East Texas in the pre-depression era, Ella Mae had no choice but to be strong. Surviving typhoid fever without access to modern medicine is a testament to her resilience. By the time she reached age 16, the Great Depression was in full force and rationing was in effect. John Dillinger and Bonnie & Clyde were robbing banks. Ella Mae even saw the procession of their dead bodies and the bullet-riddled car on the road to Dallas, Texas after the ambush in Louisiana! She was unwed and pregnant at that time with her first born son. The boy's father didn't stick around for very long. Times were very, very tough.

Ultimately, Ella Mae met and married Ben Turner, who vowed to raise her child and treat him as his own. Born on September 3, 1934, that child was Freddie King, who grew up to be one of the "Three Kings of the Blues" as we know him today. Although the effects of the Depression were easing by 1939 when Ella Mae was pregnant with her second son, it was the dawn of a new era as World War II began. A sign of the times, ration books and paper coins were still in circulation. On October 27, 1939, Ella's second-born, Benny (Ben Turner Jr.), entered the world. Times were still very, very tough.

Today, the blues and its variations are performed and enjoyed mostly for entertainment value. For Benny, the blues are something entirely different. He is one of very few performers still living who have such a history and link to the origins of the blues. His band name, "Real Blues," is a reflection of that history. A reflection of the generations of strife in his family, and the depths to which that pain pervades. Born into oppression during the days of Jim Crow laws, and uprooted at age 11 when his family moved to the big city of Chicago in search of a better life, Benny has walked the walk. His early days as a touring musician on the Chitlin Circuit were at the height of segregation and the civil rights movement. And then at age 37, the unthinkable happened when his big brother and best friend died unexpectedly. To paraphrase one of Memphis Slim's signature lines, "Speaking of bad luck and trouble, well, you know he had his share."

Freddie King's untimely death was life-changing for Benny, but turned out to be the first of a series of life events that knocked him down and forced him to reinvent himself and his career. Intensely loyal, he went on to enjoy a close friendship with Mighty Joe Young while playing bass for him until Joe's health deteriorated. After that, he moved to New Orleans for a fresh start with not much more than the clothes on his back, and ultimately worked with Marva Wright as her bandleader and bass player for more than twenty years until her death. Hurricane Katrina and its long-term effects was an unwelcome guest in his life during the New Orleans years, and continues to present challenges more than ten years later. I don't know if Benny inherited strength from his mother, or if his fortitude comes from years of necessity, but he continues to persevere and move forward with his music and his life. When Marva Wright passed away in 2010, Benny decided to take destiny into his own hands and step into the spotlight fronting his own band. The gem that had been hidden in the shadows of great rhythm sections for decades finally started to share its sparkle. This is a story of adversity. This is a story of triumph. This is the story of a survivor.

– Sallie Bengtson

INTRODUCTION

Over the course of our many lengthy, wide-ranging interviews for this book, I've learned a great deal about Benny Turner.

Benny told me about his childhood in segregated Gilmer, Texas and the loving large family he grew up in. About their courageous move to bustling Chicago at the dawn of the 1950s, a relocation that represented a whole new urban way of life for all of them. About Benny's subsequent entry into the Windy City's competitive yet supportive blues scene, when giants named Howlin' Wolf and Little Walter and Muddy Waters and Magic Sam created seminal music that will never be forgotten or equaled, and how he emerged as one of the first electric bassists on that circuit. About subsequent life on the road with hitmaking R&B singer Dee Clark, when they stormed the chitlin' circuit together and starred at the world-famous Apollo Theatre, and the gospel-belting Soul Stirrers (Benny was their first electric bassist at a time when the instrument was brand-new to the sanctified arena).

And Benny told me all about his big brother, blues legend Freddie King, who was much more than a sibling to him. He was also Benny's irreplaceable best friend, a strong-as-an-ox protector and a loving mentor from day one, and Benny's elastic bass lines were the backbone of his band during the '70s. Freddie left him way too soon when the powerhouse guitarist unexpectedly died in 1976 at the age of 42. That tragedy dealt Benny a horrible blow that might have ended the career of a lesser man. But after a prolonged period of mourning, he triumphantly came back and resumed his career with yeoman help from Chicago bluesman Mighty Joe Young, who simply wouldn't let Benny give up.

The Windy City couldn't hold Benny forever. After Young's career was truncated by physical maladies, Benny packed up his belongings and relocated to New Orleans. He basically started over, settling into his new digs and eventually joining up with force-of-nature vocalist Marva Wright, who needed a bandleader that intimately knew the blues and found one in Benny. Even Hurricane Katrina couldn't destroy their musical partnership, although it did keep them apart for awhile. Only a series of strokes silenced her for good.

After that, Benny returned to the front man role that he briefly investigated in Chicago during the early '60s, when he made three singles for a local label. Benny issued his first solo CD in 1997 and has unleashed several more since then, acclaim for his contemporary output steadily building with every release. It's taken much too long, but the world is finally getting hip to Benny Turner's considerable legacy.

This isn't one of those alleged musical autobiographies where you never get the feeling that you're actually reading the words of the artist himself. Benny was a hands-on participant in the telling of his story for this book; rest assured my input was minimal. What you're reading is Benny Turner's story the way he wants it told.

I'd like to thank Sallie Bengtson for giving me the opportunity to collaborate with Benny on his memoir, and to Deacon Jones, Edd Lively, Bob Riedy, and the late David Maxwell for speaking to me about Benny's high-energy exploits during Freddie's '70s heyday. Most of all, thanks to Benny himself for being so patient and generous when answering my endless queries.

As rock-solid as Benny Turner is as a bassist and singer, he's even more solid as a human being. He has an incredible story to tell you, one full of famous bluesmen and family ties and and heartwarming human triumph. I hope you enjoy reading it as much as I enjoyed helping to put it together.

– Bill Dahl

DEDICATION

These memories are dedicated to my entire
family with love, from Benny

ACKNOWLEDGMENTS

Special thanks to Bernard Allison, Fannie Allison, Gene "Daddy G" Barge, Betsie Brown, Linda Cain, Handsome Lee Carson, Flora Hart Carson, Sheila Carson, Debra Clark, Otis Clay, LeRoy Crume, Nella Daniels, Carla Davis, Freddie Dixon, Mabel Dee Fields, LeeAnn Flynn, Robert Griffin, Willie Guyton, Clyde Hart, Mose Hart, The King Family, Lee King, Mary Kirby, Deacon Jones, William Jones, Jimmy D. Lane, Edd Lively, David Maxwell, Valerie McCreary, Willie and Melba Moore, Kathy Murray, Stephen Nicholas, Joyann Parker, Katherine Peoples, Bob Riedy, Eddie Shaw, Dick Shurman, Benita Turner, Yvette Whittler

TABLE OF CONTENTS

1

GILMER

Gilmer, Texas sits about 125 miles east of Dallas, in Upshur County. That's where I came into the world on October 27, 1939.

Baby Benny

Mother and Me

My older brother was born there too. If you're reading this book, you've probably heard of him. Freddie King would eventually be acclaimed around the world as one of the greatest guitarists in the history of the blues, a genuine Texas legend. I played electric bass with him for a long time. He was five years older than me, and he was always big physically. When we were kids, Freddie took me everywhere he went. We were absolutely inseparable, just like Laurel and Hardy.

Ben Turner was my father's name, and legally I'm Ben Turner, Jr. Freddie's dad was J.T. Christian, who was with my mother Ella Mae King before my dad met her. J.T. deserted her after Freddie came along. Then my dad met my mom, and he took her and Freddie and raised him as his own. My mother gave Freddie the name of King. That's what's on his birth certificate. Although some reference books claim otherwise, he never had the last name of Christian.

My father's father had been a white plantation owner, and Dad and his brother Willie were half-white and half-black. They both had straight hair, and Willie's features were even more white than my dad's. One day, after my dad came home from World War II, he was in the bathroom shaving. He was standing there looking in the mirror, and I looked up at him and said, "Who was your father?" Without hesitating, he said, "Richard Fields." Of course, Richard was who my grandmother was married to at that time, but he wasn't my dad's actual father. Richard Fields was a black man, and his children were black with curly hair.

With Uncle Richard Fields, 2014

The difference in their hair alone let me know that something wasn't right about that, but I never could make my father tell me anything different. When I asked him, he never would answer. I always knew that there was something different between him and his brothers, because they looked different.

There's a discrepancy about the identity of my dad's actual father. I was always told that his name was Buster Mathis. Recently I asked my father's brother's wife (Mabel Dee Fields), and she said that my father's mother told her that the guy's name was Reese Covin, so I'm really not

Cousin Katherine Peoples, Mabel Dee Fields and me. Diana, TX, 2014

sure. The Mathis connection would explain why I've long been told that the legendary pop vocalist Johnny Mathis, who's another native

My paternal grandmother

of Gilmer, is my cousin. When my father passed away, me and Freddie came down to the services from Canada. At the funeral, Freddie told me again, "You look like your homeboy Johnny Mathis, that's your cousin!" He and I do kind of look alike, so I never questioned it.

Clora Fields, my father's mother, had lived a life of servitude, although slavery had officially been abolished by that time. She didn't talk to us much about that, although she

3

did mention how the white men would get on their horses and ride at night and take a black woman. She was a quiet woman, especially around people she didn't know. My mother always told me she had 25 children, so she had a hard life in many ways. On the weekends, my dad and I would walk about 15 miles round trip to see her, and we did it every week. It took a whole day to go there and back. My father brought home a .45 automatic from the war and gave it to her. She would say, "Oh, I'm safe because everybody knows that's here," and she'd point at that .45.

My grandmother's house, as it remains today. Diana, TX

We lived out in the country when I was little, about twelve miles outside of Gilmer. It was just me and Freddie and my mother and father at that point. We lived on the property of a man named Jim Lester. My dad worked for him on his spread, and he let us move into a little house that was located right across the road. My mom worked as the Lesters' housekeeper. Mr. Lester and his wife didn't have any kids, so Mrs. Lester babysat me. She loved me. I stayed with her more when I was little than I did with my mother. She treated me like I was

My parents, Ella Mae and Ben Turner

her own, which was a little unusual for white people back then. Mr. Lester owned horses, and he had a corral. They had a silver saddle, and Mrs. Lester would put me on that pretty saddle and let me ride one of their horses around the yard.

One day some of our neighbors came over to the house to shell peas. I was only a couple of years old, just old enough to walk but already nosy and curious. Me and Freddie didn't have anything to do but sit around. Finally I got bored, so I said, "I'm going to go find me a snake!" I was gone for awhile, and my mother said, "Fred, you'd better go see about Junior." My family called me Junior. When they found me, I was face to face with a big diamondback rattlesnake. Just a little bit of his head was sticking out from under the house, and the rest of his body was underneath. Not only was I face to face with him, every time he'd stick his tongue out, I would hit it with my finger.

Freddie came around the corner and he saw this big snake, and my finger was almost in its mouth. The snake had his eyes closed. He was kind of like playing with me. I guess he took a liking to me or something. So Freddie ran back, and even though he was almost out

Mrs. Lester and me

of breath, he shouted, "Mother! He found a snake! And not just any

5

snake--he found the biggest snake in Texas!" My mother freaked and said, "What? Where's he at?" So they went around the corner and peeked, and there I was, sitting with the snake. My mother whispered to Freddie, "Go get the garden hoe." When Freddie came back, she said, "Just sneak over and pull him back. When you reach and grab him, I'm going to come down with the garden hoe." So Freddie eased up, and he grabbed me and pulled me back. My mother came down with the garden hoe and chopped that rattlesnake's head off, just as she had planned.

Freddie picked cotton after he got old enough so he could start earning money. Of course, since we were inseparable, I had to go along with him. He'd come out with this eleven-foot cotton sack, and I sat on the sack while he'd pull it along and put the cotton he picked inside it. He'd keep me right there with him because otherwise I would go out and dig up worms and snakes. One time there was a big green worm that had to have been about two inches long. I had gotten off the sack and was look-

Freddie picking cotton with me riding on the sack. Illustration by Valerie McCreary.

ing for a snake. Freddie decided to teach me a lesson, so he went and got the worm and put it down my back inside my shirt, and it stung me. After I cried out, he said, "Now, that's a snake!" You can bet I didn't go looking for a snake again! A p-scale was used to weigh the cotton after it was picked, and to this day I keep one hanging on my wall as a visual reminder of where I came from. When I feel like times are tough, it's a symbol of what hard times really are. Keeps everything in perspective!

P-scale weighing my bass P-scale

I still have an inch-long scar on my right cheek from an accident when I was maybe four years old. My mother told Freddie to go out and chop some wood for the stove. We burned wood in there to cook with, and used the stove for heat as well. Freddie was annoyed that he had to do it, so he stormed out of the house and wasn't paying attention to anything around him. As usual, Freddie and I were together, so I was only a few steps behind him.

My cheek scar

He wasn't looking where he was swinging that axe, and when he drew it back to chop the wood he hit me right on the cheek bone. You can imagine how shocked and upset he was right after he hit me. He quickly threw the axe down, grabbed me and ran to the house. They sat me on the stove, and they turned one of the burners over because you had to take that iron thing off when you put the wood in there. They removed that and flipped it over, and they got some soot off the bottom of the stove and rubbed it in the cut with their fingers to stop the bleeding.

Soot was only one of many home remedies that my mother used on us kids. The doctors were all white and didn't give a shit about black people, so we had to figure out how to take care of ourselves. I guess even if the doctors would have helped us, we were too poor to pay the bills and too far away anyway. I can remember when Freddie had the mumps. He was in so much pain. My mom rubbed sardine oil into his jaws and wrapped his head with a hot towel. Quinine and Vicks salve were also used for sickness. Same with mullein, a plant that was boiled and used for healing. If you can believe, we also drank cow chip tea, which is boiled and strained cow manure. Yes, my mother gave us that when we were sick. I didn't know anything different so I didn't object, and I would have gotten a beating anyway if I didn't drink it, so that was that.

My mother did a lot of cooking on that stove. I can still remember the cabbage that we ate at supper. We liked fried fish, and we loved cornbread and biscuits. Her chicken and dressing were really good, too. Nobody can come close to her cooking as far as I'm concerned. My father enjoyed cooking salmon croquettes, and he was real good at making gingerbread. That was my favorite, hot gingerbread fresh from the oven, right out of the iron skillet.

When we wanted a special treat, we ate dirt. Not just any dirt, but Texas red clay dirt that was really fine, like talc. Believe it or not, we were too poor to afford candy, and red dirt was our substitute. It wasn't sweet. It has a distinct mineral taste, but for us it was a treat. Again, we didn't know anything different, so we never gave it a second thought. Guess that's what they mean when they talk about being dirt poor!

Out in the country, you had an outhouse instead of indoor plumbing. For some reason, the black widow spiders that lived around that outhouse really liked me, and I was always turning up with bites on my skin. I still have scars to this day. We got our water from a well, and we used kerosene lamps for light. Since there wasn't any electricity in the place where we lived, refrigerating food was a bit of an ordeal. We'd put food like chicken and dressing that would spoil fast in a bowl and wrap the bowl up in a towel so we could tie the rope from the water bucket around it and ease the bowl down into the well. The bottom of the bowl would just touch the water so it wouldn't be submerged. It sat on top of the water, and that would keep it from spoiling. We never got sick, but you couldn't do that for more than one day so leftovers had to be consumed within 24 hours. Later on we did get an icebox. You'd get 25 pounds of ice and put it in the top of the box like Jackie Gleason did on **The Honeymooners**, then place the pan down at the bottom to catch the dripping water. Maybe once a week we'd get ice.

Number 3 washtub

Taking a bath was no easy task either. You'd get out that old number three washtub and fill it up. They made bathtubs out of the same metal as the number three, but we never had one. There was often no bath in the mornings because it was too cold. Most times when me and Freddie had to go out, we would draw the water from the well, waiting to wash our faces before we caught the bus to go to school. A lot of mornings, we would have to go out there and break up that ice--remove it from the water and then wash our faces with cold water. It would be a big deal to make hot water, because you had to bring it in and build a fire, and we didn't have time for all of that.

Me and Freddie slept in the same bed all the way until we moved to Chicago. He used to tell me stories and read me comic books. We especially liked the ones with cowboys in them. Sometimes he would sing me to sleep using Bob Wills' country song "Roly Poly" as a lullaby. And Freddie would tell me ghost stories. He'd make them so real that I would have nightmares. After I dozed off, Freddie would go to sleep and snore. He had a major snore. I got used to it over the years, so it wasn't a problem. He would be snoring for a while, then all of a sudden he would stop. And when he would stop and be quiet, that would wake me up. Then he'd go back to snoring, and I'd go back to sleep. It was like in reverse from a lot of people.

During the time when we were living on Jim Lester's property, my dad's biological father died. A group of white people came to our house and knocked on the door. When my dad answered, they asked if he would serve as a pallbearer for their family member, who had died. He agreed to do it without hesitation. A few days later, there was another knock at the door. My father opened the door and my mother stood behind it. The white people were back, with an incredible confession.

They told my father that they had actually asked him to help bury his own father, but had done him an injustice by keeping that from him at the time. They offered to make it up to him, if he would allow it, and promised that he, his kids, and his kids' kids would never have to work again. When my dad realized that he wasn't good enough to be told he was burying his own father, he was so angry that he stepped back and slammed the door in their faces so hard that my mother saw dust fall down from the ceiling. My mother told me this story when she thought I was old enough, and my reaction was, "Was he crazy? He should have taken the money and then slammed the door! Can't we go find them?" Her response was, "Some things are better left alone." My father was a proud man, and I do understand.

Eventually we moved from that house to another one in a little place called Diana, about eight miles east of Gilmer. We lived on a man named Robert Taylor's land, and my dad's job was clearing the land. He was a hard worker, but he wasn't the primary disciplinarian in our household. In fact, he was pretty easy-going. My mother was the one you had to watch out for. We kids always came first with my dad, and Freddie came before all the rest of us. My dad would show my mom that he was putting his best foot forward with Freddie and that there was no favoritism toward his biological children. It's true that we were half brothers, but that word was never spoken in our house. If we did, not only did we get the shit beat out of us, but we had to go and cut our own stick to get beat with! Although my father did his very best not to show any favoritism with us, I will always remember that Freddie got shoes before we did. There's a picture of me and Freddie as kids where I've got braids in my hair. Freddie's got shoes and I don't. So it's pretty obvious that Freddie came first.

Freddie and me

Racial segregation was the law of the land in Gilmer and the surrounding areas. Robert Taylor had a daughter named Eva Lou. She was about my age, and they would let her play with me. That was a real rarity; black people and white people didn't interact back in those days. But they were nice people, and she was my playmate. Her little brother Buddy and I used to play sometimes too. We would spit on the ground to see if my spit was black and his was white, but of course there never was any difference. We were just kids who liked to play and didn't understand any of it.

One day my dad was out clearing land and he plowed up a big pickle jar about two feet high. I think they usually kept pig knuckles in a jar like that. It had a lot of $20 gold pieces in it, V nickels and black dimes with the woman spinning wool. He probably could have retired on what was in that jar. There was a guy that was working with him, and he ran down and told Robert Taylor that my father found this money.

Mr. Taylor came busting through the door and he looked at all the money piled up on this table. He raked that money into a bag after brushing a little off to the side for my dad (about five or ten dollars) and walked out. My dad was so furious that he kicked his friend out and told him he didn't ever want to see him again. He cussed that whole night long, and probably kept on cussing for the rest of the week. His cussing never did rhyme the way it's supposed to. He would just put a bunch of words together, like his favorite saying, 'Son of a bitch to hell!' It was hard not to laugh sometimes (Freddie and I would be cracking up), and I still laugh about it.

Things were tough during our days in Diana. Freddie and I had to get out and hunt sometimes, chasing rabbits down. As usual, I was only a few steps behind Freddie running as close behind as I could. We wrapped gunny sacks around our feet to keep them warm, and then we'd go out looking for tracks to lead us to the rabbits. We had this fork stick that Freddie would use to trap them. We would chase the rabbit into the tree trunk, and he'd jab that fork stick in there to trap the rabbit and then twist it to bring the rabbit out.

I wouldn't eat those things —no rabbits or possums or coons or chitlins. I ate everything our mother made for us but that. She couldn't pull that on me. She would tell me, "That's chicken." I'd say, "That's not chicken. I saw you make it!" My mother loved to fish. She took Freddie fishing with her, and I also went fishing with her. They would give me a fishing pole and I would sit there for a little while, but I'd get bored and wander off. It just wasn't my thing. Freddie loved fishing, all the way up to when he died.

Fishing with Freddie. May 1969

My father served in the Army during World War II. He went over to England on the Queen Mary, which had been turned into a troop carrier. While he was away, my grandfather on my mother's side, Arthur King, would come by and check on us. He always came for Christmas, too. He'd bring Freddie cap pistols because he knew he liked the cowboy movies. He was crazy about Freddie. My grandfather was a mean man. When he was around, my uncles changed from grown men to obedient little boys. Even Posey Seagull, the Gilmer policeman who hated black people, didn't mess with him because he was known to shoot you. And you did not trespass on his property! He lived in the bottom, as they say. They didn't have any reason to mess with him, but they knew not to.

When my father came home from the war, he was carrying a big duffle bag on his back. Me and my mother saw him walking down the road and recognized him, even from far away. We ran down to meet him and my mother gave him a big hug, right in the middle of the road. I asked him, "Did you shoot any Germans, Daddy?" He set his sack down and pulled out two big blue books that he brought back with him and he gave them to me, but he never would answer when I asked him what he'd done in the war. He'd just hand me those books and say, "Look through that." I looked through those books so many times that the pages started falling out. Later on I figured out that he didn't want to talk about the war.

Uncle Felix King

Uncle Wille King

I was so happy to have my dad home that I was constantly underfoot. Then it got to be bedtime, and he said, "Go to bed!" I said, "No, I want to talk! I want to talk! I want to talk! Tell me about the war!" He said in a louder voice, "I'll tell you tomorrow. Go to bed!" I said, "No, I want to talk!" And then he pulled off his GI army belt that was cloth with a metal buckle and metal tip. He popped me with that belt and yelled "I said, 'Go to bed!'" I said okay and cried myself to sleep that night. My feelings were so hurt, but now I know why he wanted me to go to bed--he hadn't seen my mother in a long time. He didn't want to fool around with me; he wanted to fool around with my mother!

Uncle
Leonard King

My father wasn't musical at all. He couldn't sing or whistle, and I never saw him pat his foot. He had no musical ability whatsoever. But music ran deep on the King side of the family, my mother's side. She played very good guitar, and my uncles did too. She had four brothers. Felix King was the

Uncle Leon King

oldest, then Willie King, Leonard King, and Leon King. Every one of them could play guitar. They were singing in a quartet, and they'd harmonize. My uncles gave my mother the nickname of "Sang" for a very obvious reason: because she could sing. She played Robert Johnson and Lead Belly songs on the guitar, the same as my Uncle Leon did. He was an influence on all of them. It's funny—Uncle Leon was the youngest, but he was the leader. He was really good all the way around when it came to singing. You know how you have one guy that will inspire everybody? He was the one.

Uncle Leon was crazy about me. He wanted me to spend the night with him one time when I was three years old, so they left me with him. Then I cried, like kids do. So he got up in the middle of the night. It was raining. And he threw me across his shoulder. I could hear his heels digging in the wet grass. I still remember that sound. It was like marching. He walked about two miles, and took me home. He didn't say anything. That's how cool he was. He walked through the door and said, "Here he is!" And then he walked back out.

On a Saturday night when they felt like having a good time, my mother and her brothers and their friends would get together at our house at night. They would set a number three washtub on the back porch, and they'd fill it full of big tall bottles of beer. They'd kick me and Freddie out onto the back porch because they'd get a little raunchy with their singing and dancing, second only to what you would find at a juke joint. So Freddie and I would stay in the back and we'd lay on the floor of the porch, looking under the door at them having a ball playing and singing and dancing. Freddie knew then that he wanted to play the guitar. Freddie would lay close to the number three wash tub and every once in a while he would manage to sneak a swig out of one of those big bottles of beer. Then he'd make me take a drink too so I wouldn't tell. I couldn't have been more than six or seven years old.

Out of the blue, my mother would yell, "Fred go down to the spring and get some water!" There was one time she asked us to get water after Freddie had snuck some of that beer, and he couldn't carry the bucket alone because he was drunk. We got the water bucket and we put a stick through the handle, then put that water bucket on it and raised the stick. He got on one side and I got on the other. And that's how we got it back home. By the time we stumbled back, half the water was gone. Guess where we had to go? Right back to the spring!

Since we didn't have access to a guitar, we made what was called a diddley bow to make music on. Like all kids do, we wanted to imitate what the grownups did. Freddie was around 10 years old, and I was about five. We took a piece of baling wire maybe three to four feet long and nailed one end up on the side of the house over our heads, and then the other end down towards our knees. Then you got two small bottles or cans, and you'd slide one bottle in one end and the other one in at the other end. If you pulled that string, you'd get a tone because you tightened the string. You'd get a little stick or something, or use your finger.

diddley bow

One day in 1946, Uncle Leon decided to take a drive and borrowed an old Lincoln Zephyr from his friend Henry. An old white man named John Hancock lived just past Lake Providence School on the left. When Leon drove past, Hancock must have thought it was Henry, and backed out in front of him. We always thought that he didn't like

Henry. My uncle tried to duck him and flipped over in a ditch. He was thrown out of the car, and it rolled over him.

In the meantime, Henry was at my house looking for Leon because he was late. I was in the front yard when an ambulance passed the house going in the direction of the accident. I went in the house to tell my mother, and she said quietly, "Something happened to Leon." Henry reassured her that everything was going to be okay. As the ambulance drove back past our house again, I saw Uncle Leon lying in the back. Someone came over to tell Henry about the accident, and said that Leon was going to be alright. My mother said, "No, he's not going to be alright," and she was right. He died before they reached Gilmer.

Leon King was only 26 when he died. He and his brother Leonard had been Buffalo Soldiers, riding horses in the U.S. Cavalry. When he came home from the service, he brought a bugle with him and gave it to us. My mother hung it on the wall. The night that he died, that bugle fell off the wall. He was the baby of his family, and he was well-loved by his siblings. My mother was so distraught over his death that she never played the guitar again. If I pushed her to show me something, then she might have demonstrated a chord or two, but she'd put it right back down.

I was too young to really understand what segregation and racism were all about until the day I went up to Gilmer with Robert Lewis "Bay" Fields, my uncle on my father's side. He asked me if I wanted to go for a ride. I jumped in the car and we went up there. We were going into the store, and there was a white guy wearing worn-out overalls standing there drinking a Coca-Cola. My uncle got out of the car and was going in the door, and the white guy said, "Hey, boy! You want the rest of this Coca-Cola?"

My uncle says, "Yassuh, yassuh, yassuh!"

And I was looking at my uncle thinking, "What the heck is wrong with you?" I never heard him speak in that tone of voice before.

"Yassuh, yassuh. Thank you, sir."

I was thinking, "What are you doing?"

As young as I was, I knew something was wrong, and I didn't know what it was. But that was the first time that I had a clue something was amiss between blacks and whites. Uncle Bay, who served our country in the Navy, just kept saying in a loud and grateful voice, "Yassuh, yassuh. Thank you, sir," as he drank the Coca-Cola.

Lake Providence was where me and Freddie went to school. Miss Ruby Granville was my first teacher. Miss Ruby's husband, Alton Granville, was the principal. He was tough. Miss Ruby wasn't so tough, but he sure was. Freddie did something wrong, though I'm not sure what it was. So here comes Mr. Granville, dragging Freddie. He said, "Okay now, kids, I want you to look up here. This is what happens when you don't do your lesson," or whatever it was that Freddie did wrong. And he took out this long switch and beat Freddie in front of the class. Most teachers would have you hold your hand out and hit you with a ruler, but they did that to Freddie instead. I didn't like it. It scared me. I didn't want that happening to me. But Miss Ruby was better. She was nice.

Miss Ruby Granville. 2014

Miss Ruby taught several grades at the same time in that Lake Providence classroom. It seated maybe four rows across, and those rows went back maybe eight deep. I didn't really have a favorite subject in school, but if I had to choose one, it would have been math. I kind of liked that and history. When we'd get out of school, they let us play ball, and that was about it as far as sports went. We didn't have a regulation bat, so we had to use a stick.

There was a guy there at school that played piano. His name was Shorty, and he was a mechanic. There was only one piano at Lake Providence School. If they gave a special function there, he would sit down and play that piano. When he got through, all of the white keys had oil on them. So if there was any doubt that he played all of those keys, that solved it right there.

My father had an account at the company store across from the school, a bill that was never paid in full no matter how much you worked. It was like that line from Tennessee Ernie Ford's hit "Sixteen Tons," "I owe my soul to the company store." More than once, Freddie put some cheese and crackers and candy on my father's bill. My dad went down to pay on the bill one day, and the shopkeeper said, "Your son came in and bought this and that." So my dad came back and cornered Freddie. He asked him, "You went down and did this here?" Freddie said, "Yes sir, yes sir."

My dad ordered him, "Go cut me a stick!" They made you cut your own stick to get beat with. So me and Freddie went down to the woods to cut him a stick. Freddie's crying, and I'm walking along behind him. So he reached down, and he's trying to find one that he's going to cut. He found what looked to me like a small tree. I said, "How come you've got to get one so big?" He said, "Well, if I get a small one and they go to beating me with it and they break it, they're gonna make me go back and get another one. If we get this one, we'll make one trip do!" I learned a lot about what not to do by growing up and learning from Freddie's mistakes.

Our family attended church on a regular basis, but we never sang in the choir there. Freddie took me to church for the first time. It was the one time I had some decent clothes to wear. I finally had a suit and shoes. He took me to church, and I was goofing around and there was a big mud puddle right by where we were standing. I tripped and fell face down in the mud puddle. I know I embarrassed Freddie but if it wasn't for bad luck, I didn't have no luck at all!

We had a big extended family that mostly lived nearby, and folks were dropping in at our house for a visit every day. One Sunday out of every month, everybody would bring their cakes and things to church, and everybody would come around and eat out of the next person's spread. If one person brought a cake, then you'd get yourself some cake from this person, and if another guy cooked a turkey, you'd get a turkey leg from him. We would go and do that even after we were grown up and went home to visit. It's a tradition that continues to this day.

My mother cooked and cleaned for a white man named Maxie Floyd who lived across the road from us. She would go over there to his place and work, and she would sneak food in her little knapsack and bring it back and give it to us. She fed us a lot like that. Floyd lived in a big white house and owned property. All of the white people around there had property. He had cattle too. He sold vinegar, and milk from his cows. But he was a bigtime redneck.

One day my mother said, "Junior, go down there to Maxie Floyd's and get some milk." I was walking across the road, and he was sitting on his porch cleaning his shotgun. Shining it, rubbing it up and down. When I got to the driveway, he pointed the shotgun at me. When he pulled the trigger, he made the gun snap back just like it would if he had really shot me. I didn't think anything about it at the time, but when I grew up, I realized that was a terrible thing to do to a child. But that was a way of life then. You'd just take it because you didn't expect anything better from a bigtime redneck like him.

I had a pet hound named Mackie. He was black and white, and I thought he was the prettiest dog we ever had. His tail was half white and half black. Mackie didn't like anybody to touch me. In fact, when my mother got ready to beat me, she had to tie the dog up. When Maxie Floyd walked by the house, the dog would go crazy. One day we woke up and found Mackie dead in the yard. There was some hamburger meat nearby, and we knew right away that Maxie Floyd had poisoned our dog. He was the only one that the dog didn't like. Smart dog!

Freddie and I both loved movies so much so that we would walk seven miles into town to see cowboy films. He loved Allan "Rocky" Lane, and I liked Eddie Dean. He used to make fun of my cowboy and made me mad. "You got a sorry cowboy," he'd tease me. "Rocky Lane, he's tough!" I loved Eddie Dean because of his clothes. Rocky Lane just wore Levis, but Eddie Dean was sharp. After watching the movies today, I have to admit that Freddie was right; Rocky Lane was the better cowboy!

The theater we went to when we saw those cowboy movies was called the Strand. They'd sit all the black people in the crowded balcony upstairs and the white people had plenty of room downstairs. We were witnessing racism at that time and didn't know it, because it was just a way of life for us. We'd claim our seats and stay there all day, because once you move you lose. At the end of the day, we would walk on back home, sometimes even in the dark.

There were two movie theaters in Gilmer. The other one was named the Crystal. That's where my mother would go, because she

My brother Michael

liked the love stories they showed there. She was carrying me in her arms when she went to see a movie called **Duel in the Sun**. It was adults only, but because I was little enough for her to carry, she took me in the show with her. When I became of age and had the opportunity to see that movie again, I still remembered parts of it.

Our family was growing fast during those years. I now had three younger brothers—Michael Turner (born in February of 1943), Bobby Turner (born in August of 1944), and Jerry Turner (born in May of

1946). Bobby and Michael, they were really close together. They could have been twins. Michael was more like my father. He couldn't hold a tune. But my brother Bobby, he ended up playing bass and guitar when he grew up. We were like clones, he and I. Jerry had cerebral palsy, but he was sharp as a tack mentally. His brain was sharp, but his body wasn't. He couldn't walk well, but he did good. The three of them mostly played among themselves because there was a big age gap between them and I. Me and Freddie were mostly together, and it remained that way throughout our adult lives.

Me and my clone, Bobby, backing Dee Clark. I'm playing Dee's guitar and Bobby is playing my bass. Look at our outifts, hair and shoes. Look how far back he played on the bass.

We left our house and moved across the road to a bigger one. By that time, me and Freddie were already getting into the blues. We used to go to school and then rush home for 15 minutes of a radio program out of Laredo, Texas called ***In The Groove***. We were listening to Louis Jordan, Charles Brown, and Hank Williams. We loved Hank. He was one of the big three with us. Hank had his own thing. He was about as close to blues as you're going to get from a country guy.

We'd only get about 15 minutes of the blues on that station, but a person could listen to country music all night on the radio. Our radio worked on a battery that was as big as a car battery. You had to run the ground wire down to the ground, stick it into the ground, and pour water on it to cut down the static. My dad could only afford a new battery once every two or three months. When one of those things ran out of juice, we were out of luck.

We lived better in that house because it had so much more room. Lots of company would come over, and my mother would cook for them. Instead of a wood stove, this place had a stove that burned kerosene. One day when I was about eight years old, my mother had some friends over. I believe it was a Sunday. She was using that kerosene stove. She'd put the kerosene in a glass container, and she'd flip it over and place it in the little cup. When she'd do that, the plunger would push the kerosene to come out. That day, the kerosene container wasn't seated properly when she placed it down, causing the kerosene to leak onto the stove and the floor without her realizing it.

Before long the stove caught fire and the burning kerosene droplets hit the floor that was already drenched with kerosene. People started screaming and mother yelled to me, "Junior! Get some sand!" By the time I got back with it, it was too late. The whole kitchen was engulfed in flames. Someone said to shut the kitchen doors to try to contain it, but the house was made from wood and the fire spread quickly. We saved what we could, but the whole house burned down.

We had about five or six mattresses that we saved from the house stacked up outside. All of a sudden, someone called out, "Where is Jerry?" and my mother freaked because we couldn't find him. We looked everywhere but where the mattresses were stacked, and we thought that Jerry may have died in the fire. Then someone said, "Let's look in the mattresses!"

My brother Jerry

23

We started pulling those mattresses up one by one. We got down to the last one, and that's where he was. He'd been lying on the first one that came out, and they covered him up during all of the commotion. He was under there and he couldn't get out. Of course, everybody was relieved. Just about that time the fire department pulled up. It wasn't a hook and ladder truck; just a small red and white automobile with a siren. I suppose they got credit for showing up at all, although they didn't even get out of the car to be sure that everyone was alright. They looked out the window at the smoldering remains, made a u-turn, and headed back to Gilmer to deal with more important things, I guess.

After the fire, we left Diana and moved on into Gilmer. Our new place was located in town, not far from the stockyards, and for the first time we lived in a community instead of being way out in the country. My dad became a Texas butcher. He did the whole nine yards—killed the cows, butchered them and made sausage, steaks, and all that. The man that he was working for happened to have a guitar. He knew my dad wanted to get Freddie one, but we couldn't afford it. He told my father, "I've got this guitar you may be interested in."

So my dad came home and told Freddie "Look, this man that I work for has got this guitar. And he says you can get the guitar, but you've got to work for it." Freddie got really excited, saying "Yes, yes! Okay, I'll do it!" So Freddie and I went down to the stockyards the very next day to get started. The job was to salt the hides. After my dad cut the hide off the cow, you'd spread it out upside down and rub the salt in, and then you folded the hide and stacked it. At that time we didn't pay any attention, but now that I look back at it, it was a pretty nasty job. But that was what we did. After a few weeks, the man gave Freddie the guitar. It was a Roy Rogers guitar, with a horse

Visiting Bruce School in 2014

24

on the back raring up. It was a cheap guitar, but the way Freddie treated it, you would have thought it was made of solid gold.

Even though I helped Freddie get the guitar by working with him, he wouldn't let me touch it. But when he wasn't around, I would get hold of it anyway. I'd get that guitar and try to play it. My mother and my uncles had already taught Freddie and I guitar, playing chords and things like that. They basically were doing back porch blues, just playing in the key of E and the key of A. I think all of those old musicians probably played like that. When I pick up the guitar, I play the same way. I've never changed. I still play their style even to this day.

Bruce School in Gilmer was very different than our one-room school back in Lake Providence. For the first time, we had classrooms and organized sports. My schoolteacher in Gilmer was Miss Marshall. She was the complete opposite of Miss Ruby, because she was big and tall, and she was a sergeant in the Army. She'd walk around wearing this leather thing—it looked like a belt, but that's not what it was. It was just a leather strap wrapped around her waist. So you were going to get beat if you didn't do your work. Freddie's teacher was Mr. Newhouse. I guess because of Freddie's size, they thought he would make a good football player. He said, "Okay, I'll try it," even though he didn't know what it was. He put on a uniform and all of that equipment and went out on the field. Those kids on the other team hit Freddie two or three times while they were scrimmaging, and as he sat down looking at his bleeding knee he said, "That's the end of football."

Visiting with Melvin Webb (L) and Norris Webb (R), some of Freddie's old classmates. 2014
Photo by Mary Laschinger Kirby

One day some construction workers were setting off dynamite blasts behind our school. They may have been putting a road in or something. I think Freddie was in the eighth grade, and I was probably in second or third grade. We were in class, and all of a sudden that blast went off, and dust dropped out of the ceiling. We didn't know what was going on, so everybody scrambled for the door.

Too many people were jamming the entrance, so I ran over to the second floor window. It was in small 12-by-12 sections, but I didn't have sense enough to know that I couldn't get out that way. My instinct was to bust out that window, so that's what I did. I couldn't get out of there that way, so I raised the window and I jumped out, and that's when I sliced my thumb. I landed in the hedges, quickly jumped out, and ran all the way home. I carry the scar from when I sliced my finger open to this day. Freddie's classmates were quite a bit older, and that blast scared them too.

The Webbs brought some old school pictures to show me, including this one of Freddie at a dance

My mother still laid down the law in our household. I remember the last beating she was going to give Freddie when he was maybe 15 years old. I was standing right there watching the whole thing. She picked up a stick, brought it down on Freddie, and Freddie grabbed her arm. She said, "Let me go, boy!" She brought it down again, and Freddie grabbed her arm again. That happened a couple times. About the third or fourth time, my mother started to laughing. It started to be funny to her. And then she dropped the stick on the floor. That was his last beating. He never got another one.

Towards the end of 1950, we said goodbye to Texas. My Aunt Corinne and Uncle Felix talked my dad into migrating to Chicago. Aunt Corinne was a leader after she married into the family. She became the person everybody looked up to. My uncle was a strong man, but he wasn't strong enough for her. What she said, that's what went. So she told my uncle, 'You know, you should bring your sister up from down there. The living's so much better up here. Bring them here.' So my uncle did what Aunt Corinne said to do and sent for my dad.

He went up there and got a job at the National Malleable Steel Company while my mother initially stayed behind with us kids. I'll never forget how she used to take all of us to the store so we could call my dad on the

I'm in back, with Bobby in front of me and Nella in front of him. Michael is next to Bobby, with Jerry in front of him. Circa 1950.

phone there. About a year after he started working at the steel company, he sent for us, buying us all tickets to ride the train to Chicago so we could live there too. The only problem was, he couldn't afford to send any money for food on the long trip.

My little sister Nella Mae Turner had just started to walk (she was born in August of 1949). She looked so cute in her little sailor dress with her long, curly hair (she took after the Cherokee side of our family). Nella Mae got antsy and wanted to take a little stroll up and down the aisle of the train. When she came back, her hands were full of money. She had collected enough cash to feed all seven of us, so that's how we ate. We got hungry again and we said, "Put her out in the aisle and let her walk up and down the aisle again!" She fed us all, all the way to Chicago.

2

CHICAGO

The Great Migration brought many thousands of African Americans up to Chicago from rural Mississippi. My state of Texas may not have contributed as many new residents to the South and West Sides of the Windy City as Mississippi, but that's the route my family took. We had no idea what we were about to face when we got off the train in Chicago in the middle of winter. Even before we arrived at the station, the snow was falling steadily. We'd all stared in amazement as we looked out the train windows at the long icicles that hung off the snowbanks along the tracks. Coming from the Lone Star state, it looked like a full-fledged blizzard to us. My dad was there at the station, anxiously awaiting our arrival. I don't remember much else after that because it was such an overwhelming experience for me.

It was Christmastime when we got to Chicago, and all the buildings were illuminated with flashing, brightly glowing lights. We thought that must have been what Christmas was supposed to be like. We had never seen anything like it. The sounds of the city were also new to us. Streetcars rumbled down Ogden Avenue. You could hear the giant coal trucks, with their huge drive chains wrapped around the axle up by their cabs, rolling down the street to deliver coal in the frigid winter months. Aside from the bone-chilling temperatures, we thought our new surroundings were cool. We were in awe. It took us a while to get accustomed to our new hometown because we weren't used to such a different, thoroughly urban way of life.

My dad already had a place rented for us in a building on the West Side that sat right on the corner at 1659 W. Adams. Six or seven families lived in our building, which was basically a slum. The owner was a blind lady named Bobbie who refused to clean or fix anything. Along with Uncle Felix and Aunt Corinne, my uncles Willie and Leonard had made the trip north before us and lived in the building too. So did my grandmother, Laura Collins, and the man she married after Arthur King, Jurdin Collins. He was just like Arthur King, tall and outspoken. I guess my grandmother liked that type of man. It was the

first time I met him, and he took a liking to me. He was in the Army and had served in World War I, and was very proud of it. He would often say, "I'm an Army man," and he wore his Army clothes regularly.

One day my grandfather took me walking with him. He stopped in a tavern to get himself a shot. He was standing at the bar, and he told the bartender, "Bring this guy a ginger ale!" Mr. Collins gulped that shot down, and I drank the ginger ale. It was my

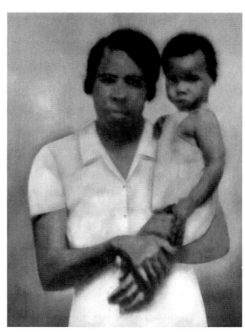

With my maternal grandmother,
Laura (King) Collins

first time in a bar, and it made a big impression on me.

Other novelties of our new city life included discovering electric lights, indoor plumbing complete with hot and cold running water, and refrigerators. We had never heard of an icebox that made its own ice. I can remember our family sitting around the kitchen table at my grandmother's, and Freddie was just dying to see the icebox magically make ice. So he got up from the table and walked over to the icebox and pulled the door open. When he reached into the freezer to get the ice tray, my grandmother said, "What are you doing?"

Freddie said, "I'm just going to make some ice water."

"Oh, you don't need ice to get cold water," said my grandmother. "Just let it run. It'll get cold enough."

So Freddie closed the icebox door and went back and sat down. I knew right away how he was feeling, because all he wanted was the experience. He didn't want the ice water. They cheated him. As young as I was, it bothered me and I really felt sorry for him because all he wanted to do was get the ice and see it. Later on, he would eventually get the ice.

We only had two rooms in that apartment on West Adams, but we made do with what we had. It wasn't pretty. My mother and father and my sister slept in one room, and we all slept in the other one on a giant-sized rollaway bed. All five of us boys (including Freddie, the oldest and biggest) would climb up on that huge bed and find our spot. Then we had to find a way to escape the noise of the city so we could fall asleep. We learned a trick from my father and used to bury ourselves under our pillows to help block the noise. It became such a habit that many times I still fall asleep that way even now.

My dad was working hard at National Malleable Steel to support all eight of us. His job was to assist with the molten steel when the big buckets came around, tipping them to fill the molds. Sparks would fly just like they were coming out of a shotgun. He would wear a protective suit, but when he got home at night we could see where those little steel pellets had burned right through his suit. So we would have to dig the little pellets out of his skin, especially his hands. He was literally scarred for life from that job. Although it was a good opportunity for him to earn more money for our family, it was hard labor and dangerous.

After settling in, the next task was to choose which local school we would attend. I don't remember what school my mother enrolled

Freddie in. He briefly wanted to change his last name, having learned that his birth father's last name was Christian. When he went and signed up for school, he came back with a little form that my folks had to fill out. The school had written "Christian" on there, and boy, did that start something! We were all hanging out in the other room when we heard my mother yell, "Fred!" in that long stretched-out way that let us know there was trouble. He went in to talk with her, and I heard every word. She said, "Listen, your daddy was no good. He deserted you. This is the man who raised you," meaning my dad. She said, "I gave you the name King, but now you have a choice. You can be a King or you can be a Turner." By the time he came out of that room, he was Fred King.

Freddie was in tenth or eleventh grade when we arrived in Chicago. But the people at the school assumed he wasn't smart enough, even though they didn't test him or anything. It may have been school policy for all the kids who moved north from the country, I don't know. They said that he had to go back to the previous grade. It wasn't fair to him, because Freddie was very smart. He was probably smarter than anybody in the class when he got there.

He went to school for awhile, even though he was unhappy about being held back from the right grade level. Freddie's days in the Chicago public school system wouldn't endure for long anyway, because he started hanging around the bars and his eyes were opened to another way of life. Once he started playing guitar and hanging out with Muddy Waters, Howlin' Wolf, Jimmy Rogers, Jimmie Lee Robinson, Sonny Scott, and Earl Payton, he jumped in that little circle and started getting some gigs. That was the turning point that started his career as a blues musician.

My mother enrolled me at McLaren Elementary School at 1500 W. Flournoy Street, which was predominantly white. I think they made a mistake letting me go there. The white boys ganged up on me, and suddenly I realized that I was facing the first of many fights in my new home. There were about 10 boys that met me on the playground after school one day and backed me up against the wall. Only one was doing the talking, and he was ready to beat me up. The rest of them had their little bats for weapons. The playground was made mostly of brick, and those kids had me backed up against the wire window screens that protected the school's windows.

I didn't know what I was going to do because I had never faced anything like that before. I had these boys coming at me. They were in my face, yelling things at me, telling me I didn't belong there and that they were going to beat me up. I was looking at the one guy that was doing the talking and figured he was the ringleader. The rest of the guys were just standing around. That's when the cowboy movies I used to watch with Freddie came in handy. They always went after the Indian chief, and the rest of the Indians scattered. So I thought, "Maybe if I grab this guy, I might have a chance." So I instinctively grabbed him, got my hand around his neck, and rammed his head into that wire screen on the window. I did it two or three times. He hit the ground, and just like in the movies, the rest of the boys scattered. So that saved me. That's when I realized I was going to have to fight to survive on the streets of Chicago.

I ran home and told my mother, "These guys ganged up on me!" And she said, "What?" So my mother went over there to McLaren, and they told her, "He's out of his district. You have to get him in Brown School." That was a black school. So they took me out of there and put me in Brown Elementary, at 54 N. Hermitage Avenue. But the fights weren't over yet. Next I had to prove myself with the neighborhood kids. One night, they decided between themselves on the corner that it was time to test me. It happened in the hall of my building. Just after you came inside, you went up the stairs, and then you had the hallway and the apartments.

They gathered around me in a circle so I couldn't get away. I had to fight the baddest boy on the block, Jimmy Wilson. He was big, black, and strong. They were standing around and they started clapping, and Jimmy came out. They said, "Kick his ass! Kick his ass! If you can't whip Jimmy you can't be part of the group!" I was the new kid on the block. Jimmy came out, and he had these big muscles. He later became a

Chicago policeman. Coming from Texas, I was strong enough, but I didn't know how to fight. Thankfully, my fear must have given me the extra edge I needed to fight this guy, because I grabbed him, and down on the floor we went. And I kicked his ass. That's how I fought my way into becoming one of the guys in the neighborhood. I was accepted then. After I beat up Jimmy, I became the new king of the neighborhood. But I think Jimmy must have been having a bad day, because he was a big dude.

Uncle Leonard's wife Maggie was the prettiest black lady that you ever saw. If you've ever seen Dorothy Dandridge in the movies as **Carmen Jones** or as Bess in **Porgy and Bess**, that was Maggie. She was from Texas, and she was fine. But for some reason, Uncle Leonard also had a girlfriend named Luvenia who lived on the second floor of our building. Maggie was looking for my uncle one night, and she kind of knew that Luvenia had something going with him. She knocked on Luvenia's door and said, "Is my husband in there?"

When Leonard heard Maggie's voice, he jumped right out of the second floor window. He hit the ground and broke both of his hands at the wrists. Uncle Felix and somebody else went out and picked him up. We were asleep in the rollaway bed when it happened. I actually heard them when they brought him in and laid him down on the bed beside Freddie. I was too scared to open my eyes, so I pretended to be asleep. I heard my Uncle Felix say after examining his hands, that he thought they were broken. So they let him rest there until they could get him to the hospital. It was bad.

Overall, it was a pretty nice neighborhood that we lived in when we first got to Chicago. But we did have one problem—a white man that lived three or four doors down from us. He did not like black people, especially kids. We would go out in the backyard and play, and he had this dog that would chase black kids. Nobody would say anything to him about it, because black folks just didn't do that to a white man. We were raised up to accept whatever white people dished out, so we used to just take it.

Freddie was up on the porch one day, and my brothers Michael and Bobby and I were out playing. Along comes the white guy with his dog. The dog chased me, and luckily he didn't bite me. But he did grab my pants and pulled me down. That was the last straw for Freddie. He came down the fire escape from the second floor and said loudly, 'FUCK IT!" He grabbed a broken tree limb, and hit the dog in the head and the dog was dead. (That rhymes, just like a blues song!)

The white guy said, 'You killed my dog!"

Freddie said, "Your dog was biting my brother!"

"I'm gonna call the police!"

The police came and questioned Freddie, and he admitted it, saying "Yes sir, I killed the dog."

They said, 'Why did you kill the dog?"

"Because the dog attacked my brother!"

So the police told the man, "You're not supposed to let your dog run loose." After they turned around and left, we looked at each other in surprise because we assumed we would be arrested. It was very unusual for the police to take the side of black people. We didn't have any trouble out of our neighbor after that. Freddie was real protective of me, all the way up to when he passed away.

Chicago was very different from Gilmer. In Chicago, you always had to keep your guard up. It seemed like there was a hassle waiting on every corner and at every turn. Somebody was always wanting to test you or to take something from you. They'd kick your ass if you let them. I had to pass under the elevated tracks to get to Brown School, and once I got there, I'd stop by a store across the street. My dad would give me a nickel to buy a snack. The store sold penny bags of potato chips, and I'd buy five little bags of chips.

Sometimes when I'd walk through the school gate, there was an older student standing there, waiting to take my potato chips or my nickel. At first, I went along with the program, thinking he was a bad guy and he was going to hurt me. He was always threatening to kick my ass, so I'd give him my nickel or I'd give him the potato chips.

One morning, my dad gave me a nickel, and as usual I went and bought my potato chips. But that morning, I was hungry. And when I got to the gate, getting ready to go into the schoolyard, there stood the same guy with his hand out, wanting my potato chips. This time I said no. He kept his word and jumped on me, but he shouldn't have done it. Down on the bricks we went as I fought him on the playground. When I walked inside the school, I had my potato chips. They were good.

I ran into the guy again during the '60s, when I was playing music on Rush Street. He was standing on the steps of the police station. I had lost my wallet, and I went there to report it. He was real nervous, looking both ways. I asked him how he was doing, and he never looked me in the eye. He just kept looking both ways. The guy's name happened to be Fred Hampton, but he wasn't the famous Black Panthers leader.

There was a huge Goldblatt's department store that stretched for almost a block located right across the street from where we lived on Adams. I possessed some talent in art (it was my favorite school subject then), and my teacher at Brown--his name also happened to be Brown--told the class to draw whatever came into their minds as a

My mother (L) and Gracie

Halloween project. I was in fifth or sixth grade. Everybody in my class drew a picture. It didn't have to depict ghosts or goblins; it could have been a picture of the weather or farming. My drawing centered around a pumpkin and a fence, and it was chosen as one of the best in my class. I can't remember if I won first prize or second prize in the competition, but four or five of us in all were honored as winners. They took a snapshot of our artwork, and then we as a group painted it on Goldblatt's window.

After three or four years of living on Adams, we moved to a considerably larger apartment building at 25 N.

Bishop just north of Madison Street. It had maybe 15 units in it. We had more space there—three rooms with a kitchen--and the accommodations were better. We would need the extra space, because there were more additions to our family: my sister Gracie Turner, born in September of 1954, was followed by my brothers Carl Turner (who was severely handicapped) and Donald Turner.

We had two rollaway beds, and Freddie and I were back to sleeping together just like the old days in Gilmer.

My brother Donald

About this time, my dad got Freddie a job at National Malleable Steel.

Although Freddie met his wife Jessie Burnett in Chicago, she originally hailed from Texas just like us. Blues legend Lightnin' Hopkins later told me that he and Jessie were cousins, which made

Freddie a cousin of Lightnin's by marriage. She was also the sister of my Uncle Willie's wife, Willie Lee. Jessie had come to Chicago to visit her sister and met Freddie. They were married right there in our Bishop Street apartment. Naturally, we were all on hand. She looked beautiful. The newlyweds moved three or four doors down on Bishop into a basement apartment.

Freddie and Jessie

Bishop Street was something. Drugs, dealers, addicts, drunks, bums, hustlers, pimps, prostitutes--you name it, Bishop Street claimed it. It was skid row, a whole city within itself. They had anything you can name there, and we were thrown right in the middle. It was nothing for me to go out of the house, take a shortcut through the alley, and find guys passed out with needles in their arms. Winos were all around. Hookers turned tricks in the alley. Me and my brother Michael happened to look out our basement window and saw some guy having sex with a woman right there in front of us. Another man tried to pay me to have sex with him. Of course, I instinctively knew how to make a U-turn and run away from him. It was just like Sodom and Gomorrah.

My brother Michael and I were exploring in the backyard behind the building one day and decided to pull up some boards that were covered with years' worth of sand and dust. After pushing aside the rocks and clearing the boards, I discovered a loaded nickel-plated .38 with two bullets missing. It had obviously been buried and hidden after someone was shot with it. Thankfully, I didn't accidentally fire any shots when I inspected it. If you were going to do something bad or illegal, that area was the place to do it. In all the time we lived at 1659 W. Adams, there were no drugs and no prostitutes, so now we were in another world.

When we moved onto Bishop, my mother and father had no idea what was in store for us, so we really weren't prepared. Luckily, I met a guy who lived in the building by the name of Melvin Parks who knew the ropes and the streets. He knew what to do and what not to do, where to go and where not to go. We were the only two boys of the same age in the building, so we quickly became best friends, and we did everything together. He taught me that when you saw the police, you went in the opposite direction. He explained, "The police do not like you. You don't have to do anything. You're black. Turn and go the other way. Anything that goes on, they'll blame it on you even if you haven't did anything. Go the other way!"

It wasn't long before I had to use Melvin's advice. One day, I had taken my brothers Bobby and Michael to the movies. We were walking home, and about halfway back two white cops pulled up in an unmarked car and said, "Where are you boys going?"

"We're going home," I answered.

"Where were you?"

"We've been to the movies."

After that, there were no more questions asked, just "Get in the car." They put all three of us in the back seat and took us home. And we were young; I was still attending Brown School, so I was 13 years old at the most and they were younger. When they got to our house, my dad was outside on the steps. The police asked if we were his boys. He said "Yes, sir." They said, "Well, keep them off the street or we'll lock you up." My dad just hung his head and walked inside. What can you do when you're not even supposed to walk on the street in the daytime? Sadly, that experience and others like it have stayed with me for the rest of my life. I still go the other way whenever the police are around.

We knew instinctively not to mess with drugs. Once I was in the dark area of the back hallway when a guy came in the door and walked over to where the washing machines were. He didn't live in the building, so I knew something wasn't right, and I stayed hidden but watched closely. He didn't see me and thought he was alone. He pulled out something that looked to me like a five-pound bag of flour. Of course, now I know it was cocaine. He spread out a little line on the washing machine, and he snorted it. When he did that, I knew right away it was something bad. Then he hid the stuff behind the washing machine and left.

As soon as he was gone, I went and got the bag and took it to the backyard. I knew it was bad and I just wanted to get rid of it, so I dug a hole and put it in there and buried it. Now as I look back, I'm sure he was a dealer and my actions probably cost him his life since he couldn't produce the dope or the money after that. They eventually poured concrete over that part of the yard, so it's probably still there, buried deep in the ground.

We enjoyed doing the Hambone on Bishop. It was like a street thing. Everybody could do it. Melvin introduced the Hambone to us. We had never seen anybody do it before. Little did I know that I would someday end up working with Dee Clark, one of the kids that sang on the hit record of that name by bandleader Red Saunders and the Hambone Kids.

There was a preacher who lived straight across the street from us. For a preacher, he was one cool dude. He drove a flashy '49 Buick with a tall antenna on the back that was decorated with a fox tail. He had gold teeth, wore a process in his hair, and was a snappy dresser. He preached with a Bible in one hand and a pistol in his pocket. He either owned or managed his building, and whatever he said was the law in there. He didn't have a church of his own, so he held all his religious meetings on the lawn. He put chairs out on the grass right in front of the building, and all of his members would come over and sit in the chairs, including his wife front and center. He'd get out there and preach fire and brimstone, and his parishioners would get to shouting.

"Church" on Bishop Street. Illustration by Valerie McCreary

In preparation for his services, the preacher would set up a table with a lamp on it. No matter what Melvin and I were doing, when we saw that we would race to the balcony of our building because we knew what was going to happen next. The preacher was involved with another woman who was living in the building, but she wouldn't come to the services. She would be upstairs in her apartment, situated directly over where he was preaching. When time came for him to preach, she would go get her oil. She would turn the lights out but leave the kitchen light on, which was way in the back. I don't think she realized that we could see her shadow from the street.

She'd sit there by the window and she'd pull her dress up, and as he was preaching, she'd get her oil. Melvin would say, "There she goes! There she goes! There she goes! Boy, look at her go!" She'd spread her legs open, put that oil in between her legs, and play with herself during the service. As the preacher would get more into his sermon, she'd work a little harder, kind of matching his pace and intensity. When he got finished, then she was finished too. She'd get up and walk on back in the back. We all knew she was masturbating, but it wasn't until later that I understood that she would climax in perfect timing with his sermon.

Before long, a guy named Rufus started to come around. Rufus took a liking to the preacher's girlfriend. I think he started making time with her. The preacher got wind of it, and he caught Rufus in there one day. He ran Rufus out. I don't know if Rufus started to lunge at him, but the preacher pulled that pistol out and shot at him. The bullet missed Rufus and hit the car of the guy that was managing the building at 25 N. Bishop, where we were living. The bullet ricocheted off the car, but it didn't hit any of us. We got lucky. Then the reverend picked up a stick and he started to beat Rufus with the stick.

Some way or other, Rufus got the preacher's thumb in his mouth. Rufus was a big guy like my uncles on the King side of the family, about six feet tall. The preacher was about 5'7", 5'8", not that big. Rufus chomped down on that thumb, and the preacher started screaming. He dropped the stick and was trying to get his thumb out of Rufus' mouth, and he couldn't do it. I saw blood streaming from Rufus' mouth. Rufus nearly bit his thumb off. The preacher finally got his thumb out of Rufus' mouth some kind of way, and then Rufus took off running. I guess that was the end of Rufus. We'd see the preacher hiding out by the building with his pistol late at night, waiting for Rufus to come back, but he never did.

Aunt Maggie was hanging out on Bishop Street too, and she was still just as beautiful and sexy as ever. She and my Uncle Leonard took the apartment right next to us. Just after she moved in, Maggie and my mother decided to take a walk up on Madison, and they crossed Bishop to get there. It was a cool day, maybe about 11 a.m. or noon, and everybody was sitting out on the steps across the street enjoying the day. My buddy Melvin and I always kept an eye out for the latest excitement on Bishop Street, so we didn't miss much that went on.

A man named Mr. Jones who lived across the street came downstairs wearing light khaki pants. He had just stepped into the street when Maggie came onto the sidewalk and turned towards Madison. She had one of these little dresses on that wiggled when the wind blew. When Mr. Jones saw her, he stopped dead in his tracks and peed on himself! My mother was in stitches, and all the folks that were sitting on the steps saw it too. He couldn't hide it. He just shook his head, turned around, and walked on back upstairs. That's how fine Maggie was.

On a more somber note, I'll never forget viewing Emmett Till's body along with thousands of other mourners after his remains were shipped back home to Chicago. He had been lynched at age 14 in Mississippi for allegedly flirting with a white woman. I didn't attend the church services, but the tragedy really had an impact on me. As guys coming from the South, we knew what could happen to you down there, but we never came face to face with it like our parents did. We saw then what my dad and mother used to talk about.

Everybody that attended the viewing was pissed off. How could they have done such terrible things to this kid, who was a couple of years younger than me? I really got mad when those killers were set free and they laughed about it. Everybody knew they did it. They didn't even try to keep it a secret. It was the way of the times. I didn't know at the time that I would later be part of a gospel group that sang at his service that day, the Kindly Shepherds.

After graduating from Brown Elementary, I attended Crane High School at 2245 W. Jackson Boulevard. I think I started there around 1954. Crane wasn't as positive of an educational experience as Brown had been. It was like the teachers didn't like you at Crane. I don't think they had any white instructors at Brown, but they had respect for the kids, and the kids liked the teachers. At Crane, it was different. Most of the teachers were white. The only teacher that took any time with the kids was the guy in woodshop. That old man, he would sit down, and if it would take an hour he would sit right there with you. He had all the patience you needed. But the rest of those people that were in charge, they didn't give a damn about us.

Crane High School

Chemistry was probably my favorite class at Crane, but what I really liked was singing doo-wop with my classmates. My buddy Melvin wanted to be a singer real bad. We hooked up with other guys at Crane because after school was when the boys would gather in the hallway and sing. You had natural echo in the halls, so that's where we liked to harmonize. Each guy had his little group. One set of guys would sing, and then another group would take their turn. The girls would stand around watching. Of course, everyone was trying to be the best. You might have had one guy standing on the side that wanted to sing and didn't have anybody to sing with. That's usually how you picked up guys to join your group.

Our group was called the Chanters. Nobody actually named it. We just got it together. We'd mimic the other groups that were out like the El Dorados and the Spaniels, and we had our own arrangement of "Swanee River." Along with me and Melvin, Joseph Moore and a guy named Larry were in the group. Another fellow called Luther came in later as our lead singer, and Robert Yates was the baritone. And we had a Spanish dude named Raymond Fabrey that became a part of it too. I was singing tenor or bass in the background. We had two or three guys that could sing lead. We would sometimes gather on the corner on Bishop Street and sing. Melvin was a good talker and convinced the Scott brothers into coming there for a competition. They had great harmonies, so they beat us.

Nevertheless, we decided that the Chanters were good enough to be on a record, so we went down to Chess Records in hopes of someone from the label listening to us. We were standing outside, and this big man walked up and said, "Boys, y'all want to see how they make records? What are you doing down here?"

We said, "Yeah, we want to make a record!"

"Well, if you want to see how they make records, come on," he replied.

I didn't know that we were with a celebrity. It turned out that our new friend was blues harmonica great Sonny Boy Williamson. He set us up in chairs, and we watched him record. I can't remember what song it was that he was recording. I always thought it was "Fattening Frogs For Snakes," but it wasn't because he did that later on. Whatever it was, it sounded good to us. We were in heaven.

Sonny Boy had an interesting relationship with label owner Leonard Chess. The band started and stopped recording their song in the studio, then started and stopped again. Leonard said, "Let's try it again, Sonny Boy."

"Now look, goddammit, you've got to get your nose out of that man's ass and run that goddamn machine!" barked Sonny Boy. Leonard had been talking to somebody, and I guess Sonny Boy thought that he wasn't concentrating enough. Sonny Boy got pissed off. That's the way he was. Our paths crossed again later on when I was playing with Freddie and Sonny Boy happened to be playing that night at a joint on Madison near Garfield Park. When I saw him, he was sitting there with his harmonica and a bottle of liquor.

We were serious about keeping the Chanters together at Crane. One of our teachers was named Galukas. I'm a full-grown Chicago street boy now. We were passing to the next grade, and one of the guys didn't make it. So we went to the teacher, and we got him in a circle. We said, "We want Larry to pass to the next grade with us!" We scared the teacher and he gave Larry a passing grade.

We weren't bad boys. We just wanted to stick together, that's all, and we talked him into it. But I think he was a little nervous. When I thought about it later on, I got to thinking maybe we shouldn't have done that. Anyway, it worked. Larry passed, and we all stayed together. But our downfall came because of the popularity of Frankie Lymon and the Teenagers and the Platters. Everywhere we went, if you didn't sound like one of them, they didn't want to listen to you. So we finally gave up.

The first established group that I tried out for was a gospel out-fit called the Wings of Heaven. Their bass singer had quit. Charles Flenard was their other tenor, and Joe Hutchinson played guitar. They were cool, but you had other guys in that group that weren't so nice. Austin Love, who tried to do things for the neighborhood kids, would come over on Bishop, pick out the young guys he liked, and try to form a quartet.

Austin was also a tenor singer. He was going to audition for the group, and I could sing bass so he brought me along to try out too. I did whatever they wanted me to do. My voice didn't sound like a lion the way my predecessor's did, but I was good. I was with them maybe three or four months until it came down to the issue of dressing sharp.

They had matching brown suits. When they got ready to go and do the programs, of course I went. But my future with the group came down to when I was going to buy my suit, and I couldn't afford it.

The guy that I had replaced decided to come back, so they fired me and hired him back again. And man, did that do a job on me. Austin knew that was going to happen, and he tried to tell me, "Don't get your hopes up that you're going to stay. Always keep in mind that you've got to move on to something, just in case stuff doesn't work out." He was trying to let me know that things don't always happen like you want. But that didn't help. When those guys fired me, it threw me for a loop because I knew I was good at the job.

Joe, Charles, and Austin said good things to me. They said, "Man, we're really, really sorry that this happened." They were the only ones that said, "If we had anything to do with it, that wouldn't have happened. We don't run anything." Joe quit, saying, "I'm just going to go ahead and work with my girls." His daughters were five and six years old. He would bring them out on Sundays. They could harmonize real well, and he played guitar with them. Joe proved he was a good teacher—his daughters eventually achieved R&B stardom as the Emotions.

I also auditioned unsuccessfully for a doo-wop outfit called the Pastels, not to be confused with the East Coast group that hit in 1959 with "Been So Long." I think it was my buddy Melvin that hooked me up with them. The audition was held in the projects over by Roosevelt Road. We didn't get that far. I just walked in, met the guys, we sang, and I left. I never heard anything from them again. I just figured they broke up or something else happened.

During my time at Crane, Freddie got busted for playing poker at a cleaners located right around the corner from the school. The guy that owned the cleaners had a back room where he held poker games. Freddie would go over there, and my brother Michael would hang around with him at the cleaners. Somebody tipped the cops off, and they raided the cleaners. Michael hid under the dry cleaned clothes, hanging on the rack, and the police never knew he was there. The cops said, "Everybody out," and they put the handcuffs on Freddie and put him in the paddy wagon.

His wife Jessie called me and said, "Man, we've got to go get Freddie out of jail!"

I said, "Jail?"

"Yeah, he got busted for gambling."

We went down to the police station on Racine and got him out. I kind of felt sorry for him when he walked out. It was kind of cold out, and he had this long coat on, like he had been sleeping on it or under it. We took him home. Freddie loved to gamble. I never saw him shoot dice or anything like that. I knew he could, but he loved to play cards. My whole family played cards. It was like a ritual.

Chicago winters were fierce. I had to walk to Crane with the wind, sleet, and snow hitting me right in the face. Although I had lived in Chicago for a few years by then, I just couldn't take that long-ass walk in the winter. I started ditching school when I was in 11th grade, and nobody bothered to try to understand what I was going through. The administrators finally got in touch with my folks about me playing hooky. My mother took me to school and sat me down in front of this white lady. I guess she was the principal. My mom was sitting there, and the principal said, "Okay, well, if you don't want to go to school, we don't want you!" And she kicked me out.

My mother was crying. She pleaded, "Why don't you give him another chance?"

It didn't do any good. The woman answered, "No, you don't get a second chance."

They didn't cut black people any slack. You made one mistake and you were out. My mother could have probably gotten me back in if she would have appealed my being expelled to a higher authority, but the principal got away with it. Nobody challenged her, so there you go. I wasn't a bad kid in school. Not at all. I was a good student. There was no reason not to give me a second chance, but they didn't.

My dad was a drinker, but he wasn't a 24-hour drinker. He was a weekend drinker. One day he was out doing his thing, and he got drunk. I don't know what street he walked down, but it was close to our place on Bishop. There was snow on the ground. He was going to cross the street, and a car ran over him. It didn't just hit him; that car ran clear over him, and the tires crushed his pelvis. The accident happened near a viaduct that separated our neighborhood from a white one. Some white kids that were there ran out with blankets and covered him, and he was taken to Cook County Hospital.

The doctors looked at him in the emergency room, and they said, "Well, there isn't anything we can do for him. Put him over there." They rolled him over to the side to die. But an Asian doctor came by and said, "What's wrong with this guy?" They said, "There's nothing we can do for him." That Asian doctor went over and looked at him and said, 'Roll him up here." He saved my dad's life.

It was two or three days later when our landlord found out that my dad was in the hospital and told us that he was about to die. My father had a habit of quietly getting on a Greyhound bus and heading back to Texas when he needed to clear his head, so we never gave much thought to it when he wasn't around. As soon as we got the bad news, we rushed to the hospital. My dad was unconscious for at least a week, but that doctor brought him back. He had a limp and walked with a crutch after that, but he was alive and that was all that mattered.

After my dad got hurt, he couldn't work anymore. There was no money coming into our household, so we had to go on welfare, or at least my mother did. Those welfare people treated you like dogs. Sometimes they'd come to your house and talk to you just like that. My family wanted me to go down and apply for welfare too. I'd just been kicked out of Crane. The office where I went to apply was down on Lake Street. There was a black guy there, and he looked at me and said, "You're trying to get on welfare."

I said, "Yes, sir."

"Why?"

I said, "Well, we need money, and my dad ain't working." He said, "Well, the first thing you've got to do is cut your hair." That's the way he said it. He talked down to me and made me feel subhuman.

Being a musician, your hair and your clothes have to look good. Then he told me all the other things I had to do. He gave me a pencil and a piece of paper, and he said, "Now I want you to walk up and down Lake Street. I want you to go in every factory there is and look for a job, and I want you to write it down and tell me who you talked to." And he gave me two streetcar tokens.

The welfare office was on the second floor. I walked downstairs after our brief meeting, and it had been raining. As I stood there recalling all the insults, I looked at the water rushing down the sewer drain. I dropped one of the tokens into the water, and watched it disappear down the drain. Next, I dropped the other one. Last but not least, I balled up that little piece of paper he gave me, took the pencil, and dropped them both down the drain too, saying, "Y'all keep those tokens company now, you hear?" I turned and walked away, and never looked back. No welfare for me.

Instead I went to a place on Madison Street called Railroad Salvage. A white family owned the place and also had a grocery store. They let their son run the furniture store, and the mother and father operated the grocery store. There was a local boxer named Larry Watson who had fought Sonny Liston and Ezzard Charles but was taking a break from the ring and working at the grocery store. Larry was my buddy, and he recommended me for a job at the furniture place.

So I went down and got the job. The son was really an asshole, although I didn't know it at the time. One day a truck came in loaded with furniture, and he told me, "Get up in that truck and unload that truck, you schmuck!" I thought to myself, "Damn, I don't know what a schmuck is. I wish I knew." It didn't sound good. So I said, "Okay, I got it." After I'd been working there for about a week or so, the son got hungry. There was a deli called Picadilly's at Ogden and Madison. He said, "Go down to Picadilly's, you schmuck, and get me a ham sandwich on rye." So I said, "Shoot, man, I've got to find out what a schmuck is. I don't even know what that is, but it doesn't sound good."

So I went and got his sandwich and I brought it back. Then I went on my lunch break and I went down to the store where his dad was. And I told his dad, "Look, I like working for y'all, but your son doesn't know how to talk to people." He said, "You're fired!" I didn't get a chance to bitch. I put up with that guy for about a week or two, and that was it.

My brother Jerry pitched in to keep our family solvent too. He attended classes at Spaulding, a special school for the handicapped. He made himself a shoeshine box in woodshop. Jerry would grab his shoeshine box and go out on a nearby street—his main corner was Madison and Bishop—and find a spot where he could stand while people walked by. He'd ask them, "You want a shoeshine?"

"Yeah, Jerry, give me a shoeshine."

Jerry would shine their shoes, then ask them, "Want some sole dressing? That'll be 50 cents!" By the time he'd get through, Jerry would polish their shoes and their socks both, because having cerebral palsy he couldn't control his hands well. But they liked him so much they wouldn't say anything.

Everyone just loved Jerry -- all except one white guy that walked by one day when Jerry was playing in front of the house on the side-walk and told him, "Get off the sidewalk, you little son-of-a-bitch!" My dad always kept an eye on Jerry while he was out, so he heard the guy say it. He grabbed his crutch, came out from our basement apartment, and he beat that guy with his crutch all the way up to Madison Street while hopping on one foot!

3

THE KINDLY SHEPHERDS AND FREDDIE

Living on Bishop Street wasn't all bad. If we hadn't moved to 25 North Bishop I never would have met the Hart family, who lived in the same building. They had a daughter named Clyde and a son, Mose. He was a few years younger than Melvin and me, but he liked to hang with us. We called him Bruh Mose. Their older daughter, Flora, was already grown and out on her own raising a family. She was married to a man named Handsome Carson who sang tenor in a professional gospel group known as the Kindly Shepherds. Occasionally, they would drop by our building on Bishop to visit the Harts.

With Bruh Mose
(Mose Hart), 2016

51

Carson was a great dresser who always kept up with the fashions. On Sundays, he wore sharp suits and black-and-white unborn calf shoes. He always drove Cadillacs, earning him the nickname "Cadillac." If he couldn't afford one with fins, he drove a LaSalle. I thought he was so cool. I just loved to see the guy come by. Melvin and I would sit out on the porch and sing, and I'd play the guitar. One day, sometime around the summer of '56, Carson stopped by while I was playing and said, "Man, you're a guitar player! I sing in a group, and we might be looking for a guitar player. Why don't you come by and try out?"

Messing around with Carson

On their next rehearsal day, Carson picked me up and took me with him. He introduced me to everyone, and they were all nice guys. I was excited, but man, was I nervous, because I didn't want to be disappointed again like I was with the Wings of Heaven. Everyone was good looking and tall and had pretty suits on. I had never played the guitar for a group before, having only sung when I was with the Wings of Heaven. I knew my chords, but every group had their own style and their own original songs.

I didn't know anything about playing gospel music on the guitar. When they would make a chord change and I missed the change, I would stop playing. They had to stop and start, stop and start. The bass singer, G.E. Eubanks, looked at me and said, "Boy, can you play that guitar or not?" The whole group looked at me as if to echo his words. When he said that, I thought to myself, "Oh, shit, I'd better get it now!" Then they started the song off again and I played it. If it came to a place that I didn't know, I just went to the one, and it worked. I passed the audition and became the first guitar player for the Kindly Shepherds. I didn't have my own guitar but they bought a Gibson that belonged to the group, and I played that.

While my musical career was just getting started, Freddie was already establishing himself and making money playing in the clubs. In 1956, he made his first record for the tiny El-Bee label. "Country Boy" was a duet with a local singer, Margaret Whitfield, and the flip side, "That's What You Think," was all Freddie. He was playing with harpist Earl Payton at the time, so Payton was on the record along with Robert Jr. Lockwood on guitar. Payton had originally hired Freddie to be in his band, but after awhile Freddie took it over. Freddie liked Payton. He was an easy-going guy, and they got along great. When that record came on the radio, we were so proud of Freddie. Remember the way the Waltons sat around the radio on that TV show? That was us, sitting around our radio!

During those early days on the local blues scene, Freddie played a Kay guitar and a Silvertone, also made by Kay. He knew I liked playing the guitar but didn't have one at the time, so he would bring it over to the house for me and let me play it sometimes. His guitar strap back then was a clothesline-type rope. One of the first places that he played at on the West Side was called the Be-Bop Bar. There was a photo of him standing on the bar there, playing that Kay guitar.

With Jimmy Rogers

Freddie always gave Jimmy Rogers, Muddy Waters' guitarist, full credit as being one of his primary influences. Jimmy turned him onto playing guitar with two finger picks: a plastic one on his thumb and a metal pick on his finger. Before that, Freddie was playing just with his fingers. He never did use a straight pick. That metal pick gave him his different sound. He had a very light touch with that thumb pick. He might not have been so light with the finger pick, but the thumb pick—if you're heavy-handed like I am, I never could play with it, because it would just come right off of my thumb. Freddie loved Jimmy and would eventually co-produce his comeback album *Gold-Tailed Bird* for Shelter.

Lockwood had a lot of influence on Freddie but Lockwood was above all the other guitar players because he knew all those chords on the guitar. Nobody knew chords. They never played chords. They just picked. Robert Jr. could do it all, so if a record producer wanted something cool on a session, they called him. But as far as Freddie playing anything that Robert Jr. played, they were totally different. Freddie liked Earl Hooker too.

Freddie's first band. LK Small (drums), Sonny Scott and Freddie.

Two of Freddie's earliest musical band members were guitarists Jimmie Lee Robinson and Frank "Sonny" Scott. I knew them both pretty well too. Sonny would sit down and play the guitar just for me. He had a gold tooth in front, and when he'd play his guitar, he'd smile and show off that gold tooth. When he would come by to pick Freddie up, we'd sit in his car and play until Freddie came out. Sonny was a nice guy. He took me for rides on his motorcycle.

Jimmie Lee was really, really good to me. I loved that guy. He was living on Washington Boulevard, up towards Homan, which was about 15 blocks away from me. I would walk there on Sunday mornings and knock on his door at around nine a.m. You don't do that to a musician, especially after they played a gig the night before and only got home at four or five in the morning. Even though he'd have his woman there with him, he'd get up, answer the door, and greet me with a smile, saying "Hey, come on in!" We'd sit in his room and he'd show me this chord and that chord. Then I'd show Freddie the chords on the guitar that I learned from him. There's an early promotional picture of Freddie where he's using one of those chords in the photo. I was proud of that. Jimmie Lee showed that chord to me, and I showed it to Freddie.

Freddie was street smart and a quick thinker. I learned a whole lot growing up with him, and it seemed like there was always more to learn. He and I joined Local 208, Chicago's black musicians' union, during the mid-'50s when I was only in my teens. There was a guy named Hillard Brown who was a well-known jazz drummer and an agent for the union, and he said he knew we were struggling. The musicians union had developed a credit union, and he kept wanting us to go down and join up and get in that credit union. I don't know why they were behind us to join it. Hillard told us, "Y'all go get in the credit union and borrow some money!" I said, "Man, why are they doing that?" Freddie said, "I don't know. Let's do it!"

So we went and borrowed the money. We went to 18th and Halsted and bought two Fender amps. We took the Madison Street bus and sat in the back, where we were most comfortable, since in Texas we had to ride in the back. At the next stop, one of the bums from Madison Street stumbled onto the bus, paid his fare, and started down the aisle. Freddie elbowed me and said with a snicker, "Look at that motherfucker." I asked what he meant, and he said, "I know he's heading right back here and he's gonna ask for some money." Sure enough, the bum made his way back to us, and just when he got close enough but before he could say anything, Freddie called out, "Hey man, can I borrow a quarter?" The guy stopped dead in his tracks and said, "Why, you son of a bitch!" And Freddie just fell over on the seat laughing. He knew exactly what was going to happen, and he beat the guy at his own game.

The amps were beige with little brown threads running through them, real pretty. We did that because we had a party to play on the South Side. We played that party, and after we got through we went to the lobby and Freddie told me, "Watch the amps while I go get the money." I was kind of in awe of all the people and everything, and I was watching them, especially the pretty girls. Freddie came back and asked me, "Where's the amps?" I said, "They're sitting right there." I turned around, and they were gone. They were brand new. Played on them one time. Somebody walked off with the amps. Freddie didn't get mad. He didn't say anything. He walked on out the door. I don't think we ever paid for them. I felt so bad, and Freddie had every right to be pissed off at me, but he wasn't. We just went back to playing with our old amps.

The Kindly Shepherds played locally around Chicago, but also did quite a bit of touring. On one of the tours we ended up in Yazoo City, Mississippi, and we got there a little early for the gig. There were no hotels involved. You played a gig and then you'd leave, because the hotels weren't that great. So when we got there, we stopped at the corner drug store. We got out of the car with our hair all pressed and processed, nice and clean, suits and everything. All the black girls started gathering around us, touching us and stuff. We told them we were singing that night, and invited them to the program. They said okay and went on their way. After they left, two little old black ladies came by. They said, "You boys have to be very, very careful!" I said, "What do you mean? Those are black girls!" She said, 'Not really—those black girls be going with these white guys, and they'll kill you!" We all looked at each other in shock because we never heard of that before, but that was Mississippi.

We stopped at a gas station down there. The men's bathroom was out of order, and the only one that was working was the ladies' room. The guy working there was a cool young white boy. He said, "Ain't nothing working but the ladies' room. You go in and use that, and we'll watch and keep everybody out." I said, "Okay." So I went in the ladies' room and went in the stall. I'm standing up there pissing, and sure enough the door comes open. The door shuts, and the lady walks over and looks in the mirror. I'm watching in between the cracks of the stall door, and there's this little old white lady standing there. I said, "Oh, shit! There's a white lady! What am I gonna do?" So I let the top down on the seat and I sat back and I put my feet up on the door so the door wouldn't come open if she pushed on it.

Sure enough, she pushed on it, but it wouldn't come open. Of course, I've got a grip on it. So she went to the next stall. And she pulled and she tugged, and she pulled and she tugged. She must have had a girdle on or something. Finally there's some trickles. She goes to the bathroom, then she pulls and she pulls. It must have taken forever. Then she finally opened the door, went to the mirror and put her purse on the sink. I was still watching her through the crack. Finally she got all duded up and walked out the door. I stayed long enough to give her time to get out to her car. Then I pulled the door open maybe about a foot and stuck my head out. In the van, everybody was looking, wanting to know if I was still in there. They asked me, "How in the hell did you do that? The lady going in there and staying there that long, and she didn't scream and run out? How did you do it?" That was one hell of a fix to get out of, and since I was a black man in Mississippi, considering what they did to Emmett Till, I'm sure they would have dissected me!

Our baritone singer, John Sutton, doubled as the Kindly Shepherds' manager. Amos Waller was one of our lead vocalists. Benny Northcutt sang first tenor, Carson sang second tenor, and I sang fifth. Our other lead singer was Johnny Meddles. Carson called him

"Nubfinger" because he was missing half of his pointing finger. We always wondered how he got his finger cut off. He would always tell a little story about how it happened, but his story would change. He never had a job, but he seemed to have money. He was very creative and came up with good ideas when we rehearsed in church. Johnny was a loose cannon, but I didn't know it at that time.

Amos broke away from the group to become a preacher. What started as his homegrown house of worship in a storefront went on to become the great Mercy Seat Missionary Baptist Church on West Roosevelt Road. In those early days it was the Kindly Shepherds' main spot to sing. Back then, Amos didn't have a public address system to preach his sermons. I've always been interested in electronics and was a collector even back then. I happened to have one of those acetate recorders that recorded directly onto a 78 rpm disc. You could actually talk through it and it would amplify through the speaker. That became Rev. Waller's first p.a. system.

We picked up another lead singer, Cleo Martley, to replace Amos. Cleo was a little guy, but he had a voice like Archie Brownlee of the Five Blind Boys of Mississippi. We were performing in Detroit and he came up and sang and floored all of us, so we asked him, "Do you want to come back to Chicago?" We brought him back, and the older guys helped him get a job and found a place for him and his family to stay. Johnny became first lead with the group, and Cleo was second lead.

One Sunday, we were off work and decided to visit another group's program. We were all dressed in our uniforms. By that time, we had hired a new manager, Len Hollands, to try to advance ourselves. He had been Archie Brownlee's manager before us. Len told us upfront that when they mentioned us, he just wanted us to take a bow. Not only did he consider that to be the professional way, but he thought you should let the people want you enough to come to one of your shows. We were feeling good though, and we wanted to sing. Johnny was outspoken and said, "I want to sing!" So we stood up and went to the stage and took a bow.

As we started to walk off, the audience started clapping and didn't want us to leave the stage. Sutton said, "We didn't come to sing today, just to listen." Everyone kept clapping for us, so Sutton said, "Alright, we want to introduce you to our newest member, Cleo Martley from Detroit. We'll sing one song for you." Cleo sang "On The Battlefield." There were lots of groups in the audience that day, including Jeannette Harris and the Chicago Harmonettes. Jeannette was married to R.H. Harris, the former lead singer of the original Soul Stirrers, who was a big influence on Sam Cooke. As we started to sing, the whole church was getting into it, and as Cleo got more into the song, people started shouting. Everybody was up on their feet shouting and singing, including Jeannette Harris. As long as I had been with the Kindly Shepherds, I had never seen them electrify an audience that way. It was such an amazing day.

I made my first two trips inside a recording studio with the Kindly Shepherds, and we had to go all the way to Nashville to do it. The group had been recording for Ernie Young's Nashboro label since 1956 and had three singles out already by the time I made my first trip down there with them in '59. At that first session I was on, we recorded "On The Battlefield," featuring Cleo, and Johnny's "Testify For Jesus," which I arranged.

The Nashboro/Excello studio at 179 Third Avenue North in Nashville was about as basic as you could get, but it didn't have a bad sound. Ernie got what he went at, and the recordings were clean, except you weren't able to go in and fix anything. Whatever take you got, that was it. Ernie had plenty of patience with us in the studio. The label and its studio were situated in the same building as Ernie's Record Mart that advertised nightly over WLAC. That was quite a setup. The place was like a junkyard--stuff was everywhere. Records were all over the place in bins and things. It was something to see.

The next time we went down to Nashville, we cut "Before This Time Another Year I May Be Gone" and "Every Night I Lay Down To Sleep. I arranged both of those songs. I was nervous at the session, and I broke my G string. I told the piano player, who was a real cool guy,

"Look, I tell you what. You play this chord to give the guys the cue to come in. When I get halfway down through this chord, let the piano come in and finish it!" Then nobody could tell I didn't have that last string. Ernie laughed. He said, "That's cool, boys!" I played the rest of that session with only five strings.

Nashboro released "Every Year Carries A Number" and "Take The Lord Along With You" (both songs had been retitled) in 1960 with Sutton listed as writer of each. He got credit for a lot of songs that the group recorded, but I'm the one that put those two numbers together. I played the guitar, created the arrangement, and sang high tenor.

For a group of black men driving the highways of the south in a shiny new car, we were asking for trouble from the police, even though we didn't do anything wrong. Benny Northcutt was behind the wheel one time, and the police were driving real slow behind us. He said, "This guy might be out here to cause us some trouble. I'm just gonna stop him." So he threw his hand out the window and flagged the police down. When he got out, Northcutt started acting crazy, like he didn't know where he was. Benny said, "I'm looking for the highway!" So the cop gave him directions. Of course, Benny wasn't really looking for anything. G.E. Eubanks was driving another time when they pulled us over. He got out of the car and shut the door, and he showed the police something, and they looked at it and said, "Okay, go ahead." He got back in the car, and the police hadn't asked him anything. I said, "What happened?" He said, "I hit him." I said, "What do you mean, you hit him?" He meant he threw him a sign, like the Masons. And they told him to go ahead.

Once when we got off the road, Johnny Meddles invited me out on the town. He said, "Okay, we're gonna all go out together. Do you want to go?" I had my first drink of hard liquor with Johnny that night when we went out on a double date. He was dating his future wife, and I was there with my girlfriend. We went to a bar, and in those days you could bring your own liquor. The waitress would sell you juice, Coke or whatever non-alcoholic drink you wanted with ice in a glass. They called it a setup. Johnny ordered a setup and a bowl of red cherries. I was eating the cherries and Johnny was drinking Scotch. Pretty soon Johnny looked at me and said, "Come on, you're a man now. Have a drink!" So I took a drink of his Scotch. And he kept filling my glass. So I kept drinking and eating cherries.

All of a sudden I started to get up, and said, "Whoa! I'm drunk!" I sat there for awhile, and then I tried it again. I was starting to feel sick, so I forced myself to get up, and I said, "I'll be back. I need some air." I went outside, and I couldn't walk good, so I was holding the side of the building to help. Then I threw up all over my new unborn calf shoes. I started to feel better after that, and made my way back into the bar. I told Johnny I needed to go home, so he took me. I managed to get out of the car. We were living in the basement apartment across the street on Bishop by then. I got inside and I made it to my room. That's where they found me the next morning, fully dressed and wearing my new shoes. Late that morning, my dad finally woke me up. He opened the door and looked in and said, "It's about time to get up." He didn't get mad, but I was really embarrassed. To this day, I find it really, really hard to down a shot of Scotch.

I knew a woman named Helen from one of the all-female gospel groups we performed with. Her husband, Levi, was a small time hustler and gambler. He also owned a cab stand on Madison Street and was looking for a helper/runner. He offered me the job, and gave me the run of his house and the cab stand. I was just like Henry Hill in the movie *GoodFellas.* I would run Levi's errands and park his Cadillac--whatever he needed while he was hustling. I really enjoyed that job because I could come and go as I please, I got more respect than I did when I worked for the furniture store and nobody messed with me. He was a big shot on his corner, and by working for him, I felt like a big shot too.

After my experience at the bar, I wanted to return the favor and show Johnny a good time, so I brought him with me to hang out one day. I took him to Levi's apartment and we had some drinks. I also showed him Levi's gun collection. We called it a day, I locked up, and we left. I didn't realize that Johnny had unlocked the back door so he could sneak back later and steal some guns. That night when Levi closed up and got back to the apartment where I was waiting, he sat down on the couch and poured himself a drink.

He looked me straight in the eye and said, "Where are the guns?"

"They're in the drawer," I said.

He told me to bring them to him. I looked, and the drawer was empty. He then asked me if I had anybody there with me, and I told him I had my friend Johnny with me. He got up, went to the back door and found it unlocked. He said, "Looks like your friend Johnny unlocked my door and came back and got my guns." He was cool as a cucumber and didn't even raise his voice to me, but I still felt awful. I was embarrassed, shocked, and betrayed. When I left that day, I never went back. I felt too bad about the whole thing. And that was just the beginning of Johnny.

During my time with The Kindly Shepherds, Freddie would often come get me and take me to all the places that he was playing. Just like the old days in East Texas, we were always together and it seemed like Freddie was happiest when I was with him. He took me to meet Howlin' Wolf one time when he was playing at a club on West Madison. After the gig, Wolf said to us, "Come on, boys, let's go eat some pork chops!" He took us across the street and bought us pork chops. I'll never forget it. We were all sitting at the counter eating, and Wolf said, "My pork chop tastes 'tainty,'" meaning spoiled, and Freddie looked up with a smile and said, "What pork chop?" He was so hungry and ate his pork chop so fast that he didn't have a chance to notice if it was spoiled or not! Wolf laughed and bought Freddie another pork chop. Freddie loved his pork chops.

Wolf was really good to Freddie and took him under his wing. One day when Freddie picked me up, he took me to this place in the projects. We went inside, and there were Willie Dixon, Howlin' Wolf, and Hubert Sumlin. They were all sitting around. They counted a song off, and Dixon started hitting that bass. This was the first time I'd been close to those guys, and it was quite an experience. The song they were rehearsing was "Spoonful." Freddie played the rhythm on it. Anything he thought I would enjoy, he'd come get me. He loved to tell every-one, "This is my brother! This is my brother!" Even though Freddie had taken me around to many of his gigs, this was the first time I thought to myself that I wanted to be a blues musician. I was hooked.

Wolf loved Freddie. We had been hanging around, and when Wolf got ready to record "Spoonful" in June of 1960, he pulled Freddie into the studio and let him play a little part. Hubert Sumlin, Wolf's gui-tarist, could have probably done it, but Wolf gave Freddie a shot. Freddie made a mistake on the end of "Spoonful." All he had to do was play the repeating riff, but at the end he went flat. He missed it and tried to make it fit, so he tried to bend that string and make it come back up. Listen to it! They didn't go back and do it again. He did it close enough for it to pass. Hubert had the guitar work on Wolf's Chess recordings pretty much cornered. His playing fit Wolf, and Freddie's playing didn't. He had a different style.

Freddie played at a place in south suburban Argo, Illinois called the Cotton Club where saxist Lorenzo Smith often head-lined. Sometimes Freddie would go out and play a one-nighter. His rhythm section consisted of Robert "Big Mojo" Elem on bass and T.J. McNulty on drums, and they were killer.

Robert was from Louisiana, and he had that funny way of talking. He didn't talk like a nor-mal black guy. He and his brother had a weird accent. Freddie loved Robert because Robert kept him laughing all the time. Just before they'd go inside to play, they would get a half a pint of Hennessy.

Luther Allison and Robert Elem

Freddie would drink half of it down and pass it to Robert. Robert would drink the other half down and drop the bottle, and they would pat and rub their stomachs and say, "Now let's go and play some blues! That's what I liked about Freddie. If somebody messed up, he didn't care. He loved to play the blues and he'd just keep that momentum going. The main thing was to get the crowd. T.J. was a great guy. He pretty much minded his own business. He didn't spend his money much. But he liked to drive a Cadillac and always bought himself one. He later owned Walton's Corner and eventually had a club on West Lake Street called T.J.'s.

Freddie and Robert were drunk one night when they decided to race their cars backwards down an Argo alley. I think Robert had a Buick, and Freddie had an old green Packard. They couldn't go side by side down that alley, but they were going backwards—and the cops stopped them. Freddie got out of his car, and the cops asked him for his drivers' license. He knew he didn't have his drivers' license, but he took all the paper and stuff out of his car and started laying it on the hood. He got down to the last piece of paper and he put his hands on his hips. "Ain't this a bitch? Ain't this a bitch? I left my drivers' license at home!" The way he did it, the cops started laughing and let him go.

Freddie also gigged at the F&J Lounge in Gary, Indiana. Singer Harold Burrage was playing at the F&J. Freddie led the backup band and had picked me up to go along with him. After the gig, we were on the highway back to Chicago. Freddie was driving his Packard with a spotlight on it, just like the police. We were driving right behind Johnny Jones, the piano player for Elmore James and Magic Sam among others, and Freddie said, "Watch this!" He turned that spotlight on, aimed it right at Johnny's car, and shook it like a policeman would. Johnny panicked and threw his whiskey bottle right out of the car window. The bottle flew around and around as it sailed through the air, the whiskey flying out of it in a little circle.

When Freddie pulled up beside him and Johnny realized it was him, he yelled, "You made me throw away some good whiskey! Motherfucker!" Freddie put it in drive and took off laughing. He loved to have fun, onstage and off. Freddie told me a story about Johnny burning his car because he couldn't get a fly out of it! According to Freddie he couldn't catch the fly, so he locked all the doors and set the car on fire.

I used to enjoy playing basketball with Melvin and Mose. One day, Freddie drove up and said, "Look, I might need you tonight. Robert Elem is sick and I think he wants the night off. I don't have a bass player. Can you come with me to the Squeeze Club?"

Otis Clay and me in front of the old Squeeze Club. 2014

I said, "But I don't know anything about playing bass!" He said, "Come on, man, try it! Try it!" So I dropped the basketball and said, "All right! Hell, yeah!" Ever since I went to the rehearsal for "Spoonful" it was my dream to play the blues, and this was my chance. So off we went.

When Freddie offered me the chance to play behind him, I grabbed it. That meant my gig with the Kindly Shepherds came to an end. We didn't make money with the Kindly Shepherds. All it was, you'd get the women to follow you, and you'd get to go up onstage and sing. The music was great, and you'd meet all the other groups and do competitions, which was cool. The other guys in the group had day jobs, so they weren't in it for the money. Everybody had money but me. Once I started getting a job here and there with Freddie and earning $15 a night with him, I said goodbye to the Kindly Shepherds.

Freddie's main joint to play on the West Side when I joined his band was the Squeeze Club at 16th and Homan. When you'd walk in the door, there was one way in and one way out. You'd come in the front door and the bar would be on your right. The place had a few tables and a little bleachers area on the left wall. It was built like a shotgun house. We usually had either AbbLocke or a guy named Cheatham on sax when we played at the Squeeze. Abb was a cool guy. He called me Junior, my family nickname. He'd tell me, "Hey, Junior, you've got to learn to read music. You learn to read, it'll take you a long way." Abb is best known for his sideman work with Howlin' Wolf. When we wanted a piano player, Freddie hired Johnny Jones. Johnny was a character. I loved him. The only thing was, at the end of the night, Johnny would be sloppy drunk, leaning on the piano. But he could still play the hell out of some blues. Every time he played with us, he sang "Dirty By The Dozen."

Freddie was never the jealous type if there was another musician on stage playing better than him. It was all about getting over and having fun. I learned that from him and now I'm the same way. Everything we did back then was adlibbed. We never rehearsed anything. We'd just get on the stage and play it. Any originals we did were created right on the stage.

Freddie had fun with the breaks on "Hide Away"when we were onstage. He'd put his guitar down on the floor right by his foot when we'd come to a break in the song, like a soldier with his rifle. Then he would kick it. The guitar would fly up and he would catch the guitar, and then we would go to the IV. It was so cool. That old Les Paul guitar of Freddie's was solid as a rock, so you could kick that thing and never hurt it. When he got the Gibson ES-345, he couldn't kick that one because it was hollow.

My brother could pick things up in a hurry. He could hear a riff and remember it. He'd hear lyrics and remember them. B.B. King sang "Sweet Little Angel," and he could sit there and listen to it and say,

"Hey, let's do that tonight!" We'd get onstage and he'd sing it. We could be riding along and a song would come on, and when we'd get to the club he would call it out. Of course, most of the things we played were 12-bar blues or slow blues or whatever, so whatever he called out, we could play it. But he could hear it, and when we got to the gig, he could sing it. He had that memory. He'd take a piece of paper and look at it, sit there and look at it and put it down and play it. He would always tell me, 'You've got to put the paper down!" I said, "No, I need the paper." I sung two or three lines and I couldn't remember the fourth line. He thought everybody was supposed to be like him. He didn't pick up a guitar, as far as rehearsing for the gig or anything. He was just smart. He was born to play the guitar.

The Fender bass hit the local blues scene in the late '50s. Very few guys owned them, but Robert happened to be one of them. That first night, Freddie got the key to the case, unlocked it, put that bass in my hand and said, "Now play!" We played in the key of E all night long, doing slow blues and shuffles. Freddie knew I understood the changes, and said, "Just follow me." Not knowing how to move around on the bass, I developed the one-string shuffle and stuck with it. I played my bass with a pick that night, and I still do to this day (Robert played his bass with a thumb pick). The next night came and we moved up to the key of G, up to A the night after, and then we played in C. By the end of the month, I had turned into a really good bass player.

I don't know if Robert got nervous, but he started hanging around the gig more. By this time I had other bass players coming in there too, trying to learn some stuff from me. Robert ended up at my house (we lived on Madison Street by then) and would say, "Hey, show me something, Doc!" He gave me the nickname "Doc," and that's what he and T.J. called me. Calvin "Fuzz" Jones, who would later be in Muddy's band, also came down to take some lessons from me. These guys had been playing long before me, but I guess they liked what they were hearing. Aron Burton, who had been coming out to see us, was so inspired that he went out and bought a brand new Fender bass and asked me to teach him some things.

I recently learned that I was an influence on Freddie Dixon, Willie's son. He told me he used to come out to watch my brother and me, and decided to drop his bass low so he could play like me. Like an arrogant rooster, I was strutting around thinking I was becoming one of the best bassists in the city, at least until Jack Myers walked through the door of the Squeeze Club. Jack sat in that night and took me down about three notches, letting me know I still had a lot to learn.

Not only was Jack a great bass player, he also had showmanship. About the time he finished, T.J. eased up behind me. He had a funny way of talking where he sniffed two times. After two sniffs, he quietly whispered in my ear, "He just cut your head, Doc!" When another band would come to your gig and play better than you, we always used the term "cut your head." T.J. and Robert didn't cut me any slack. That made me get better. Jack was the one that made me come on with the entertainment and the showmanship more, because he had the moves.

It was pretty common for the guys to do that to each other, and Freddie and I were no exception. One night, we decided to visit Syl Johnson's gig and cut his head. We had developed a little routine where I could play chords on the bass and Freddie would put the guitar down and kind of go crazy while singing a song, walking back and forth and falling down on his back on the stage. That night, Syl had a short cord on the microphone that was plugged into his amp. As Freddie finished up his routine and fell down onto his back, he broke the mic cord and everything stopped. Freddie just covered his eyes with his hands and started laughing. Syl was pissed because Freddie had screwed up his gig, but Freddie just kept on laughing, all the way out the door.

There were three main blues clubs on the West Side at that time: the Castle Rock, the Squeeze Club, and Mel's Hideaway Lounge. Otis Rush led the house band at the Castle Rock, Freddie King headlined at the Squeeze Club, and Magic Sam was at Mel's Hideaway. We would all visit each other's gigs. It was nothing to look up at the Squeeze Club and see Muddy Waters walk through the door, or Matt "Guitar" Murphy, Earl Hooker, Magic Sam, Buddy Guy or Luther Allison, just to name a few. When the "5" Royales were in town, their trumpet player stopped in, too. I met B.B. King for the first time at Mel's Hideaway, when Freddie took me to see Little Milton playing there.

If you wanted to hear real blues, you would go to the West Side. If you'd walk into a bar on the South Side and then you'd go back to the West Side, you could tell the difference right away. Those West Side guys ruled. Otis Rush and Freddie King and Magic Sam, they were spectacular players. The guys playing up and down Roosevelt, they played pretty much the same way. Junior Wells and all those other people that were on the South Side were different. Even Syl Johnson, he played guitar for a long time, but he played a little bit different from what Freddie played. Then you had Wolf and them on the West Side too. I would go see Otis at the Castle Rock on West Roosevelt. I didn't go out that much, but I would go and listen to Otis. He was killer. Mighty Joe Young was his rhythm guitarist. We crossed paths with Bobby Rush over at Walton's Corner. He was playing bass at that time. Bobby was playing around with everybody—kind of like me.

A lot of guys on Chicago's blues scene simulated the sound of an electric bass on their guitars. Before I could afford a Fender bass of my own, I was one of them. You tuned the top four strings an octave lower, which made them really, really loose. I'm heavy-handed to begin with, and I wasn't having much luck with mastering it. Odell Campbell from Magic Sam's band said, "Man, you've got to have a light touch." Odell was really good at it. He had that light touch. You almost couldn't tell it wasn't a Fender bass when he played. He said, "Come on to my house! I'll show you." We took an old guitar, and he put the strings on it. He said, "Now, look, you can't play hard. You have to use a light touch, because if you hit it too hard the strings are out of tune." So Odell showed me a technique of doing that. If you played it light, then it would be okay.

Jimmy Dawkins played at the Squeeze when Freddie and I weren't gigging there. Freddie knew him and I knew of him, but I never did go there when he played. The only thing I knew about Jimmy was he made his own guitars. He also made his own bass, and he would hide it up on top of the phone booth at the Squeeze. If I played with Freddie and Robert's bass wasn't there, I would sneak and use Jimmy's homemade bass. It didn't play very good, but I used it anyway. I preferred the Fender bass or the tuned-down guitar.

We met Tyrone Davis at the Squeeze Club. He was one of the regulars there, just a guy hanging out that wanted to do something. I can still picture him, sitting in the bleachers along the wall with his elbows on his knees, holding his face in his hands. He would listen to us every night as he tried to learn the ropes, and Freddie always brought him up to sing. Tyrone would get up and sing off time. Everybody would be laughing. We all laughed at each other's mistakes, actually, because although we took it very seriously, the main thing was to have fun. But Tyrone would keep right on trying, and Freddie had lots of patience with him. Eventually he did learn.

After Freddie got his hits and was on the circuit, he let Tyrone be his chauffeur. The band didn't like to see Tyrone coming because of his bad timing as a singer. But Freddie insisted that they let Tyrone sit in. He'd say, "Lay off that guy!" He gave Tyrone a chance to try and work his thing up. Tyrone said he had a big argument with Robert and T.J. about it in Argo. Freddie was that way because when he was coming up, I think the only guy that gave him a break was Howlin' Wolf. Muddy Waters was pretty tough. If he didn't know you, he didn't fool with you. But Wolf was different. He was a cool guy. So I think Freddie kind of put himself in that position when it came to Tyrone. Give a guy a break because somebody gave him a break.

It took a while, but in early 1969, Tyrone's recording of "Can I Change My Mind" on the Dakar label became a smash, and he was an overnight star. Mighty Joe Young played rhythm guitar on the record. The label originally planned to push the opposite side, "A Woman Needs To Be Loved," but Joe said from the beginning that "Can I Change My Mind" was the hit, and he was right. Before long, Tyrone was one of the top soul singers on the national scene.

We started doing pretty good playing at the Squeeze Club. We were making some money. One night, Johnny Meddles came to the club to hang out with me, and I introduced him to Freddie. Johnny knew that Freddie was looking for a car. So Johnny showed up one night with this Cadillac. I think it was a 1954 blue Cadillac Fleetwood. Nice car. He told Freddie, "I can put you in this car. You pay me the notes, and that's it. You've got that car and you're gone!" He had a payment book all ready and told Freddie he would finance the car. So Freddie jumped for it.

Other musicians soon learned that Johnny could get them nice cars too. Abb Locke was one of them. Johnny showed up with this pretty pink Lincoln. I mean, it was gorgeous. The first time I saw it was at the Castle Rock. It had those big long fins in the back. Abb was stepping kind of high with that car. It became Abb's ride. Johnny also got cars for other musicians. I told him, "Man, I need a car too!" He showed up with a '60 Oldsmobile, a really nice black one. He said, "You can drive it," but he never would actually get me a car, and that was strange. Then Johnny showed up at the Squeeze Club with this pretty '57 red-and-white Cadillac. I wanted that one, but he wouldn't give it to me either. Now I know why. I guess he had graduated from stealing pistols to stealing cars by that time, and he didn't want to get me in any trouble.

Me and Freddie used to drive by deejay Big Bill Hill's cleaners on West Madison and try to get his attention. He would broadcast from the cleaners. You could see him in the window. This was when Freddie was driving that stolen Cadillac. We would drive by and Freddie would honk his horn, and we would have Bill tuned in on the radio. Bill would always say, "Tail Drag!" when he saw that car. He didn't know it was Freddie. Freddie would laugh when Big Bill said "Tail Drag" over the airwaves as we drove by. Freddie would make a U-turn and drive back by the cleaners, and Bill would say it again, "Tail Drag!" Bill wasn't the only blues deejay doing live remotes. Pervis Spann would go down to Mel's Hideaway Lounge and broadcast live from there at night.

How the police got onto Johnny, I have no idea. But they did, and they pulled Freddie, Abb, and all the others in and had them down in front of the judge at 26th and California. The judge reamed them out and let them go. He said, "You aren't getting your money back, but this should teach you a lesson." Johnny went to jail. When he came out, he needed money, and I finally learned how he lost part of his finger. Every time he needed money, he would stick his hand on the railroad tracks and let the train run over it, ultimately cutting off three more of his fingers. Then he would sue the railroad. When that money ran out, he went back and stuck a little more of his hand on the tracks--at least two more times. Finally, he had lost his whole hand. He got money for that too.

Rev. Amos Waller at John Sutton's funeral

Another former member of the Kindly Shepherds also had some interesting times after I left the group. John Sutton had a '58 Buick and he had fallen behind on the payments, so the lender sent someone out to repossess it. After the man got his car and was driving away, the story goes that Sutton caught a bus and when he was able to catch up with the guy, he shot him. Sutton always had a short temper. In fact, once when we were on the road headed to Nashville, Sutton and Johnny had an argument. Sutton stopped the car, got out and went straight to the trunk and pulled out his pistol. Of course he didn't shoot Johnny because we stepped in and stopped him, but that's how he was. He was a nice guy, but you didn't want to get him riled. So he served his time in prison for the car payment shooting, and sometime after he was released, he got into a fight and was killed. I attended his funeral with Northcutt and Carson. Amos Waller preached at the funeral. I learned early that gospel singers get the blues too.

Even when I wasn't playing with Freddie I would still hang around the Squeeze Club. I got to meet some of the up and coming

L to R: Willie Guyton, me, Dorothy Turner
(Michael's wife), Freddie, Joyce Coleman
(Freddie's niece) and Jerry

With Carla and Yvette, 2016

blues players, including Luther Allison. He and I became friends and used to hang out. John Sinclair, the owner of the Squeeze Club, had a place up on the second floor. Luther knew people who were living there, and we would go up there to party after our gigs, often spending the night there.

We met a young lady named Fannie who used to come in the club, a really good-looking woman who was very outspoken and carried a gun. George Crockett even wrote a song about her called "Look Out Mabel," which he recorded for the Chief and Checker labels in 1957. One night Fannie came in and had her friend Willie Guyton with her. She introduced us, and Willie and I later moved in together. She's the mother of two of my daughters, Carla and Yvette.

Luther and Fannie Allison

Luther met Fannie and really liked her. They became husband and wife in 1966. Their son Bernard followed in Luther's footsteps and became a great guitar player. He has his own blues band with his own style and is a fine entertainer in his own right. I'm very proud of him, and I know Luther would be too.

WALTON'S CORNER
AND DEE CLARK

Freddie got a call from John McCall, who had been one of the Kool Gents. John was singing with Lil "Upstairs" Mason, whose nickname stemmed from a record she'd made by that title back in 1946. They were like a team. They needed a backup band for their gig at Walton's Corner on West Roosevelt Road, so they hired Freddie to do his thing, and then Lil and John would come on after Freddie.

Walton's Corner was a much bigger place than the Squeeze Club. They had a restaurant area and a ballroom. Lou Walton's club was upscale and four-star. The clientele had to dress up to come inside, so the band had to look their best too.

The ladies would wear their gowns or suits or whatever. I'd say it was the classiest place on the West Side. Walton even had Chinese cooks on hand to prepare Cantonese food for an authentic experience. They had a published band schedule and club security.

Freddie at Walton's Corner

It was like a new scale for Freddie and better pay, so he jumped at it. He would go over there to Walton's and play, and he eventually became the house band. Lou even bought a Fender Precision bass for me to play. It was a brown one, just like Robert's. He kept it locked up in a closet right by the bar. I'd come in and he'd pull it out of the closet, and I'd get onstage and play. Then he'd lock it back up. When I first went to play there, Lou said, "Get him out of here!" in his high voice because I was underage, and I had to play from outside the back door using a long cord. Finally, he accepted me.

Standing with Otis Clay where Walton's Corner used to be

Lil and John had to go up to Milwaukee to do a gig, and they took off from Walton's Corner. Robert was playing bass with Freddie that night and I wasn't doing anything, so they asked me to go with them and I jumped in the car. As soon as we got past the outskirts of Chicago headed to Milwaukee, they pulled out some marijuana. I never had been around it that much. I didn't like it, because I knew that marijuana, black people, and police was a bad mixture. I didn't want anything to do with the police.

I was sitting in the back of the car and watched them all pass the joint around. Sure enough, the next thing I saw were flashing red lights. It was none other than Johnny Nab, aka the police. They pulled us over, and when the driver rolled the window down to let the smoke out of the car, wouldn't you know that the smoke blew right on me. I was sitting there shaking and thinking to myself, "I'm in trouble now!"

The guy that was driving our car must have been affiliated with the police in some way because he met the cop before he got to the car, talked to him, and everything was alright. So we went on our trip. But that was a scary moment for me. When we got to Milwaukee, I pulled John to the side and said, "Say, man, what are you doing? You're a cool dude. You ain't got no business with marijuana!" I must have sounded like a fool, trying to get him off the stuff. I had good intentions, and I was right. John, he was a cool dude. He just sat there with that little smile that he had, that natural smile. He said, "You're right, you're right, you're right. I dig where you're coming from. You're cool." I know it went in one ear and out the other because John never stopped smoking it.

Slide guitar legend Elmore James was kind of weird. He sat in with us a couple of times, once at the Squeeze Club and the other time at Walton's Corner. Or at least he was going to sit in at Walton's. Freddie introduced him, "We've got Elmore James!" Elmore pulled his guitar out, and as he was coming towards the stage Abb Locke started to play "Pop Goes The Weasel." Elmore got on the stage and was getting ready to hook his guitar up, and it dawned on him what Abb was playing. Elmore said, "Take my guitar down! Talking about 'Up Popped The Geezer!'" Elmore didn't play. Oh man, I wanted to hear Elmore play that night. Not only was he one hell of a blues player, but he looked just like my grandfather, Arthur King. As it turns out, I never had another chance to hear Elmore because he passed away not too long after that.

After we would get off at three or four o'clock in the morning, we sometimes headed over to Maxwell Street, also known as Jewtown, Chicago's open-air market on the West Side. That's where you would find a lot of the musicians, right on the corner of Maxwell and Halsted. I met pianist Sunnyland Slim there and too many more to mention. Across from the hot dog stand, the blues musicians would set up on Maxwell Street. They would set up their little bandstand and play right there. Around the corner, if you walked off of Maxwell Street onto Halsted and made a left turn, a couple of doors down there was a music store.

On Sundays, all the merchants would bring their goods out onto Maxwell Street to sell. That was the coolest thing. You could find real bargains there. I liked visiting the Maxwell Street area clothing stores like Smokey Joe's. When we had our band Operation Soul during the late '60s, me and my brother Bobby bought our first matching suits there. I loved to haggle with the old guys that worked there, and they had fun doing it with us. They were masters. After they figured you weren't going to go any higher than you said you were, then they'd give it to you at your price.

I didn't think it was as dangerous out on the far West Side as around Maxwell Street where I was living, but I got robbed there one night while standing on a corner waiting for the bus after visiting my girlfriend's house. I was riding the bus because I didn't have a car at the time, and I was all dressed up, wearing my brand new shoes and a real nice watch. Two guys came up posing as police officers and stuck me up. I tried to get away from them, but they tackled me and knocked me into the hedges. That was on Ogden Avenue. They stuck a knife to my throat and stripped me of all my stuff--my money, my shoes, and my watch.

As soon as they walked away, I managed to get out of the hedges and went straight to a phone booth to call Freddie. He was onstage at Walton's Corner and dropped everything, saying, "My brother's in trouble!" He put down his guitar and the guys got off their instruments and came running to help me. Within five minutes, I saw three Cadillacs come roaring up like in the gangster days. You could hear their tires squealing. It was Freddie, T.J., and Robert, and Tyrone Davis came with them in his car too. They really made me feel special. I knew they had their pistols, but by the time they got there, those guys that robbed me were long gone. I got in the car with Freddie and he took me back to Walton's Corner. Anyone else would probably have called their parents at a time like that, but I called Freddie because we always had each other's backs.

I took a little break from working with Freddie to play bass for Chicago-based R&B singer Dee Clark. Dee was one of the biggest stars on the roster of Vee-Jay Records, chief local rival to Chess. He'd had his first national hit in 1958 with "Nobody But You" and enjoyed more the next year with "Just Keep It Up" and then "Hey Little Girl" and "How About That" in 1960, all on Vee-Jay's Abner subsidiary. He moved over to the main Vee-Jay label after that.

Photo from cinematreasures.org. Uploaded by Tom O'Neill.
Licensed by CC 3.0

The first time I saw Dee was in 1959. My family had moved into a larger apartment in a two-story building at 1433 West Madison Street. We lived above some commercial businesses on the first floor. I had my own room. There was a movie house, the Century Theater, situated four doors down, and my sister Nella was the candy girl there. Freddie's oldest daughter, Wanda, used to hang out with my sister there. That's where Nella met her husband, Danny Daniels. He was a Chicago policeman at the time. That was her first love, and she married him.

Me and my brothers Bobby and Michael used to hang out at the Century also. The guy that ran the projectors took a liking to us, and he taught us how to run them. The Century had two projectors, and we

learned how to switch from one reel to the other. The guy got really comfortable with us, so at about seven or eight o'clock, he would go home and we'd run the show. The janitor at the theater was named Samson, and he became a good friend of ours. He loved the guitar, and he knew that we played guitar. So after he'd clean up and all of the people were gone, we'd put an amp in that little ticket booth window where the ticket lady would take your money and give you your ticket. Then we'd get a guitar and we'd sit in there, playing into the wee,

My sister Nella and her husband, Danny

wee hours of the morning. Nobody would give us problems. I told Samson, "I've got a brother that plays!" and he said, "Let's get him out!" So Freddie would come by and he would play too, right in that little booth.

Anyway, I was sitting in my window one day and I saw a pretty white Cadillac Eldorado convertible drive down Madison with the top down. It was gorgeous—white on white with the big fins in the back. A guy was sitting in the car with a process hairdo, all clean and everything. It turned out to be Dee Clark, but I didn't know him at the time. We actually met when I was playing at Walton's Corner with Bobby King, a Chicago blues guitarist who was unrelated to Freddie. Robert had gone back to playing bass in Freddie's band, so I picked up the gig with Bobby. We wanted to try something different that night, so Bobby said, "I'm going to get up on the piano, and then I'm going to get on your shoulders. You just walk around, and I'm going to play on your shoulders!"

So I went over by the piano. Walton's Corner had one of those little spinet pianos. Bobby climbed up on the piano and got on my shoulders. I was walking around, and Bobby was playing his guitar while he was up there. It was really cool, but we probably should have thought about how he was going to get back down. Now how was he going to do that? "Okay, wait," he said. "Back up to the piano, and then come down easy!" It sounded like a good idea, but I couldn't tell when I was low enough to let him off my shoulders. I got down low and I thought he was off or about ready to get off, but he wasn't. So I leaned back to let him off my shoulders, and over behind the piano he went! Bobby went one way, and his guitar went another. I can still see him laying on the floor and laughing with one leg pointed towards the east and the other facing west. You could hear the guitar playing by itself with the strings twanging as it fell. Everybody in the crowd was laughing.

Dee happened to be in the club that night. Before he became a solo star, he'd been the lead singer of the Kool Gents, so he came by because John McCall was working there. Dee was laughing at Bobby's antics, saying, "Man, that's funny!" Then he said, "Come out to my car with me." Dee had a '60 Fleetwood Cadillac and a big bottle of Scotch. He sat down, opened the bottle, and gave me a drink. Then he took a drink and said, "How would you like to go on the road with me?" I paused for a minute to think, because I wanted to go on the road with my brother. He had just recorded "Hide Away," and I knew it wouldn't be long before he started touring. Cheatham, who would sub for Abb Locke on sax, used to always tell me, "Blood thicker than water. Blood thicker than water." But I wasn't convinced. Robert had been playing bass for Freddie full-time and I thought he would be the one.

Not wanting to miss my big chance to go on the road, I jumped at the opportunity and said, "I'll give it a shot!" So we got to talking about this and about that, and Dee introduced me to his guitarist, Phil Upchurch. A couple of days later, the three of us took off from Chicago, and my opening gig with him was at the Apollo Theatre, with me on electric bass. Man, I went from chitlins to steak! And it turned out that I made the right decision because Freddie didn't take any of us on the road with him. His booking agency sent new acts out to play with the house bands at the venues where they performed, so he went on the road by himself.

Artist photos from the Apollo

Singing with Dee Clark at the Apollo

The day before our gig at the Apollo, Dee, Phil and I arrived for rehearsal. We walked in the back door and went right downstairs to the rehearsal room. I walked in wide-eyed and innocent, not knowing what to expect. Rather than rehearsing with a small band, I discovered that we would be playing with a full orchestra led by Reuben Phillips, something I had never experienced before. They made you come in the morning, and the whole orchestra was set up. All the acts were there. Then each act took turns rehearsing with the orchestra as we looked on. The rehearsal was laidback and I was still unsure how everything would unfold, so I didn't ask questions and just played it cool.

The next day, bam! It was show time! Lights, orchestra in full dress, all of the acts in their stage outfits, and a theater packed with people. I felt like I was in the middle of Hollywood! For this show, Phil directed the band, but I would become the band director for our future gigs. After the show, Apollo stage manager "Honi" Coles and his crew would visit each dressing room to let the acts know if they cut the mustard and got to stay, or if they had to go. They would give their opinions on everything from our clothes to our performance. Everything was fair game. He told us it was a nice show and we did a great job, so we got to stay for the week. It was a full schedule, because we played three or more shows per day. Many years later when my friend Otis Clay and I were reminiscing about the Apollo days, Otis told me about his first experience with Coles. He told Otis that he was a great singer, but the next time he came he had better be dressed, meaning in a full suit instead of the jumpsuit that Otis had worn that night. I guess I was lucky to get a good review from Honi my very first time there.

Carla Thomas, the queen of Stax Records, was on one of those early '60s Apollo bills with Dee. Her mother was her chaperone, but Carla and I used to go behind the big movie screen at the Apollo and make out. I also played the Apollo with the original Coasters, who at the time were Dub Jones, Billy Guy, Earl "Speedo" Carroll, and Carl Gardner. I first met them there, and then I backed them at the Howard Theater in Washington, D.C. and the Regal Theater in Chicago (I don't think Dee was on the Regal bill). I played guitar behind the Coasters on those shows, and I was their only accompanist right then because they had the orchestras of Red Saunders in Chicago, Reuben Phillips at the Apollo and Rick Henderson at the Howard to play behind them. I loved playing with the Coasters and was very, very fortunate to work with them.

When we weren't playing and the movie was showing, I'd walk out of the Apollo's stage door, turn left and go to the corner, turn left again, and there was a little restaurant there. Comedian Pigmeat

Markham, a fixture on the Apollo stage, used to hang out in there. When he talked, his voice would resonate through the whole room. The people would look at him, and they'd get kind of annoyed. But I was enjoying it, because I was a big fan of his. One of the waitresses said, "Pigmeat, why don't you shut your mouth?" But I was thinking, "No, let him talk! Let him talk!" He was funny, even just having a normal conversation.

Dee and I were together for a good little while. I played that Bo Diddley beat powering "Hey Little Girl" lots of times with him onstage. His voice reminded me a lot of Clyde McPhatter, who founded the Drifters and sang lead for them prior to starting his solo career. Phil Upchurch had an instrumental hit of his own, "You Can't Sit Down," so he wanted to go out and capitalize on that for a bit. I had learned more

At a party with Dee Clark, doing The Twist

guitar from watching Phil. He taught me a few things, including how to play Dee's smash "Raindrops" so I was ready to pick up the guitar and play R&B on it. I went to the Apollo with Dee three or four times to play as his guitarist. He was a great guy, just like Freddie. He never got pissed off about anything.

I went along with Dee when he appeared on Dick Clark's *American Bandstand* in Philadelphia and watched as a member of the audience. I was sitting there on the little bleachers where the kids were sitting. I didn't play behind Dee on the program, because they mimed to the records. Back home, my sister would get up and imitate the people dancing on *Bandstand*, so it was a kick to be there on the set to see it. I did play behind Dee on another television show hosted by Jim Lounsbury, however.

Me and Dee spent a whole lot of time on the road together, just he and I. And we'd kind of run out of things to talk about. We got to talking about National Malleable, the steel mill, and how everybody worked at National Malleable. I asked Dee, "I guess you worked at the steel mill like everybody else, huh?" He replied, "No, man, I didn't work at the steel mill." I said, "Well, what'd you do?" He said, "This is between me and you—I was a chicken plucker!" He didn't tell everybody that. He showed me how he did it, how he would get the wings of the chicken and pull the wings around the back and hold the wings and pluck the chicken and then hang it up on a hook.

I've long had a sixth sense that's come in very handy at times. It kicked in one night when we were staying at some hotel on the road. Something said, "Go down the hall and knock on Dee's door!" And I did. The old black hotels we stayed in weren't the greatest, and they used little gas heaters in each room. You're always advised to sleep with a cracked window when using gas heaters to let the fumes escape. Wind had blown into the window and blew the gas heater out. The room was filling up with gas fumes that you could have cut with a knife while Dee was sound asleep. My knock woke him and Dee came to the door, and he said, "Man, I like to have been gone if you didn't knock on this door!" My sixth sense doesn't work all the time, but I'm glad it worked that time.

At one point during one of our tours, we were with some of The Jarmels and Marvin Gaye. I can't remember the exact details, but I do remember spending time with Marvin. We hung out together backstage at a Stevie Wonder concert during the time that "Fingertips" was on the charts. He told me that someone had

Backstage with Marvin Gaye

stolen his money, and showed me the new pistol he bought to prevent that from happening again. Years later, when Marvin Gaye was shot by his father with the pistol he had given him, I wondered if it was the same one he had shown me. That was such a tragedy.

Dee never did achieve his dream to star at the Copa in New York, but we played all the major theaters, including the Howard in D.C., the Uptown in Philadelphia, and the Royal in Baltimore. Honi Coles was mild compared to the reviews we got at the Royal, because the audience thought nothing of throwing bottles at the stage if they didn't like the show! At the Uptown, I witnessed Jackie Wilson's comeback show after he recovered from a gunshot wound. Man, they didn't call him "Mr. Excitement" for nothing! I was fortunate to watch from the wings as Jackie did everything from throwing his gold pinky ring into the audience to actually free-falling right into the crowd! He set the bar for later acts who would imitate his flamboyant style. There was one time that me, Dee, and his girlfriend were waiting for the elevator, and when the doors opened, there stood Mr. Excitement himself. Dee's girlfriend was so in awe that she started saying, "Oh Jackie! Oh Jackie! Oh Jackie!" It was a little embarrassing and I felt bad for Dee because he was a star, too, but he stayed the gentleman that he was, and shook hands with Jackie.

Dee's show got better and better as the tour went on. I remember when the orchestra would take a solo during "Raindrops" and Dee would walk back as Phil and I walked forward from both sides and up to the edge of the stage. The lights would shine on us and our suits sparkled, which made the girls go crazy. As they were yelling and screaming, I got my first taste of how it must feel to be a rock star on stage.

One night we were in the car with Dee when a very familiar melody came on the car radio, broadcast over clear-channel WLAC-AM in Nashville. It was Freddie's recording of "Hide Away," on its way to becoming a big hit. I was so proud. I started boasting to the rest of the guys in the car, 'That's my brother! That's my brother! That's "Hide Away!"' That was the first time that I heard the song on the radio.

Freddie ended up on Federal Records with the help of their A&R man Sonny Thompson. I don't remember Sonny coming into the clubs where we gigged, but he was a guy that hung around the studios, so that's probably how he met Freddie. In any event, Sonny drove Freddie to Cincinnati for his first Federal session in August of 1960, which turned out to be a good move. Thompson used the label's house musicians for Freddie's Federal sessions, with Sonny himself on piano.

I got to do a little recording while I was with Dee. I played bass on "I Want To Love You," the rocking flip side of his biggest hit of all, 1961's "Raindrops" (Dee wrote both songs). We cut "I Want To Love You" down south somewhere while we were touring with Gladys Knight & the Pips, and we used the same band on the session that was playing with everyone in the show, led by tenor saxist Bobby Scott. I was on the B-side of a huge hit record! Freddie also toured on a package show with Gladys, so I was fortunate enough to be on a tour with both Dee and Freddie for awhile. Me, Chuck Jackson, and the Drifters all went to Gladys' house when we came through Atlanta. They made dinner for us.

During that time, I would ride with Freddie so I could spend the time with my brother. Road-weary after spending the whole day driving through the Appalachians, we arrived at the gig to see Gladys in the middle of a heated argument with her Pips, who numbered four at that time. Freddie jumped out of the car and ran and grabbed one of the Pips by the collar, saying loudly, "You all know better than this!" and broke the tension. The fourth Pip, Langston George, left the group soon after that.

The Drifters were one of the headliners on an Apollo bill that Dee was on, when Rudy Lewis was their lead singer. Billy Davis, the Drifters' guitarist, was a strange dude. He drank boiling water, and he could hypnotize you. That's why they called him Abdul. We were in the dressing room downstairs, and Bobby Scott had a toothache. He said, "I don't even think I can go on. It's killing me. I can't do this." So Abdul is sitting in a chair. He said, "Now, look at me." He had a cigarette. He said, "Look at the cigarette. Now when I touch your forehead with this cigarette, you're going to sleep." He brought the cigarette slowly toward Bobby's face, and he touched his forehead with it. And Bobby went to sleep.

We had the driver from the Harlem Globetrotters as our chauffeur at that time. His name was Pepper, and he was the cousin of Leon Hillard, who played for the Globetrotters and eventually became their coach. I looked at him and said, "Pepper, man, I don't know, man!" So Abdul looked at Bobby and said, "Raise your hand!" So Bobby started raising his hand. Abdul said, "But your hand's heavy. You can't raise your hand." So sure enough, Bobby is struggling, trying to raise his hand. And Abdul would knock it back down. He'd try to raise it again. And Bobby could not raise his hand. So Abdul stood there, and now he's got a safety pin. He stuck it in Bobby's arm. He pulled it out and blood came out. Abdul wiped the blood off, and he said, "That feels good, don't it?" Bobby started laughing!

Messing around with Pepper in the basement of the Apollo

Then after he was sure that Bobby was under, Abdul took his finger and put it in Bobby's mouth. He rolled it around and said, "That feels good, don't it?" Bobby said, "That feels good!" He pushed his finger in his jaw, where Bobby's sore tooth was. Then after a little while, he said, "Okay, now, I'm going to bring you out of it. You ain't going to remember nothing. You're going to go upstairs and you're going to play. You ain't going to feel no pain." So Abdul counted to three, and Bobby took up his conversation where he left off. I didn't think he could do it, but we looked at each other and said, "Damn, man, Abdul's a bitch!" And Bobby went upstairs, played his horn, and kicked ass. No pain or nothing. That was strange. I never saw anybody get hypnotized before.

Pepper didn't believe Abdul had hypnotized Bobby so he hypnotized Pepper too.

Bobby's band was really good. They did tours backing five or six acts, and you had to be good to satisfy all of them because everybody had their own little thing. They pulled it off. But I think it was Bobby's band that didn't show up one time for a Dee Clark and Jerry Butler show, so me, Phil Upchurch, Curtis Mayfield, and Leo Morris, a drummer who later changed his name to Idris Muhammad, got to play together as a band. It was the coolest thing to me, and one of the best and most memorable nights I ever had. Curtis and Leo were in Jerry's band at the time, although Dee had originally picked Leo up from New Orleans singer Joe Jones. Then Leo left Dee and started playing with Jerry.

I was playing in the Bronx with Dee at a club that guitarist Mickey Baker either owned or fronted called the Blue Morocco. We were with King Curtis, and the saxman found out I was Freddie's brother. We hit it off right away. We were sitting in the back, talking and talking and talking. He said, "Man, you're Freddie's brother!" I said, "Yeah, I'm Freddie's brother." He said, "Man, he's got a song I like called 'Hide Away.'" I said, "I can show you how to play it!" So we sat down with the guitars, and I showed him how to play it. And he played it. He said, "Man, I love this here! I wanna record this with your brother." And he later did, for Cotillion Records.

King Curtis and I also talked about hairdos. He asked where I got my hair done, and then told me, "Look, I tell you what. I'm gonna take you where I get my hair done." We were wearing processes. So King came by the next day and picked me up. And we went and we stopped at Sugar Ray Robinson's barber shop. It was on 7th Avenue, close to 125th Street. He said, "This is where it is. Come on, man! Come on!" He took me to his barber, the guy he liked. And he told the guy, "Look, man, this is my friend. Fix him up!" And I got in the chair, and the guy was combing my hair. I've got my head down, like how you do when you get your hair cut, looking down towards the floor. Then all of a sudden I saw combat boots standing there, and a firm voice said, "Hey, man, you're sitting in my chair!" I said, "What?" And he said, "You're in my chair!" I said, "Oh, shit!" I looked up, and it was Sugar Ray Robinson standing there with a big grin on his face, and King burst out laughing. Then Sugar Ray patted me on the shoulder and said, "I'm just kidding, man. I'm just kidding. Go ahead on!" Turns out I was in Sugar Ray's chair getting my hair done by his personal barber!

Temptations lead tenor Eddie Kendricks and I became friends after we shared the bill with them on a number of shows. Roy Hamilton was on one Apollo show with us and Eddie and I were both fans, especially of Roy's big hit "You'll Never Walk Alone." Not only was Eddie shy, he was so popular that he couldn't go out into the audience. So if Eddie and I wanted to see somebody perform, we'd go up on the catwalk. As soon as you'd walk in to go to the stage, there was a ladder right by the stage. If you climbed that ladder, there was a little platform up there by the catwalk where you could overlook the stage. Eddie was mesmerized by Roy's performances. I don't think he moved the entire time!

Sometimes we'd go out of the stage door between shows, walk directly across a narrow street behind the Apollo and play basketball. The last time I played there, it was with the guys in the Temptations. Melvin Franklin, their bass singer, had the basketball, and he was pretty aggressive. He was dribbling, and I was supposed to guard him. I didn't want him to go left or right. For some reason, he straightened up, and I was directly over his back when he raised his head up. He hit me under my chin, and since I had my tongue out, he almost made me bite my tongue off. I said, "Damn, Melvin. He was apologetic--"Oh man, I'm sorry, I'm sorry!" It was rough. We didn't play roughhouse like that in Chicago.

One time when Dee and I were driving to the Apollo, we got snowed in. We wanted to get to the Breezewood exit for the Pennsylvania Turnpike, because once you got to that exit, you weren't far from New York City. The biggest part of the drive was over. But we didn't quite make it to the Breezewood exit that night, and we had to check into a hotel. We shared a room that night, and boy, did we have a time. Dee had a bottle of Wild Turkey, and I had one too. We felt every ounce of that 100 proof liquor after drinking it! We told stories and ended up on the floor playing our guitars and singing Beatles songs. The next morning, it was back to reality when the car was frozen and wouldn't start. Dee had loosened up the night before, but now it was back to business. When we finally got to the Apollo, we actually did one of those Beatles songs onstage, sharing a mic for "She Loves You."

Rick Henderson, the saxist who led the house band at the Howard Theater in D.C., fought with almost everybody that came in to play the place, including Jackie Wilson. He just didn't like anybody. Dee always wanted to have his own musician be the musical director, but Rick wanted to direct the horns and things even though he didn't know the dramatic parts of Dee's arrangements like I did. He came to the dressing room and told Dee, "Look, I'm the bandleader here. He's not the bandleader!"

I said, "I'm Dee's musical director!"

"Yeah, but I'm the bandleader!"

He was a mean guy, and he pissed me off. He walked out of the dressing room and I pushed the door behind him, and he came back in that door and came at me. My brother Bobby had been using my equipment, and he left a razor in my amp. I knew it was there, and when Rick came at me, I threw that razor up, and he stopped. He said, "Well, I'll just go get my gun then." He turned around and left, like he was going to get his gun. James Sheppard of Shep and the Limelites heard the commotion. He said to one of his Limelites, the shorter guy, "Go back to the hotel and get Junior," which was his pistol. So Shep was the one that cooled him down. Shep protected me. Henderson lost the battle, because he tried to get me kicked off the set but he couldn't do it. The management knew how he was, so I walked on and directed the band like I normally did.

There was a restaurant across the street from the Howard called Gladys's. There was a side door directly across the street from the stage door at the Howard, and it was a popular place for the performers to eat. When you walked through that door, it was nothing to see stars like Diana Ross, the Coasters, the Temptations, or James Brown having dinner between shows. It was a really unique setup because the Howard was the only theater we played where we would all stay in the immediate area in rooms rented from the local neighbors. You could walk down the street and see the Coasters sitting out on the front porch or one of the Temptations taking a stroll with his girlfriend. We were all like a little family when we played there.

Visiting the Howard Theater in 2014

When my grandmother passed, I flew to Chicago for the funeral while Dee went on to Alabama for a gig in Gadsden. I think Jerry Butler was there too. When I got through with the funeral, I flew back down to Alabama to meet Dee. I got in this cab driven by a white guy, and I asked him, "Can I get a ride?" He said, "Yeah!" He didn't ask me where I was going. When we got to the outskirts of town, he said, "I've got to drop you here." I said, "What do you mean, you've got to drop me here?" He said, "I can't take you into town. Martin Luther King's people are in town, and they're causing a ruckus. This is about as far as I can take you, you being black." So he dropped me at the edge of town. I had to walk all the way in from there carrying my suitcase and find my way on my own.

I finally found the hotel where everybody was staying, including Harry Belafonte and Marlon Brando. I don't think Dr. King was staying in the same hotel we were in, but it was full of his people. We played our gig, and it went nice. As soon as we were finished, one of the guys from Dr. King's movement got up on the stage and yelled, "Are we ready?" Everybody was gathering around, and they screamed back, "Yeah!! We're ready to die!! Yeah!!" So we all looked at each other and said, "Man, this is getting scary! I'll tell you what we're gonna do—we're gonna pack up and get out of here!" All you could hear was the drum cases going "click, click, click," and the guitar cases too. Everybody was hurrying, closing up fast to get out of there. We left, so I don't know what happened after that.

Dee had a roadie named Joey, a light-skinned black guy. Joey was popular and knew lots of people. It was nothing to see Little Anthony, who scored many a hit with his Imperials, knocking on our door. Joey came in handy one time when we were down South and couldn't find a hotel willing to let us stay there. We went all over town, but nobody would rent Dee a room. Dee decided, "Let's send Joey in!" Sure enough, we went back around to the same places we had been turned down and sent Joey in this time. Joey went in and got a room right away. He got rooms for everybody. Joey swung the door open, and he was so happy he was jumping up off the ground, shouting, "I got the rooms! I got the rooms!" The man looked outside and saw it was us. Bam! That's it. No rooms.

The Holiday Inn chain was just getting started back then. They were one of the nicer chains that started allowing black people, and they only charged $8 a night when you could find one. One of our drivers decided to go swimming in their pool. He jumped in and was swimming back and forth, not paying attention. All of a sudden his chest starting scraping the bottom of the pool! Then he raised his head up and looked, and the water was gone! They pulled the plug on him and drained the pool. Hey, you can't ask for everything. We got a room. You couldn't ask to swim too.

Not only did I get to rub shoulders with some famous musicians while I was with Dee, I also had the chance to be stylist to the stars. My days on the gospel scene helped me develop more than just musical skills; I also learned how to process hair. Back when I was living on Madison Street, Rufus Crume was one of my best friends. He was tight with Clady Graham and Major Robinson of the Pilgrim Jubilees, a well-known Chicago gospel group. Clady and his brother Cleve were their lead singers, and Major had a barber shop. I started hanging out with Major, and I learned how to process hair at his shop. I waved the hair of R&B stars Brook Benton and Bobby Lewis while on the road with Dee. I especially liked hooking up with Bobby because my dad loved his song, "Tossin' and Turnin.'" When the Pilgrim Jubilees were getting ready to send a demo to Peacock Records in Houston on a song called "Stretch Out," they invited me to sing on the demo session with them. They said, "Come on, Junior, go down with us and sing on this record!" So I went down there and I sung on it. They sent that demo to Peacock, and they got on the label right away. It was a good tune.

While I was touring with Dee, Gladys and the Pips, Chuck Jackson, and Jerry Butler, there was a road manager on that show named Levi who was aware that I wanted to try to be a singer. I had these songs I wrote, and Phil Upchurch had this nice little Wollensak tape recorder. He'd play, and I'd sing. Levi wanted to manage somebody. He happened to know George Leaner, who owned United Record Distributors, Chicago's leading black-owned distribution company, with his brother Ernie. The Leaners also ran their own label, One-derful! Records, which had a national hit with its first release in 1962, McKinley Mitchell's "The Town I Live In." Levi took the demos that I'd made with Upchurch down to One-derful!, and George said, "Yeah, let's talk to him!" That's how I got hooked up with One-derful! as a singer. They brought me down, they started to work with me, and they put me on a record.

Milt Bland, also known as Monk Higgins, arranged both sides of my One-derful! debut single in 1962. I think we cut it at Universal Studios, Chicago's leading recording facility. I had to have Al Duncan on drums, who played on Dee's hits for Vee-Jay and Jerry Butler's too. I loved Al. He wasn't fancy, he just played the beat. Al wasn't loud or anything. He just had that nice little beat, and he didn't overplay. Al could use the

Norma Joy Price

brushes and be funky. Norma Joy Price had her singers there, and they did background work for most of the artists, including Harold Burrage on his "Master Key." She and I met at One-derful! and she and her singers sang background on my records. I had my first daughter by her. Her name is Benita.

Benita and me

Milt was the pianist on the date. He could play piano, and he could play sax too. He and I were very tight. We'd get back there in that room, and he'd put down everything that I said. If he liked it, I'd see those teeth. And I saw teeth most of the time. He liked what I did. We worked really, really good together. I was down as writer on both sides of my debut single, which paired "Come Back Home" and "When I'm Gone," but the latter was actually written by Terry "Buzzy" Johnson of the Flamingos. Buzzy sang it to me and I recorded it. He played guitar with Dee for a minute, not very long.

I got to know the Flamingos' lead singer Nate Nelson when I was playing with Dee in New York. He came by the Park Sheraton Hotel. That's where I liked to stay, where Jackie Gleason had his headquarters. Nate came over and hung out there the whole day. Nobody was in the room but just me and Nate so he sang his ballads, and I played Dee's green Guild guitar. Nate said, "Man, you've got a good ear!" I could follow along. I was no picker. I could just play chords, because that's what I was doing with Dee. But I had a pretty good ear at that time. And I had fun playing with Nate.

The Park Sheraton was a great hotel when we stayed there. A lot of people in the music business didn't have steady work, and many had no work at all. The key to getting hired was to look important, so the people who didn't have gigs hung out on the corner downtown at an Italian restaurant with a newspaper under their arm and a toothpick so they looked like they were reading the **Wall Street Journal** and had just finished a veal parmesan dinner. In reality, they were starving. A lot of people did that because they knew the street.

I didn't have another single out on One-derful! as a singer until 1964. That was probably because I was on the road with Freddie, and I wasn't hanging in Chicago much. The label moved me to its M-Pac! subsidiary for that one. I had to split my writer's credit on "Love Me," the A-side, with Verlie Rice, who was George Leaner's wife (she had nothing to do with the song's creation, which was often the case for musicians and songwriters at that time). The Leaners repurposed "When I'm Gone" for the flip side, retitling it "You Gonna Miss Me" and putting down Jeanne Dodd, Ernie Leaner's wife, as my new "co-writer."

Milt put his Monk Higgins alias down as my co-writer on my other M-Pac! 45 later that year, "Good To Me." He helped me with the music, so I didn't really care. I didn't even care if my name was on the record as a writer, to tell you the truth. I just wanted my name down as the singer. Verlie Rice was again my alleged co-author on the other side, "I Don't Know." We didn't care about writers' credits. If we could hear a song that we were doing played on the radio, that's all we wanted. Later on, though, you thought about it. Like most musicians back then, I didn't know about publishing rights and benefits, and was swindled out of money because of it.

I knew Harold Burrage, who was one of M-Pac!'s top artists, very well. Back in 1959, he had made the tune "Crying For My Baby" for Vee-Jay. Harold heard it on the radio two or three times, and according to Freddie he went down to the recording company and told them, "I want my motherfuckin' money!"

"Harold, they played it two or three times!"

"I don't care," said Harold. "I want my motherfuckin' money!"

Harold and I were going home one night from a gig, and he went somewhere else. I think he had separated from his wife or something. So I had the girl I was dating at the time with me, and this guy was going to give us a ride home and drive Harold's wife too.

The guy pulled into an alley and pulled out this big .45. He pointed it at my date and me and said, "You two get out of the car!"

"Say what?"

"Y'all get out of the car! Get out of the car!"

So I grabbed my girlfriend and said, "Come on, let's get a cab." And then he drove off, with the gun pointed at Harold's wife's head. We raced to a phone booth and called the cops, but they didn't catch him, and he raped her. But he made a mistake and let her go, and she knew who he was and had him arrested. The next thing I know, Harold was coming by. "Hey, man, look, I want you to go down to the police station with me so I can identify this guy!" We went down to the police station, and I said, "That's the motherfucker!" So they had the trial. They put me on the witness stand. They were going to try to mess up my testimony. And I said, "Look, let me tell you something. If you've ever had a rusty .45 pointed in your face, you're never going to forget it. And you're never going to forget who had it!" So they sent his ass to jail for years. That's how well I knew Harold.

I always like to say Harold was the one that was most likely to succeed. Tyrone Davis was the one that was least likely to succeed. Harold was one of the best singers, if not the best, in Chicago. Tyrone couldn't even keep time. The outcome didn't match the talent. Harold didn't have many hits, and Tyrone left everyone spinning in the sand with all of his smashes after Harold died. They were really good friends. Tyrone said that Harold was actually on the way to his house and made it to his yard when he died of a heart attack in November of 1966. Tyrone was living three or four blocks from me on the West Side at the time. I could walk it real fast. I was living on Lavergne Street on the West Side, and Tyrone was on Jackson. I would go by Tyrone's place every once in a while and he'd tell me, "Man, Harold died in my yard."

After my third single for One-derful!/M-Pac! failed to hit, my first stint as a solo recording star was over. Nothing like that really discouraged me because I felt that better things would be waiting for me down the line. I had my bass playing skills to fall back on, so I just went on my way, to tell you the truth. I didn't try to contact them anymore.

But George Leaner was great. He liked to drink J&B Scotch. When he was drinking J&B, he'd get a little loud on you. He'd tell you what he thought of you. George was nice to everybody, but you didn't want to piss him off.

5

THE SOUL STIRRERS, FREDDIE, DAVE MITCHELL, AND OPERATION SOUL

I transitioned back into gospel music when I met LeRoy Crume and Richard Gibbs of the Soul Stirrers. We were playing in Miami, and they were down there touring with the Staple Singers and the Caravans. LeRoy had been Sam Cooke's right-hand man when Sam fronted the Soul Stirrers. LeRoy, who was the group's high tenor and guitarist, and Richard, who sang baritone and was married to Inez Andrews, said, "Man, we're talking about adding a bass player. Our manager, Jesse Farley, is big on the idea, too. You think you might want to try it out?" And I said, "I don't know."

So I went out with them that night. It was a big night in Miami. Sammy Davis Jr. was at the Fontainebleau. George Rhodes, his conductor, was hanging out with us. Even the Rev. C.L. Franklin, Aretha's father, was in town. I went and sat in with the Soul Stirrers, and came back and said, "Man, I like this!" Sam Cooke really didn't think electric bass belonged in gospel. He didn't want it, and he told Jesse, "No, man." He wanted to leave it like it was. Sam said, "You start adding the bass and then you change everything. We want it real." You have to give Jesse Farley the credit for having the foresight. He'd been a Soul Stirrer since 1936. Jesse said, "Sam I can see it. It's going to happen, so we want to be the first. We want to jump on this. I'm going to hire this guy!" So Jesse hired me, and I was the first bass player in a gospel group. I was kind of like a pinball in my early days. I'd do whatever I liked. So I arrived in Miami with Dee and left with the Soul Stirrers.

Although I hadn't met LeRoy before that, I'd seen him perform with the Christland Singers. When I was living on Bishop Street, if Melvin and I and our other friends found out somebody was singing or playing, we would always try and go see how they did it. One time we found out the Christland Singers were going to be performing over at a storefront church on Lake Street, which was a trip because the elevated train would go by overhead and drown out the music. But those guys were big time and the train noise didn't make a difference!

The Christland Singers were led by R.H. Harris, who had been the primary lead singer of the Soul Stirrers prior to Sam Cooke's arrival. Sam picked up a lot of his vocal tricks from R.H. Also in the Christland Singers was a guy named Rev. Dowdy, who was just as good as Harris. They were all dressed in pretty suits, and LeRoy was the guitar player. He caught my eye, sitting in his chair. They were all sitting down. And LeRoy had his head thrown back and his mouth wide open singing. That impressed us. In fact, I have to say that the first gospel group that influenced me was the Christland Singers.

Like LeRoy before me, I never dreamed that I'd end up in the Soul Stirrers. We played mostly churches. We did schools as well, using the school auditoriums. The Soul Stirrers would perform at DuSable High School for Mother's Day every year. At one of the first gigs we played up north, Sam showed up and sat in the back to listen. This was the first time that he actually heard the bass with the group, and he gave it his stamp of approval. Sam still had his hooks into the Soul Stirrers. Even though he wasn't singing with them, they still relied on him for a lot of things. The Soul Stirrers gave everyone a salary, because they played guaranteed gigs. In addition to my salary, they had a Christmas fund. At the end of the year, the group split the Christmas fund.

I had my required uniforms that I wore onstage with the Soul Stirrers, and my brother Bobby loved them and wanted to wear them too. I told him, "Bobby, don't mess with my suits! Those are not street suits. I have to work in those!" But as soon as I would leave the house, he would grab my suits. My dog Pompey, who was given to me by the Flamingos' Buzzy Johnson, was very protective of my things. When Bobby would reach for those suits, Pompey would grab hold of the leg or the arm or whatever and try to take them away. He knew they were mine, and he would grab them from Bobby and pull them under the bed, tearing them in the process. He was very smart to do that, but it ruined the suits.

Along with LeRoy, Richard, Jesse, and I, the Soul Stirrers were rounded out by Paul Foster and Jimmie Outler, who was one of our lead singers. Jimmie was a little wild, which earned him his nickname of "Outlaw" because he would fight at the drop of a dime. He would occasionally try to pick fights with me. He jumped on Rev. Ruben Willingham with the Swanee Quintet, and I think he even jumped on Farley. He was a loose cannon, but I didn't know it at first.

We went to shoot pool one night when we got off the road. Black hotels were in the ghetto, and they were like rooming houses. Out in back of the hotel, there was a little fence, and across from that was a little pool room. So me and Jimmie were shooting pool, and these guys were at the next pool table. Me and Jimmie had our hair processed and were looking good, and they thought we were gay. They said, "You guys must be some of them sweet guys from Chicago!" When Jimmie would get mad, you could tell he was getting mad. His nose spread about two feet wide, so I knew they were pissing him off. But the last thing to cross my mind was Jimmie hitting the guy.

Next thing I know, Jimmie picked that pool stick up and hit that man across the head. Out the door we ran, and I jumped the fence because the hotel was right across the street. Jimmie was right behind me, and he jumped the fence too. Just about the time he got to the top of that fence, a pool ball hit him right in the eye! It busted his eye like a fighter, like someone hit him with a right cross. So Jimmie went to his room. Jesse Farley was having a meeting with somebody, but his door was open. I didn't want to interrupt him, but we had to make a decision about whether Jimmie needed stitches or not. So I kept walking back and forth outside in the hall, looking into his room. Finally, Jesse started laughing.

"What's wrong?" he asked me. "What's wrong?"

I told him, "Jimmie started a fight and got hit in the eye!"

Jesse came and looked at Jimmie, and blood was running down his face. We decided against taking him to the hospital, but looking back I think we should have because the next day when we were performing and he started to perspire, the blood would run down his face. Jimmie was always quick to fight, and ultimately he was stabbed and the word out was that he was killed by his own brother.

The Soul Stirrers were in Philadelphia for a show at The Met and also to audition a guitar player named Sonny Mitchell. While we were there, I ran into the Rev. Julius Cheeks for the first time since I last saw him in New York. We had talked about playing together, and he asked if I wanted to be part of his program that night, and I said yes. So I grabbed the Soul Stirrers guitar and we had a hallelujah good time. It was just me, Julius and his wife Margie on keys. My favorite song we played that night was "I Believe I'll Run On." That was a real honor for me, because he was one of the baddest dudes out there at that time.

Eventually I started to miss Freddie so I quit the Soul Stirrers after a couple of years and started back playing with him. You couldn't play gospel and blues at the same time. You had to do one or the other. I wouldn't have had time anyway, because the Soul Stirrers were constantly on the road. Freddie was on a gig in Chicago with B.B. King and Bobby Bland when I caught up with him. Freddie was doing his set and I eased up behind him and took the bass and started playing. The minute I hit the first note, Freddie turned around and started laughing. He was happy to see me. Freddie said, "I can tell when you pick up that bass!"

I went back on the road with Freddie and started doing some of his chitlin' circuit dates as his bassist. Freddie had a show at Chicago's

Regal Theater in the spring of '64 on the same bill with Dionne Warwick, Solomon Burke, and Smokey Robinson and the Miracles. He was on the show with all these big name people, and they put him on first. I think Dionne went on second, and Solomon went on after Dionne. Freddie hit the stage and was tearing it up. He was probably at his best because his family was in the audience. He'd start up with those blues and they would shut everything down but the blue lights. Freddie made it so hot up there for Dionne that she switched spots on the bill. She said, "You've got to get me from in between Freddie King and Solomon Burke. These guys are too tough. I'll open the show." So Dionne opened and Freddie followed. He was really getting hot, even co-starring at the Apollo with James Brown.

I was a big fan of comedienne Moms Mabley. My dressing room at the Regal was right next to hers, and I had to pass hers to get to ours. Moms had the cutest little maid named Joy working for her. Everybody looked at Joy. I would stop at the store on the way to the Regal and get me an apple. I was eating one and I passed the dressing room, and Moms was sitting there. She said, "Son?" I backed up and looked in. She said, "That sure looks good!" These were big apples. I just loved them. Moms said, "I sure do love red apples!" So after that I started bringing her a red apple every day. And then I'd get to go in and see Joy and talk to Joy. I never tried to hit on her or anything, but Joy was fine.

Another time, we were on a package show on the road with Little Willie John and the Upsetters (Little Richard's old band) and a young Otis Redding. Willie John was onstage, I was sitting in the dressing room, and Otis was sitting across from me. I was cattycorner from him. He was in one corner and I was in the other, but he was facing me and I had the newspaper up hiding my face because I wasn't in a talkative mood that night. Then Otis said, "Hey, man! How you doing?"

"I'm doing alright," I answered. "How you doing?"

"Oh, I'm alright."

I went back to my newspaper. It was kind of like when you're on a plane and you don't want to talk, so you give short answers. He said, "My name is Otis Redding!"

I said, "Glad to meet you." I put the paper back up.

"I got a hit record!" he said. "My name is Redding. Ain't you heard of me? I got a record out!"

I said, "Well, I haven't heard of you."

"You haven't heard it?"

"No, I haven't heard it."

By this point, Otis was determined to make me know who he was. Little Willie John and the Upsetters were kicking up a fuss onstage. So Otis got up out of his chair, came and got in my ear, and sang the whole song. I'm probably the only guy in history that had a concert from Otis Redding, one on one! Then he raised up and said, "Ain't you heard of me?" I said, "Is that you?" I'm messing with him now, just to get rid of him. He said, "Yeah, I told you I had a hit record!" I said, "Man, cool!" So I went on and got in the car the next day, and his song came on the radio. And I said, "I'll be damned! The cat does have a hit record!"

We met Emily Smith, later immortalized in Leon Russell's song, "Sweet Emily," at a wedding Freddie was hired to play in Tulsa. She talked us into going back to her house afterwards to jam. Later we learned that Leon was part of the group at her house that night. Emily was serving Johnnie Walker Red and by the time we left, we were all like a blind man reaching though an open window--we weren't feeling any "pane!" Emily gave us a case of Scotch for the road and sent us on our way.

It had been raining that night and the roads were slick. We were all tired and trying to get back to Dallas as quickly as we could, and Freddie was pushing about 105 miles per hour on the speedometer. The northbound lane of the Interstate had been shut down and we were traveling south (there must have been signs posted that the lane closure was coming, but we weren't aware of it). Freddie liked to drive in the passing lane, where the northbound traffic was diverted. The next thing I knew, we were facing an 18-wheeler coming straight at us, but it didn't register at first. Freddie's brother-in-law, O.C. Phillips, was in the back seat with my dog Pompey. Suddenly, O.C. yelled out loudly, "Freddie! You're gonna hit that truck!"

Freddie panicked and turned the wheel hard to the left. We ended up sliding down the highway sideways as the truck passed us by. Then we hit a barricade on the passenger side where I was sitting that knocked my door open, and the car landed in the ditch between the north and southbound lanes. Freddie reached over and grabbed me so I wouldn't fall out of the car. I looked out and saw the mud kicking up from the ground as the car spun around and around. My dog freaked out and ran to the back of the car to hide behind the amps. When the car finally came to a stop, Freddie was still holding me with one hand while he patted the dashboard with his other hand, saying, "Whoa, baby!" He still had me by the arm. I said, "You can let me go now, Freddie!" We took the dog chain and used it to tie the door handle together, and then went on to Dallas. I truly believe that the wet roads helped save us that night. If those roads had been dry, we would have had more traction and the car would have become airborne instead of sliding. We were very lucky.

At a gig in Austin, Sweet Emily and her friends came out to hear some blues. After that, we hooked up with Jimmy Reed and set out for some engagements in Louisiana and Mississippi. As hard as we tried, we couldn't talk the girls out of riding along with us. Emily didn't see black and white; she just saw great music and loved the blues. So we said, "Okay, let's go," and we hit the road. All of a sudden our worst nightmare came true when we saw red lights flashing in the rear view mirror and knew we were getting pulled over by the cops. As our car hit the soft shoulder, the gravel hitting the car woke Jimmy up. He came to and said, loudly, "What the goddamn hell is going on?" Our driver said, "The cops done pulled us over." Jimmy said, "Don't nobody move!" Walking toward us was the spitting image of that sheriff with the sunglasses in the Dodge TV ads that said, "You're in a heap of trouble, boy!" Jimmy opened the door, got out, and announced, "My name is Jimmy Reed. 'Ain't That Loving You Baby!'"

The cop stopped in his tracks and said, "You're Jimmy Reed?"

"Can't you hear? I said my name's Jimmy Reed. 'Ain't That Loving You Baby!'"

"I've got all your records!" the cop said. "I love your music!"

Suddenly Jimmy Reed's signing stuff for him.

"Y'all go ahead!" said the cop. "Y'all go ahead!"

When we got to the gig, the black people wouldn't let the girls in. So they went and woke up the mayor, who was friends with Emily's father, a well-known construction business owner. The mayor called down to the club and said, "Y'all let 'em go up in the balcony and watch as spectators." They couldn't come downstairs and mingle, but at least they could sit upstairs and look down.

The road had its pleasures, but it also had its downsides. I remember once early on when we were headed back to Dallas from Florida, it was really hot. A guy named George Scott was driving. We all wore processes, and you put that black scarf around your head to hold it in place. The window was down, it was scorching hot, and we didn't have air conditioning. Freddie was asleep in the back and sweating, and his head scarf had come halfway down and was hanging off his forehead. A white night watchman had noticed us driving, and he decided he was going to play police because he had his uniform on.

He signaled us to pull over to the side of the road, just like the real police would, and George complied. Freddie said, "What's wrong?" George said, "The goddamn motherfuckin' police pulled us over. Bitch motherfucker!" The night watchman got out of his car with an arrogant little step, holding his gun. We looked at his badge and it said "Security," so we knew he wasn't an actual cop. So just about the time he got up even with the car, Freddie raised up out of the back seat, looking pretty rough and mad with that headrag halfway down off his head. Freddie was sweating, and big. That

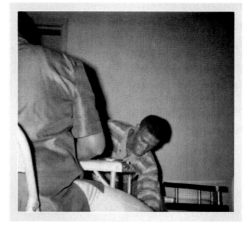

Freddie and George Scott at the poker table

night watchman took one look in the window and said, "Y'all go ahead!" Freddie scared the shit out of him. At the time we were pissed off about the whole thing, but now when I look back it's pretty funny because Freddie didn't even have to say a word!

Jimmy Reed was drunk every time I saw him. When we were somewhere in Indiana, Jimmy couldn't find any water to put on his hair, which he needed because when you wear a process you put water on your hair to relax it. "Where the goddamn hell's the water?" he growled. I was drinking a Coke, and he told me, "Pour that goddamned shit in my hand!" I poured it in his hand, and he put it all over his head and combed his hair. "There, goddamn it!" Then he said, "Next time, I'm gonna kick that damned guy if I don't have no water. I'm gonna hit him just like this!" He threw his fist like he was going to hit me in the face, telling me how he was going to do the man. I could feel the air passing my face with every swing. Freddie was standing there laughing, and he said, "He come kind of close, you know?" He came mighty close, because some of the Coca-Cola that was on his hand hit my face.

I met up later on with Jimmy on the South Side of Chicago in some club. Junior Wells was there too, and we were drinking in the daytime. I was sitting on the left, Junior was on the other side, and Jimmy was in the middle. We were just hanging out. All of a sudden, Jimmy looked at me real funny and grabbed my right arm in a vise grip. He was having a seizure, and I didn't know it. He started leaning back off the bar, and he held on to my hand. Junior had the other side, and we let him lay on back. He had one of those nasty kicking seizures. He bopped and kicked down there for a long time, and then all of a sudden he came out of it. He got up and brushed himself off, got his handkerchief out and wiped his mouth. He yelled to the bartender, "Pour me a goddamned drink!"

There was a little black motel in Dallas called the Green Acres that was right out in back of the Empire Room. Everybody stayed there when they played at the club, and I used to stay there when we weren't touring. It later changed its name to the New York Ballroom, the place where Freddie played his last gig. It was a popular stop on the chitlin' circuit for the blues and soul acts. One time Jimmy had been drinking, got drunk and fell asleep at the Green Acres. His manager, Al Smith, went into his room and went into Jimmy's pockets and got some of his money. But when Al pulled the door open to walk out, Jimmy woke up. We were all out on the sidewalk. Jimmy came out of the room half asleep, wiping his eyes, looking like something was wrong. He said, "Goddamn it, somebody's just been in my room, and went in my pocket and got my goddamn money! It looked like Al Smith. It walked like Al Smith. Goddamn it, that was Al Smith!" There were lots of people that I really enjoyed over my career but there are two that really stand out: Jimmy Reed and Little Walter. They definitely had their own style.

Not only did I meet Ray Charles when we were all staying at the Green Acres, I played dominoes with him there. He was maybe a couple of doors down from me. Ray would just sit around his room, and I'd go in and talk to him. He said, "You play dominoes?" I said, "Yeah, I play dominoes!" He said, "You can't play dominoes!" I said, "I can play!" "Okay, okay—let's play!" So I went and got my dominoes. You wonder how he could play dominoes? Ray would turn them upside down and feel the spots on the domino, and then I'd just have to tell him what was on each end. And the dude was fast! I'd say, "Well, you've got a six over here, a five over there, a one over here." And he's say, "Okay, well, now—bam! 15!" Because he'd count 5-10-15-20-25-30. I messed around and beat Ray the very first game, and he had that old funny laugh—"Heh, heh. Yeah, well, I always let the chumps beat me the first one." And do you know he beat me every game after that? Every one. And I was a pretty good dominoes player. There were only two people that could beat me: Ray Charles and LeRoy Crume.

I got to sit in on bass with Texas blues guitar pioneer T-Bone Walker one night at the Empire Room. He'd do his shuffles, and then do slow blues. He was easy to play with. I had some sandals on that were cool and comfortable, and I loved them. But one of them had gotten snagged on the side, and my toe was sticking out. Freddie was in the audience, and instead of watching the people, he was looking at my toe and laughing. He said, "Man, have you looked down at your feet?" He watched my toe more than he watched T-Bone.

I finally got to record with Freddie at King Records in Cincinnati on August 26, 1964. Freddie did a dozen songs with me on bass and my old friend Bobby King on rhythm guitar, including his instrumentals "Man Hole," "Funny Bone," and "Cloud Sailin'" (all named, no doubt, by Sonny Thompson, who was on piano as usual).

We were all proud of Freddie because he was the first person in our family that succeeded like that TV sitcom family, the Jeffersons: he moved on up and got to be somebody. His dream was to get out and make money so he could pull his family and his parents' family out of the ghetto. Then he got on Federal Records and had some hits, and it looked like it was going to happen. But the record company was squeezing him out of his money. I always thought it was Sonny Thompson. Then after having a talk with Freddie's oldest daughter Wanda, I found out it wasn't Sonny so much. It was actually King Records. They did what was normal in those days with black musicians. Freddie didn't know anything about the record business or about publishing. He had no idea he was stepping into a fish bowl full of piranhas.

That was along about the time Freddie moved back to Texas. He'd had a disagreement with his wife. They wanted to buy two houses, but the record money didn't roll in like he expected it to. So Freddie and his family ended up moving to Dallas. He couldn't look after all of us too. He could only look after his immediate family, so that's what he did, which was understandable.

Freddie's house in Dallas

I really didn't like the road that much, so I started playing bass around Chicago. I was playing at Globetrotter's Lounge at Madison and Damen on the West Side with my brother Bobby and a drummer named Willie Nolan. He was the bandleader that got us the gig there (Luther "Guitar Junior" Johnson was another of the club's head-liners). The guy that owned the club told me, "I know a guy that you might be good with. I want you to come down to the Rush Street hotel where I'm gonna be working, and I'm going to introduce you to him." I went down, and it was saxist Dave Mitchell. Me and Dave sat down and had a talk, and we hooked up and got to be good friends. I played with his band for a long time.

On drums, we had Casey Jones, who later became famous when he played with Texas blues guitarist Albert

Dave Mitchell and the Flames. L to R: Paul Brownlee, Casey Jones, Dave Mitchell and me

Collins. Paul Brownlee was our guitarist. He came from the gospel world. Dave pulled him into the group, and he was really good. Dave loved to have fun, and I like people like that. He had this carved wooden tongue that was about ten inches long. He'd take that tongue and go around teasing the women with it.

Paul was funny too. He worked at the post office and he played at night, trying to support all the kids he had. He had a lot of kids. It was driving him crazy, and he would drink. At the end of the night, he would have to drive all the way back to the suburbs, sleep a couple of minutes, and get up and go to the post office. One night we got off work, and Paul got in his car. He had a white '61 Cadillac. He was driving down the Dan Ryan Expressway and was too sleepy to drive, so he decided to pull over and park and sleep a little bit and then continue on. Thinking he had pulled over to the side, he had actually pulled up in the middle of the Dan Ryan, put the car in park, turned off the lights, put the seat back and went to sleep! Of course, he got hit, but he came out of it alright. He could have gotten killed. It must have been pretty funny even to the cops, because they let Paul get away with it. When they asked him why he stopped in the middle of the road, he said, "Well, I was just a little fatigued!" They let him go without a DUI charge.

We had to rehearse sometimes, because we needed to get those Top Ten R&B songs like "Knock On Wood" down. We all sang, except for Paul. We played as a unit for a long time, because we had a nice little group, although we didn't make any records. We performed on Rush Street for the tourists, as well as working at parties and bars all over the city. Dave was pretty connected. We played at the Scotch Mist on Rush Street with the Treniers and Tommy Hunt, formerly of the Flamingos, who got out on the floor, jumping around dancing and doing the splits. The Treniers were funny onstage, but they were strictly business off it. Playing on Rush Street gave me great opportunities. Redd Foxx was doing his act there at the club in the hotel. I got to meet Louis Armstrong there. He used to hang out in the back. I met Joe Williams there from Count Basie's band.

I'll never forget January 7, 1966. It was the day that my car note was due, and I had my daughter Carla in my arms when I went over to Fohrman Motors at 2700 W. Madison to make my payment. The Fohrman Brothers were really famous locally for bringing Saturday night wrestling to local television (the program was hosted by Cubs announcer Jack Brickhouse). The Fohrmans sold a lot of Cadillacs to black guys who wanted them but couldn't get a loan anywhere else, including me. But things went sour that day for the Fohrmans. A disgruntled customer who was an ex-convict came into the showroom and shot to death two of owner Benjamin Fohrman's sons who worked there, as well as Albert Sizer, the guy that sold me my car.

I heard the gunshots, and just as I got up to the door to go in, I saw a skull lying in the window. It looked like a coconut shell. I said,

"What is a coconut shell doing lying in the window?" Then I looked at this pretty black Eldorado on the showroom floor, and I saw brains lying on top of that. I thought to myself, "Something ain't right here!" But somebody getting his head blown off never crossed my mind. Somebody told me, "No, you can't go in right now. There's been a shooting." Things were still unfolding when I got there. Fortunately, I was just about two minutes late--otherwise I'd have been inside right when it took place.

I was in a band for awhile with harmonica genius Little Walter, Bobby King and Gene "Daddy G" Barge, the great saxophonist. We had a gig at Pepper's Lounge, and Bobby said, "Oh, man, I don't want to be bothered with Walter tonight." Walter wasn't your average guy, but I loved him. I said, "I like Walter, and it's my car! And we're going to pick Walter up." He was one hell of a musician. I would have walked over glass to play with Walter, but he never did learn my name. He told me, "You're a motherfucker on that bass!" I said, "Well, thank you!" And the name stuck. I was "Motherfucker" from then on. Eddie Shaw had a place right around the corner from where my mother lived called the 1815 Club. We had moved over by 14th Street. I had my own place by then. One time I left Eddie's club and I was walking, it was about a block away from Ashland Avenue. And I heard, "Motherfucker! Motherfucker! Hey, Motherfucker!" And I looked over and there was Little Walter on the other corner, jumping up and down.

I went over there, and Walter said, "I got this gig! I got this gig at Vi's Lounge." It was down on 14th and Ashland. Walter said, "She's going to give us 15 cents ($15). I'm going to try to get 17, but I know I can get 15. You want to play it?" I said, "Yeah, I'll play it, Walter. It made me sad for a guy who made as many hits as Walter to be playing a $15 gig. Unfortunately, I didn't get the chance to play that gig with him. That was about the last time I saw Walter before he died. He was quite a dude.

Before that, Walter and I played together at Johnny Pepper's place in Robbins, way out in the southern suburbs. I think that's the last time we played together, out there. Gene may have played that one.

I liked Gene even before I found out who he was. I loved his playing. King Curtis was the other saxist I really loved, and I got to meet them both. I wish I could remember the details of the song I recorded at Chess with Gene and Maurice White on drums. I never got the record or even knew the name of it. I'd like to have it just to hear it, just to say I played with Gene and Maurice of Earth, Wind & Fire. Gene later told me I kept Bobby King straight. Bobby and I didn't have no big quarrels, though. He always looked at me like I was his brother. In fact, he used to introduce me on stage as his little brother, just like he heard Freddie say so many times.

During that time, trumpeter Paul Serrano and I dreamed about having a recording studio. He went on to achieve his dream by opening PS Studios, one of the most influential recording facilities in Chicago. I ran up on Paul one day and he told me, "Man, I've got two Crowns!" He was talking about Crown tape recorders with the big reels. Paul put together a little studio during the mid-'60s and called me one day. He said, "Hey, come out! I've got this guy that wants to record this song. I want you to come out and play bass!"

So I went out there, and the session was with veteran comedian Stepin Fetchit, whose real name was Lincoln Perry. He wanted to do an answer to "How Much Is The Hound Dog In The Window." In his answer song, that dog turned out to have the mange! It was a big thrill to be in the studio with someone who had worked with the biggest names in Hollywood, including Oliver Hardy, Will Rogers, and Shirley Temple. Stepin Fetchit was different in person than he was on those shows he did. I really didn't care for how he portrayed himself in the movies, but then I looked at his track record. The guy knew everybody and had been with everybody with that little thing he was known for in the movies. He was a different guy in person, more business.

I was going to play bass on the session and learn all these notes and everything. Paul put the tape on and we started the song, and my fingers didn't know what I was doing. I was playing all these notes, and Paul and the rest of them came out of that control room, yelling, "Hey, whatcha doing? Whatcha doing?" They embarrassed me. He said, "This is a Stepin Fetchit song!" From that day on, I learned how to track. On a track, you play with a drummer. You play simple, and I learned that less is more. I learned discipline from Paul. Even to this day, if I'm singing and somebody gets loose, I can't take it. It has to be a simple beat, a straight beat. I learned that from that session.

The assassination of Dr. Martin Luther King, Jr. in April of 1968 set much of Chicago's West Side ablaze. Madison Street, one of its leading commercial thoroughfares, was burning, but the neighborhoods themselves weren't. It was hard trying to get home from my gigs, but I had to work because I had two little girls to take care of. That was when I was staying around the corner from Tyrone Davis on Lavergne. I had to try to get home the best way I could at night, and sometimes I had to come through the alleys. I remember coming out of the alley in my '59 white Cadillac and trying to get around the corner fast, and I clipped some guy's car. I didn't hurt his car, but I bent one of the back fenders on my Cadillac. I was so pissed because it was such a nice car. When I would get off work, I would roll all the windows up and put classical music on because it was so quiet in that car.

Operation Soul L to R: Bobby Turner, me, Rick Howard (drums),
Robert Griffin (trumpet), Jose Ivy (saxophone) and
L.C. "Pig" Carr (vocals)

My younger brother Bobby had learned to play guitar by watching me, so after I left Dave Mitchell, we decided to put a band together that we called Operation Soul. Bobby had a group of his own, and we all used to play down on Rush Street, so we took some of the guys from Bobby's band and some from my band and put them together. That's when organist Melvyn "Deacon" Jones came into the picture. He'd been a charter member of Baby Huey and the Babysitters from when they first formed in Richmond, Indiana. When we met, he was working in an A&R capacity for Curtis Mayfield at Curtom Records. Robert Griffin doubled on organ and trumpet, and Charlie Robinson was our drummer.

L.C. "Pig" Carr and Bobby Turner

Operation Soul got hooked up with a big local booking agency. They got us a gig on the North Side at some theater, and we actually opened for Wayne Cochran. We looked up and saw our name in lights up on the marquee with Wayne Cochran, and we said, "Man, we're doing alright!" Cochran was a little nuts onstage. At the end of his act, he was throwing chairs up in the ceiling, all over the band. I met him again a few years later in Toronto when I was gigging at the El Mocambo. I went to his room and we sat down and talked about hats. He loved hats and I like hats too.

Deacon would go out and play gigs with Mayfield when he wasn't working in the studio (Curtis gave him his nickname when he was introducing the band onstage and forgot Melvyn's first name). He was playing with the Impressions, and he was taking gigs with us in Operation Soul. Curtis needed a band, and Deacon said, "I know where you can get a whole band, ready!" So he introduced Curtis to Operation Soul. Of course, they knew me already from my days with Dee Clark. Curtis wrote us a song called "The Other Side Of Town," and we learned it. He and Eddie Thomas wanted to record us, but they never did. It seemed like Curtis was always busy doing something. He finally sang the song himself on one of his albums.

We went with Curtis and the Impressions for some gigs down South. After that, we ended up at West Point in New York. The Impressions' asses were on the line because Curtis was running late and they were unable to go on without him because there were just two other members, Sam Gooden and Fred Cash. So they came to where we were and said, "Look, can y'all go out and do something?" We were all looking at each other, and we said, "Yeah, we can go out and do something!" Marvin Gaye had just come out with his hit "Too Busy Thinking About My Baby." We came out onstage and hit Marvin's song, and the place went up. After that, we sang Brook Benton's new smash "Rainy Night In Georgia," written by Tony Joe White. The audience went nuts. After we finished our little set, they gave us a standing ovation. Then the Impressions went on, and they couldn't come from behind us.

After the show was over, the manager came in the dressing room and said, "That's it, baby!" We were thinking it was time to go.

"No, no, that's it!" he replied.

"What do you mean, that's it?"

"That's it! You're fired. Y'all can go home."

Deacon remembers, "They'd just gotten mad at our singing. Benny and Bobby, they could sing like nightingales!"

We all left with our tails between our legs, and decided to stop at the Apollo before we went back to Chicago. I got everyone in backstage, and there was my old friend Tyrone Davis from the Squeeze Club, singing his very first hit, "Can I Change My Mind." Talk about good timing! We felt right at home. We returned to Chicago and started playing gigs again.

Operation Soul wasn't fated to last for long. Freddie was in town in late 1969 when we were playing at the Turning Point on West Madison. He'd get in touch with me whenever his back was up against the wall, as far as needing musicians. So he came out with his guitar and sat in with us, and he loved the band. Afterwards, I asked Freddie

"What do you need?" He said, "Man, I'm having a little problem with my band. I think I need you." I said, "Okay!"

So I jumped on a plane and went down to Austin.

BACK WITH FREDDIE

Freddie was using our cousins, Sam and Lee King, as his band when I got there. Their father, Levester King Sr. was a first cousin of our mother. Lee played rhythm guitar, and Sam was the drummer. They were good. They're still out there on their own right now doing their thing, out in L.A. I played with them behind Freddie in 1969-70, but when they left I pulled in the members of Operation Soul to work as my brother's band.

Unlike Freddie I never did officially move back to Texas, although I was down there a lot. I just went back and forth whenever he asked me to play with him. Freddie would put me up in a hotel, or I would just stay with him. Then if I'd get tired or there wasn't any work or if I missed my kids, I'd go back home to Chicago.

But I did want a house of my own in Chicago once I started playing with Freddie pretty regularly. He said, "Well, go get you one! Just go get it and let me know." I called him and I said, "I found a house!" He said, "What do you need to get in it?" I said, "$2500." He said, "It'll be there tomorrow. Go to Western Union and pick it up!" So I went and picked the money up and bought the house. It was in Markham, a southern suburb. If it had been anybody else asking him, they wouldn't have gotten the money because Freddie was real tight with it. He came from an era of musicians being taken advantage of and he was skeptical about trusting people when it came to his money. I lived in that house in Markham until I moved to New Orleans.

In part due to his two King Curtis-produced albums for Atlantic's Cotillion label during the late '60s, Freddie was on his way up. He had just made the transition out of the chitlin' circuit, and he was drawing big crowds. When I came down to the Armadillo World Headquarters in Austin to join him, that place was packed. Then I started doing festivals with him, and they were packed too. Freddie liked playing for everybody, but he really came alive when he played for white people because they showed a great appreciation for him. When he looked at their faces in the crowd, it actually fired him up.

The chitlin' circuit was no cake walk, to say the least. You had to work hard for every single dime, and surprises seemed to be waiting around every corner. Freddie was having problems with his manager at the time and really wanted to take the next step and start working with Jack Calmes. Jack became his manager and Freddie signed with Shelter Records.

My old Freddie King/Shelter Records t-shirt

That decision turned out to be his biggest blessing, and it never would have happened with his manager from the chitlin' circuit. From that day on, everything fell in place, and Freddie blues-rocked his way right into the Rock and Roll Hall of Fame!

Signing with Shelter gave Freddie the opportunity to reach a different audience. It was just a matter of time. Leon Russell was just becoming a star himself after more than a decade of playing with other people, including a lot of studio work. With Don Nix, Russell produced **Getting Ready...**, Freddie's first album for Leon's new Shelter label. Leon was a good writer and had a good feel for soul music as well as blues and gospel. He was a super guy to work with.

Later on we were in Long Beach, California, and we were going in the auditorium on our way to perform. Somebody yelled out to Freddie "Are you going to play 'Going Down' by Jeff Beck tonight?' Freddie looked at me as we walked together and said, "Man, that's a goddamned shame," because that's a Freddie King song (from the album **Getting Ready**). We got inside, and he got up on the microphone: "Ladies and gentlemen, I got a request to do a tune, 'Going Down,' by Jeff Beck! Everybody thinks Jeff Beck recorded this so it's a Jeff Beck song, but that's bullshit!" And when he said that, he counted it off. And boy, we hit that song and the place went up!

Freddie had started going to London in the 1960s, because that's when Eric Clapton was recording Freddie's songs. That's what made the people in England want to hear Freddie so he went over there. I didn't go with him during the '60s, but I did play all of his '70s gigs in England. One time when we were in London, I hung out with Leon in the hotel room. Everybody had gone out that night, and I always took a nap when I'd get in off the road. So I went to sleep, and when I woke up I called Freddie and didn't get an answer. I called the rest of the guys. No answer. I called Leon, and he picked up the phone. I asked him, "Hey man, where's everybody?" He said, "They've gone down to the speakeasy." I said, "The speakeasy? Well, I've got a bottle of champagne! Would you like some?" He said, "Come on up!"

So I went up to Leon's room, and we sat there and talked about this and that and drank that champagne. That's when I found out he had great respect for Freddie. He asked me, "Who do you think is the best gospel group?" And I said, "Hands down, there ain't but one, as far as I'm concerned—it's the Mighty Clouds of Joy." He said, "Are they a good group?" I said, "Yeah, they're a great group, man!" Later on, he went and hired them to play with him on some of those shows. After we finished the champagne, Leon got up and said, "Let's go down to the speakeasy." So when we got to the club, Leon walked right past the ticket booth and just went on in. Nobody even asked him for a ticket! I was right behind him, saying to myself, "So this is what it's like, being a rock star!" Leon liked to party like everybody else, but he was pretty much a business dude on the road. When he got onstage, he was stone cold serious. We did some gigs with him in the United States too.

During this period, Freddie started doing more funky-type things. I think that was due to Leon because with him and Leon getting together, it changed his style. Before that we were basically blues— "Sweet Home Chicago" and all that stuff. But then Freddie kind of changed. Jack was pushing us. He wanted Freddie to change, to try to get the commercial crowd, to try to bridge it. So they started doing different things like "Going Down," which was not traditional blues. When Freddie got away from the chitlin' circuit, it turned into a higher-energy situation.

While touring in the U.K., I met Henry McCullough of the Grease Band and we became good friends. Henry always greeted me with a smile and treated Freddie and the band with respect. There was one member of the Grease Band who didn't share Henry's sentiments, and I really think it was jealousy, because Freddie was on fire as usual. One day while we were all out having a stroll, Freddie and I walked past Henry and that particular band member, who spit across in front of Freddie. Henry was so mad that he broke his hand hitting him. He actually finished the tour playing guitar with a cast on his hand! I lost contact with Henry, but last I heard he went on to play with Paul McCartney and Wings.

We liked "Palace Of The King," one of the new songs that Russell and Nix brought to **Getting Ready…,** but we never played it that much. I remember we were sitting in the dressing room with Leon and a lot of them, and Freddie had an acoustic guitar. He started playing the old-time blues, just playing that old shuffle on "Sweet Home Chicago." So everybody was patting their feet, and everybody was listening to Freddie playing. On the stage, he'd sing those old songs. He liked the old songs. People wonder why we did those, but they never understood. Even the younger generation doesn't understand why we still play those songs. It's because those songs put food on the table. Those songs made the rent. And those songs gave you a job. Those songs were embedded into us. Those songs fed us, and that's why we did them. We pick up a guitar, we're going to play one of them. I still do Guitar Slim's "The Things That I Used To Do" and Eddie Boyd's "Five Long Years" nightly.

Freddie made two more albums for Shelter, **Texas Cannonball** in 1972 and **Woman Across the River** the next year. Although Leon continued to use his band to back Freddie at his sessions, we did cut versions of "I'm Tore Down" and "Dust My Broom" in November of '71 at Hollywood's Capitol Tower (the songs were made for radio broadcast and weren't released at the time). By then, Dino Neal was our drummer, and my Operation Soul bandmate Robert Griffin had become our organist (he doubled on trumpet).

When we got Dino he didn't have anything. And at that time, he had to get in the union. So I took him down on Madison Street to a pawnshop and bought a set of drums. Freddie said, "What do you think?" I said, "Well, he can play a good backbeat, he can play a good shuffle, and he can play funky." He said, 'Good—we'll take him then." He went down and got in the union, and unlike when Freddie and I joined Local 208 a decade-and-a-half earlier, Dino had to take a test to join Local 10. Then we took him out with us on the road.

On stage with Deacon Jones

Freddie also did a session with us at A&M in December of '72 where we recorded a blazing instrumental that we called "The Boogie." Magic Sam had a version of the song, and I liked it. Freddie picked it up, and that's why he started playing "The Boogie." Like "Hide Away," we put our version together right on the stage (by then, we'd brought Deacon Jones and Charlie Robinson from Operation Soul onboard). I changed some things in it, coming from the IV. We were steady changing it. Despite its sky-high energy level, our recording of "The Boogie" was shelved at the time, even though it was a prominent part of our nightly shows.

Singer D.J. Rogers came into the studio while we were recording "The Boogie." D.J. said, "Hey, man, you're a bad dude on that bass. Sly Stone's bass player just quit. I think I can hook you up with Sly Stone!" I considered it, to tell you the truth. But then I remembered that Sly was supposed to play Chicago's Grant Park a couple of years earlier, and he didn't show. There was a riot there as a result. And I said no.

In Hollywood, playing "movie stars" L to R: Charlie Robinson, David Maxwell, me, Robert Griffin

Jimmy Rogers had a lot of influence on Freddie during his early years. Freddie repaid him by producing Jimmy's Shelter album **Gold-Tailed Bird** in early '72. Half the album was cut in Chicago with the Aces (Louis and David Myers and Fred Below), the same trio that played behind Little Walter on many of his early hits, backing Jimmy. The other half was done in Hollywood at Paramount Recording Studios with a young rhythm section from Chicago behind Jimmy. Pianist Bob Riedy was the only sideman to work both sessions. Riedy remembers his young band touring Texas with Rogers prior to their arrival in Hollywood for the session, where they were entertained during their off hours by a movie crew filming **Blacula** at their hotel.

Freddie flew me out to L.A. because he was having some problems in the studio, and he knew that I had an ear for good sound and how to arrange and produce music. When I arrived in Hollywood, he told me to sit in the hotel room by the phone, because he might need me. I didn't end up going to the session, and although Freddie kept me updated, he never said exactly what the problem was. The one thing I know for sure is that Jimmy and Freddie weren't having problems with each other.

We were on the road all the time during Freddie's Shelter years, and we still encountered our share of bigotry when driving through Texas. We pulled into a gas station one time to buy some gasoline. Freddie had a Coca-Cola and he drank a lot of it while the guy was gassing up the car. He went to set the bottle down because you'd leave the bottle behind when you'd pull away. The man said, "Take the bottle with you." Freddie said, "What?" He replied, "Take it with you. We don't want it." Freddie took a nickel out and slammed it on the Coke machine and said, "Well, there's a nickel for the bottle." And he walked out. I said, "Man, Jim Crow ain't dead. He's just gone underground."

When WAR first hit the scene, we did a concert with them in south Texas. WAR had their whole entourage with them. We opened the show for them, just Freddie, Dino and I. We tore up the place, and when Freddie got through, WAR didn't have nobody to play to because most of the audience was Freddie King fans. They didn't want to be booked with us anymore after that, because they felt like if Freddie could do that with three pieces, he must be a bitch with his whole band! We ended up on another show with them in December of '72 at the Santa Monica Civic Auditorium, and they were not happy. Our dressing room shared a bathroom, and one of our band members overheard them complaining about it. They were saying, "I told them not to book us with Freddie King anymore!" We really were hot at that time. Deacon remembers that WAR waited a whole hour before they took the stage to let it cool off.

We toured with Creedence Clearwater Revival and Tony Joe White, and John Fogerty was something like Grand Funk Railroad's Mark Farner. They could sing all night long at their high range, and they never lost their voices. It was the damnedest thing I ever saw. John was comfortable playing with three pieces. He was great. But Fogerty's crowd and Freddie's crowd were different. We'd play a big auditorium, and when time came for us to play, the Freddie King crowd would come to the front. And then when Freddie was finished and it was Fogerty's time, the crowd would change and Fogerty's crowd would come to the front. Freddie covered CCR's "Lodi" (which he called "Lowdown In Lodi"), but I think that song was brought to Freddie rather than learned first-hand. I don't think we even listened to Creedence most of the time because we were too busy playing poker.

One time we were coming out of an auditorium we had just played with Creedence. They had their big truck parked right by the stage door. They were rubbing their guitars down. Freddie and I always walked together. He looked at me and said, "Look at them rubbing on their guitars. When they're finished there, ain't gonna play no better! Ain't gonna sound no better!" I never saw Freddie rub on a guitar. Never. Freddie was strong and he used to break that little E string of his all the time. I would try to fix the bridge on his guitar so his strings wouldn't break. I'd work on his guitar, and one day I picked it up and it had dirt all under the strings. So it ain't the guitar. It's the player. He could put a new string on and tune it fast. He'd always pat himself on the back at how fast he could change that string. I never did understand why he didn't just put two guitars on the stage. I would have. If I'd have thought about it, I would have told him to and he would have did it. But we didn't think like that.

Along with Carlos Santana, we performed across the Pacific Northwest and Canada. It was a great time because he and Freddie were well-matched. The crowd liked both of them. I also learned what a cool guy Santana was personally. We always wore boots, and Santana especially liked my boots because they were unique. One night we played an auditorium, and our bus was parked way across the parking lot. I was pissed off about something, and when I'm pissed off, I'm gone. I'm off to myself. I don't know what I was angry about that night. But I went across the parking lot and got on the bus. I was just sitting there. All of a sudden, I heard a knock on the door. It's Santana. He steps on the bus and says, "Hey, man, you didn't speak to me tonight!" I said, "Oh, man! I'm sorry, man. How you doing?" That immediately changed my whole mood. I got off the bus and forgot what I was mad about and went back inside with him. It was such a cool thing. For as big of a star as he was, he stayed very humble. I got that feeling again later on when I had chats with blues piano legend Charles Brown. He had that same humble vibe.

L to R: Freddie, me, Deacon Jones. Illustration by Kay Johnson

Then there was our tour with Grand Funk Railroad. We played Madison Square Garden with them, and they apparently really enjoyed touring with us. Their song "We're An American Band" was about Freddie. When they sing, "Up all night with Freddie King, I gotta tell you that poker's his thing," that was a true story. They played poker with us in Little Rock. I think Little Rock might have been during the last part of the tour. We all got together and played poker that night. That's what inspired that song.

Freddie and I never played against each other, because one of us would always win when we played in the same game, so we stuck together. My ankles used to get sore from Freddie kicking me under the table when he wanted me to turn down. But he knew if he kicked me and I didn't turn down that I had a winning hand, so he would turn down instead. We played many variations of poker: five card stud, seven card stud, low hold, deuces wild, and spit. We had our own card nicknames that the dealer used. Aces were "ice cream cones upside down." Twos were "two 'til Lou get through." Threes were "three days in the county jail." Fours were "before you go think of me." Fives were fever—"went to the doctor and he said fever." Sixes were "seasick and water bound--can't swim, you're bound to drown." Sevens were "hard-hearted Hannah." Eights were "eight, skate and donate." Nines were "niney-biney." Tens were "Big Ben sit and grin." Jacks were "fish hook," Queens were "Queen Esther," and kings were "Cowboy Dan from the Rio Grande." If the pot was $400-$500 and it came to the showdown at the end of the hand, that's when you threw your big money in. But if it was just the two of us left, Freddie would throw in a quarter.

We did a lot of poker playing on our tour bus. Freddie had picked up a 4104, an old Greyhound. We had it redone with a table installed right in the middle for our poker games. Our longest poker game was from Chicago to L.A. We played from Chicago until we took a break in Denver. In Las Vegas, we had a 39-cent breakfast—Las Vegas was giving away stuff then, but they aren't doing it now—and got right back on the bus and continued playing clear on to L.A. That was our longest poker game.

Sometimes the stakes in those poker games were high. I won a car in one game, and Freddie won a car in another. Deacon remembers one guy who claimed he was going to jump off a bridge after we cleaned him out during an all-nighter in northern California (he didn't). I picked up a '68 Toronado from somebody at a game in Dallas. Freddie won a car from a cocky promoter somewhere in Texas. This guy came in and said, "I heard you guys can play poker. I want $100 from Benny, I want $100 from Deacon Jones, and I want $1000 from Freddie King!"

So we all sat down to play poker. We had a way of playing to make you think that you had a good hand. We called it goosey-loosey low-hold. Say you've got two cards down, and if you can match those cards, they're wild. So this dude had five kings. Freddie knew he had five kings. And Freddie had five aces with no ace showing. So the man made a big bet. I mean, we're talking about thousands. Freddie looked over at the man's hand. He said, "Damn! You done hit them five kings. You better have 'em!" The guy said, "But it's gonna cost you to see it!" And Freddie said, "Call, and I raise $1000." The man said, "I don't have any more money." Freddie said, "Well, you have a car! Throw the keys in!" The man threw the keys in, and Freddie said, "What else you got?" The man said, "35 cents." Freddie said, "Throw that in." The man put his last dimes and nickels in and said, "Sorry, Mr. King. I hit them five kings." He went to reach for the money and Freddie said, "Hold it! Them five kings win in China. I've got five aces!" The man was completely shocked. He didn't say a word as he got up and walked to the door. He opened the door and turned around and said, "I heard y'all could play poker, but I didn't know you were that good!" He slammed the door and we never saw him again.

Our poker game with Grand Funk had been fun, because they were gentlemen players. We weren't out to cut nobody's throat. If you lost, you lost. But this other guy had come in to actually cut our head. That's what he wanted to do. That man had gone to the ceiling with his bet, and he ended up with nothing.

Cain's Ballroom in Tulsa was one of our favorite places to play because we had lots of fans there. It was like the Armadillo for us. Whenever we played there, a lot of people came out to see us and it was like a big party. I remember one gig at Cain's in particular where Freddie was a different guy. He had a look on his face, like he was thinking, "I know I'm in command, and I can do whatever I want to do!" Maybe he was high or something, because I had never seen him like that. That was one of his best shows I ever saw. Sadly, Cain's Ballroom was the last gig we were scheduled to play in 1976, but we never made it.

Whenever we got out to Los Angeles, we hung out with blues greats Lowell Fulson and Shakey Jake Harris. Although he was on the Chicago blues scene during the '50s, I met Jake out there. I can't remember how long I knew Lowell but I knew him longer than I knew Jake for sure. Jake could get his harmonica and sit there in his chair and play for me for an hour, laughing and singing. But when he'd get onstage, he'd get nervous. Freddie said that's why they called him Shakey Jake.

Rock luminaries weren't our only high-profile co-stars. Freddie was one of the headliners at the 1972 Ann Arbor Blues and Jazz Festival.

Miles Davis was supposed to close that night, and we were slotted next to him. Miles was apparently pacing from one end of his dressing room to the other end with his horn, barking "Get him off the stage!" because we were fired up and Freddie was kicking ass. I think Grand Funk came to see us that night, because we had just finished our tour with them. Freddie got on the microphone and announced to the audience, "We've got Grand Funk Railroad here with us tonight!" Nobody out in the crowd said any-

On stage with Freddie at Ann Arbor Blues Festival, 1972

thing, other than a few scattered groans. It was definitely a blues crowd. Freddie repeated loudly, "*I said*, we've got Grand Funk Railroad here!" Finally, the crowd responded with cheers. Then we hit our opening song. I think we did "Big Leg Woman," because that's what Freddie always liked to play first.

There was another memorable night when we played at an outdoor festival. It was hot and muggy and everyone had been out in the sun all day. It was getting to be toward the end of the day, and everyone in the crowd was overheated. We hit the stage hard and were fired up as usual, and the crowd started chanting, "Make it rain, Freddie! Make it rain! Make it rain!" So Freddie hit one of those high notes and pointed his guitar toward the sky. Next thing we heard a big crash of thunder followed by rain! Everybody started cheering. It was great.

We played the 1973 Montreux Jazz Festival, and I did double duty by also playing bass for piano legend Memphis Slim, who didn't bring a band with him. That was an experience! His voice was so strong he could perform without a microphone. We used Freddie's drummer, Charles "Sugar Boy" Myers, and we had the great Mickey Baker on guitar (like Memphis Slim, Mickey had left the States behind long before that to live in Europe). That was when the Watergate scandal was raging, and Slim sang "Watergate Blues" to commemorate the occasion. The performance was recorded and came out on a record called ***Memphis Slim Very Much Alive and In Montreux!.***

Freddie knew Slim because he'd played with him just before Slim moved overseas. He'd gone on the road with Freddie and gotten sick up there somewhere. I think it was in Michigan. Every time we played in Paris, Slim would pick us up in his Rolls-Royce and take us out. Willie Mabon, another expatriate Chicago blues pianist, would hang with us too. I'd first met Willie back home when I saw him playing the local clubs.

I never was a marijuana smoker, and I'm still not. But when we played Gainesville, Florida, everybody around there was pulling and toking on marijuana cigarettes. They kept telling me, "Come on, man, you've got to try this here, man! Get in the groove. Get in the groove!" I told them, "Okay, okay, I'll get in the groove."

Album credits should be Charles Myers on drums and me on bass

Not only did I smoke marijuana for the first time that day, I smoked the best marijuana they had. We've got about four or five thousand people out there, and we're on the stage playing. We're all doing our thing as usual. Freddie 's out there doing his thing, and the music is supposed to stop, and I do a solo on the bass and then everybody comes back in. So Freddie's playing and then stops--and nothing! He's still looking out at the people, waiting for my bass solo.

Freddie finally realized that there wasn't any music coming from behind him, and then he turned around and looked at me. I was standing there scratching my head and thinking: "How in the hell does this thing go?" I was thinking and thinking and I could not remember how the thing went, despite having played it for years. So Freddie realized that I had forgotten it. He came from the microphone all the way back to where I was standing, got in my face, and started to sing and tell me how it went! I was looking at Freddie as he gave me the "Boom, boom, boom" beat with his eyes wide and his jaws flapping up and down with each "boom." I started laughing, which made Freddie start laughing. Then, bam! It came to me, and I started playing. Man, all of those people in the crowd went up! It was the best part of the night. This is just another example of how Freddie was on the stage. He liked to have fun.

My brother smoked cigarettes for years, and his cigarette of choice was Viceroys. I never will forget it. Freddie would tell me, "Go get me a pack of Viceroys." I said, "Freddie man, you know how you're coughing? That's why you're coughing, because of those cigarettes." He said, "Man, you know, you might be right." And then he'd come in smoking. I'd say, "Man, you didn't put the cigarettes down." This went on and on and on and on. Finally he said, "Okay, okay, I'm gonna stop." So he put his cigarettes down, and he would chew gum instead. If he wanted a cigarette, he'd get him a piece of gum and he would chew it. I got him off the cigarettes. In the Leon Russell days, Freddie came by the hotel to pick me up. We were going somewhere. I walked out of the hotel, and I had a cigarette in my hand. He said, "Ain't that a bitch?" I said, "What?" He said, "You done got me off the cigarettes, and then you're standing there with a cigarette!" I threw that cigarette away, and I took the package and I threw it away too. And I never picked up another one.

The baddest band we ever had was me, Deacon on organ, Charlie Robinson on drums, and David Maxwell on piano. We were in

Boston, and we had just played the Jazz Workshop. Maxwell had come out to see the show and asked to sit in. Freddie said yes. David started playing, and I said to myself, "Goddamn, this man can play!" After the show, Freddie asked, "What do you think about him?" I said, "Man, I thought people that played like him, all those guys were dead!" He said, "Yeah, man, we'll just take him." So we hired David right there.

Maxwell stayed in trouble. He was just like Dennis the Menace, but we loved him. We were getting ready to go play with B.B. King in Las Cruces. And he and Ernest, our organist right then, were in Denton while we were in Dallas. So Freddie left first, and he said, "You bring the band up." I said okay. We had an old Dodge van. So I got everybody that was leaving from Dallas in the van, and then we went to Denton to pick up Maxwell and Ernest. When we got there, Maxwell was in a local bar, playing the piano drunk. I told him, "Maxwell, it's time to go. We got a ways to drive. We ain't got much time. It's time to go."

"I'll be there," said Maxwell. "I'll be right on."

We sat there for about five or ten minutes, and he and Ernest are not coming. So I go back. Maxwell was on the piano, playing a blues song that he liked to sing, something about a Greyhound bus that he had written. I said, "Maxwell! Let's go, man!"

"I'll be out! I'll be out!"

"Okay—well, you've got ten minutes."

So I go back, get in the van, start the van up. Ten minutes go by, no Maxwell. I said, "Y'all lock the doors." Click, click. I took off. I left them there and I went on to the gig. When we arrived, Freddie was standing outside with both hands on his hips. He said, "Where's Maxwell?" I told him, "Maxwell's in Denton. I left him in Denton because I waited around for 30 minutes and he wouldn't come." He said, "You did the right thing." So two of B.B.'s band members played with us that night, filling in for Maxwell and Ernest. They finally did get there. They had driven up in Ernest's beat-up old van, with the engine knocking when they arrived. But Freddie said, "Y'all got here on your own, you're going back in that too." I don't think Ernest's van even made it back to Dallas. It wasn't in good shape. I'm sure they learned a good lesson.

We had fun, but we had rules. Maxwell wasn't the only one who got left behind over the years.

Maxwell had a beef at one gig, and he and I got into it. Freddie said, "That's between them." So he stood outside the door while me and Maxwell were inside. Well, of course I kicked Maxwell's ass. I'm not going to say why we were fighting. I'll just say we had a misunderstanding, and we fixed it. But Freddie stood outside the door until we fixed it. He didn't allow anything outside the family. So he stood out there, and we didn't let nobody in the door. Then when it was over, it was over. Maybe some of the guys in the band knew, but nobody else did. We argued it out right there. We were professional about whatever we did. We had fun, but we were professional.

Jack Calmes always wanted us not to dress like your typical blues band, and he would compliment us if I wore a top hat. He'd say, "That's the way you ought to dress, like that!" When we played on the television program ***Don Kirshner's Rock Concert***, Maxwell had a zebra suit on that his girlfriend had made for him. I had tall boots where you could flip them down, like power boots, and I think I wore a cape, although I might have taken it off. We had platform shoes on, including Freddie. It was a sight!

When we were gigging in Campbell, California, Maxwell had been drinking as usual. Freddie was dancing around on guitar. He was playing "Hide Away." Maxwell was playing, and all of a sudden Freddie looked around, and Maxwell wasn't

Freddie wakes up Maxwell. Illustration by Kay Johnson

playing anymore. He was sitting there at the piano with his head down and was sound asleep. Freddie danced all the way over while he was doing "The Walk." He tapped Maxwell on the head with his guitar, and that woke him up and he fell right back into the groove!

Kay and Virginia Johnson, the Native American women who designed Freddie 's belt with the naked ladies on it as well as some of his jewelry, were there. They made an illustration commemorating the occasion. We laughed about that for a long time, including Maxwell too! Maxwell left Freddie's band during the summer of '73.

"Benny was the anchor. He was sort of like the de facto band-leader," recalled Maxwell shortly before his 2015 death. "Benny kept the band together rhythmically. He really kept it driving."

Charlie Robinson

Charlie got fired after a gig at the Cotton Bowl in Dallas. I have no idea what happened between Freddie and Charlie. Freddie was a heavy drinker. Later on, when he was sick and had to tell the doctors about his habits, he was drinking a bottle of gin a day. But I never saw him off-center or anything, except at the Cotton Bowl. When he came there, he staggered once or twice. I thought to myself, "What's wrong with Freddie?" I'd never seen him like that. He was pissed off about something, and something went down between him and Charlie. So after the gig, he sent Charlie home. I can't remember if we ever got him back. I hated to see Charlie go, because with myself, Charlie, and Deacon, we were the fire behind Freddie.

We got Calep Emphrey, Jr., one of Charlie's successors on drums, from Little Milton. Musicians followed the best-paying gigs. Milton wasn't paying that much and Freddie was paying better than Milton so he came with us. He drove all the way from Mississippi to Dallas to audition for the Freddie King band. Freddie would always come and ask me, "What do you think?" I watched how Calep did his hi-hat. Everything was on time. He was a very good drummer. I loved Calep. I said, "Man, this guy's a bitch!" Freddie told me, "Okay, we got him.

We're hiring him!" So we took him overseas. Calep later spent a long stretch with B.B. King's band.

Just like the first time I played with Freddie back in Chicago, we never brought a set list onstage. We'd just call out a tune. Nothing was organized. Everything was strictly ad-libbed. We took on a female singer named Sexy Bull at one point, and I rehearsed the band for her. But Freddie and the band never, ever rehearsed. You jumped on the stage and you'd start playing.

We had many rhythm guitar players over the years. Most were great, but a few were not. Our least favorite had gigged with James Cotton for a minute before he played with us at the Armadillo in Austin, although later on he tried to make people believe he had played a whole lot with us. His name sounded a lot like that of Greg Poulos, a guitar player out of Sarasota, Florida who played with us at the end, and this other guy took advantage of that. Anyway, he got onstage with us at the Armadillo that night, and he kept rushing time. His timing was bad and I told Freddie, "I can't play with the dude. He rushes time." Freddie didn't like rushing either. He said, "Well, we're not going to take him to England then." The guy later tried to sue me and Freddie because we didn't want to take him to England.

Not only that, but I was down at the Armadillo one day with a couple of the guys, working on a song I had just written to get ready to do my first demo, and this same guitarist walked in, got onstage, and played with me even though I hadn't invited him. When he walked up with his guitar, since he was part of the band right then, I just figured, "Why not?" We usually played a run of two or three nights in a row at the Armadillo, and saxophone great David "Fathead" Newman was with us that time too. Alvin Hemphill was on keys.

Fathead offered to help after he heard my ideas, and he brought a friend of his because he thought we needed two horns. He and I drove all over Austin in his Cadillac talking to his fellow horn players and looking for someone who was available. I still have the demo around somewhere. Anyway, the guitar player ended up demanding money for being on "Benny's first album," in addition to the money he wanted from Freddie because he allegedly bought uniforms and things to go to England as well as for breach of promise. Man, we went through a deal. He filed a big suit. He had a claim as thick as a Chicago phone book. Of course, it didn't go anywhere, but what an ordeal, man. That was one of the guys that couldn't play.

When we played at the El Mocambo up in Toronto, we had a roadie, a white guy from California, who was pissed off because all the girls were chasing the band. I wasn't the only one they had their eyes on, but he was particularly pissed off at me. We were in the dressing room getting ready to play, and he pulled a knife on me. I had just gotten up to go do our set, and he drew the knife back as if he was going to throw it at me. I put my bass in front of me for protection and I told him, "If you miss, then I'm gonna kill you with this bass!" So I drew it back like a batter in a baseball game, and he ducked. I said, "I mean what I'm saying!"

So he folded up his knife, which was a big one, and put it back in its holster on his belt. We went on and played our show. The next night, we were coming from the hotel to the venue. Me and Freddie always walked together. Out of the blue, he said, "How come you didn't tell me that guy pulled a knife on you last night?" I said, "Ain't no big deal. I took care of it."

"Yeah, but I don't want nobody pulling a knife on you."

I said, "It's alright."

He said, "Yeah, but I don't want nobody pulling a knife on you!"

"Okay, okay, okay."

So we went in and played our set. Everything seemed alright. Then we went down to play at the place where we first saw Maxwell, the Jazz Workshop in Boston. We were going to pack up to go to London the next day. The same roadie was still with us, and he was throwing the drum cases around. Freddie said, "Watch out, man. Those are instruments." Then all of a sudden the guy threw a guitar case and pushed it to the side, and Freddie said, "I told you—do not throw the instruments around!" That roadie stood up and said, "Well, fuck, man!" As it turned out, Freddie was still pissed off about that incident with the knife, and this was his breaking point.

Freddie picked him up by the neck about two or three feet off the ground, walked into the bathroom with him, and he had the guy up against the wall, choking him. I went into the bathroom right behind Freddie and when I saw the look in his eyes and the way he was gritting his teeth, I knew he was going to kill the guy. So I grabbed Freddie's hand and started to peel his fingers away, one by one, all while quietly saying, "Freddie, don't kill him. Don't kill him."

Just before Freddie let him go, he slapped him. Freddie wore a big turquoise ring on his pointing finger. He slapped that guy so hard that his ring flew off his finger, hit all four walls, and bounced right back to him. Then he let the guy go, and the guy dropped to the floor. Freddie looked down at him and said, "If you ever pull a knife on my brother again, I'll kill you!" And he walked out. That was the end of that guy's job as a roadie with us. He didn't know how close he came to dying. Well, maybe he did. Even today when I think back, it scares me to think how close Freddie came to killing that guy. Freddie was a fun-loving, great guy, but don't fuck with his family. It's pretty funny that I ended up saving the life of the guy who wanted to hurt me to begin with!

Jeff Miller, who was Leon Russell's roadie, decided to go to work for Freddie. We had a cube van where two people sat in front and all the equipment was stored in the back. Jeff pulled it into the parking lot of the Holiday Inn on Lake Shore Drive in Chicago, and not paying much attention to what he was doing, he opened the back and got our clothes and whatever else we wanted out of the van. Instead of him backing the van into the wall, he just left it out like that, not knowing that the parking lot attendants were watching. Then I went home to Markham. One of the guys called me the next morning and said, "Hey, man, somebody went in the van and got all of our stuff!" They got our guitars. They got everything but one of Freddie's snakeskin platform shoes. Freddie picked up that shoe, walked out into the middle of Lake

Shore Drive, and threw it down the road, yelling, "Here's something you missed!"

That wasn't the only time we got ripped off. I had a maxi-coat, a denim coat that I had sewed myself, and man, it was really, really nice. It was made of different colored denim patches, and it went all the way to the floor. I had people in the airport stopping me, even designers, asking, "Where did you get this coat from?" I said, "I made this coat!" We went in for sound check at a college in Brussels, and I put it in the room with Freddie's coat. The lady that was the concert promoter, she had a sable coat. Freddie had a briefcase there full of money, and there was other valuable stuff around. But this particular thief wanted my coat, and that sable coat that the lady had. He raised the window, slipped inside the room we were dressing in, and stole my coat and her sable coat and left everything else. That was a heartbreaker. I'd made it myself, and it was one-of-a-kind.

We also lost all our gear in Boston, but it wasn't to thieves. We were in the dressing room of a club where we were headlining, playing cards as usual, and Freddie had a bottle of gin on the table. The owner was up there too. He said, "Well, how are you doing, Mr. King?" Freddie said, "I'm doing alright." Freddie had already gotten the word that this guy may pay you, and he may not. So Freddie decided to ask for his money every night after the gig. I think we were playing two or three nights. He said, "I play this gig tonight, I want that amount of money," and then he wanted to be paid the next third the next night, like that.

The guy said, "I don't pay like that. I'll pay you at the end of the engagement."

Freddie said, "No, no, no. I want my money every night I play. Just give me my money, what I've got coming that night."

"I'm not going to do that!" he replied.

Freddie said, "Look, I told you--if I play, I want to get paid nightly!"

The owner had something of a temper, and he picked up that bottle of gin that Freddie had on the table and banged it down on the table and busted that bottle. Freddie said, "I don't care how many tantrums you're gonna have, but when you settle down, I want my money."

We went over to the hotel after the show, and about nine o'clock that morning, Mighty Joe Young, who was scheduled to play the place after us, knocked on my door. "Hey, man!" Mighty Joe said. "How y'all doing?" I looked out the door and said, "We're doing alright." He said, "You better get on down to the club, because it's on fire!" I said, "What?" He said, "The place is on fire! Y'all left your stuff in there, and I think it's gonna get burned up!"

So we jumped in the van and went down there, and sure enough, everything burned up, Freddie's guitar and everything. The neck burned off my bass. It was a fretless bass, and I was proud of it even though it was always out of tune. I went and got what was left of it and put it on the bus, and then we left and went to New York because we were supposed to play Carnegie Hall. Of course, we didn't get to play because we didn't have anything to play on. We were at the gate for the load-in and expected to find our gear but it didn't arrive on time. We were disappointed because it would have been cool to play Carnegie Hall. Instead, we went on to the next gig after that, where Jack Calmes had full gear waiting for us.

Armadillo World Headquarters, Austin, TX

When we'd roll into Austin to play the Armadillo, all the other shows around town that night would just shut down because they knew everyone was coming to see us. We stayed at the Austin Motel right down the street, and the people that would come see our show would nearly fill it up. One night we were getting ready to go to the gig. Me, Deacon, and Freddie always went together. Deacon's room was next to mine, and we were walking towards Freddie's room, which was

139

on the second floor. Deacon had a Canfield's 50/50 bottle that he mixed his gin and Cokes in. He's walking and carrying that, and we're all dressed up and headed to Freddie's room. There was a good old boy standing by the Coke machine. He called out to us, "You niggers sure look good tonight!"

Visiting the Austin Motel, 2016. Photo by Derek O'Brien

We kept on walking, talking about this and that, paying no attention. Then Deacon and I stopped at the same time and looked at each other. "What did he say?"

And the guy said, "That's right, you heard me! You niggers sure look good tonight!"

Meanwhile, there was a car waiting on the guy with two of his buddies inside, and the passenger door was open. I had a Coke, so I threw it up and hit Freddie's door to get his attention. He came out and said, "What's goin' on? What's goin' on?" I said, "We've got a couple of guys down here messing with us!" Freddie said, "Just a minute!" He walked in his room for a minute and came back out shooting. He was shooting to the left, shooting to the right. He was just shooting. The eyes on the guy by the Coke machine got as big as can be. He said, "Goddamn!"

Then the guys in the car yelled, "Come on, let's go!" They started to drive away with the door open and the guy running alongside, trying to jump in. In the meantime, me and Deacon were running behind the car. I said, "Deacon throw the bottle!" He said, "But man, I just mixed this!" I said, "Throw the bottle! Throw the bottle!" He said, "Yeah man, but this is my gin!" Just as the car was getting ready to leave the parking lot, Deacon stopped and said, "Fuck it!" He threw the bottle, and it sailed like a football. It went right in the car, straight across the dashboard, and busted the windshield. It was the perfect shot! The guy finally made it inside the car, tires screeching and everything as they made their getaway. We went on down to the Armadillo and we played. Freddie had left his brown Cadillac at the motel because we didn't need it. Sure enough, when we came back later that night, all four of the tires were slashed.

Another time when we had just played the Armadillo, Fathead came on by the Austin Motel. You could park around back. We had decided to come on back to the motel and get the poker game going, and just as we made a left turn to go around to the back, we heard a car horn blaring. I said, "Damn, what's that?" A Cadillac horn was loud. We turned the corner to go into the motel parking lot, and there's Fathead in his Cadillac. All the doors were open, the lights were lit, and he's lying in the seat with his knees on the horn and all of his clothes off. I jumped out of the car and I went over and shook him. "Fathead! Fathead! He woke up. "Huh? Huh?" He started searching his pockets, which wasn't easy because he didn't have his underwear on. There was a little ditch right behind the car, and Fathead had not only thrown his clothes in that ditch, he'd thrown his horns in there too. So he had to go fishing. Normally the neighbors would call the cops for something like that, but I guess we got lucky that night.

Freddie's pistol got him in trouble on another occasion. We had just played somewhere in New Mexico, and he and I got up to go to catch the plane. I don't know what happened to the band. They may have taken the bus and left on their own, and Freddie and I were going to fly. Freddie got to the airport before I did, and got into line. Before long, I got a call from him: "Man, they got me locked up down here at the airport. I forgot that my pistol was in my bag, and they arrested me." So I went down there to the airport, and he was in a room. I told him, "Well, I tell you what—I'm not going to leave you here. I'm gonna go back and hang out in the hotel room, and you just let me know when you're ready, and I'll come back and get you." And that's what happened. He knew he had made a mistake, so he wasn't pissed off or anything.

Even dropping by a party could be dangerous. We were in San Antonio, staying at different hotels, and I was supposed to pick Freddie up in the morning. I had the car. I pulled up to the motel where Freddie had been partying and hit the horn. Freddie peeked his head out the door.

He said, "Hey, man, bring me some clothes!"

I said, "You got clothes!"

"Man, bring me some clothes!"

"You got clothes! Put those on and we can change later."

I got inside, and Freddie didn't have a stitch. Someone had taken Freddie's clothes, coat, and briefcase after he fell asleep and walked out. I said, "That must have been some party you had last night!" We laughed about that for years.

One time between tours when everyone went home to rest, I was back in Chicago and feeling really good to be off the road for awhile. I had a habit of getting in my car and taking a drive to relax not long after getting home. At this time I was driving a practically brand new 1972 Cadillac Eldorado. I was enjoying a nice drive around town when all of a sudden I heard sirens. So much for relaxation--I was getting pulled over. The cop came up to the door and I rolled down the window. First thing out of his mouth was, "Hey boy, where did you steal this car?" And do you think I had any chance of defending myself? Needless to say, I ended up in jail. Not 24 hours earlier, I was on stage rocking in the spotlights, and now it was back to the harsh reality that Jim Crow was still alive and well.

Freddie's contract with Leon and Shelter eventually ran its course, and he signed with Robert Stigwood's RSO Records. London always did have a soft spot for Freddie. Jack Calmes put the deal together. It was a good one, and they were nice people. Stigwood loved to party, and he took care of us when we came overseas, chauffeuring us around in limousines. He'd also sit down and try to play poker with us. Notice I said "try." I think the last time I played poker with him, it was when we played the Bottom Line in New York. That's where I met Richard Pryor. He was real polite. He called me sir: "Hello, sir."

There was a song on ***Larger Than Life***, Freddie's first RSO album in 1975, that I really liked called "It's Your Move." Freddie loved "Big Leg Woman" and usually called it out as his opening number onstage. I said, "I know what I'm gonna do. I'm gonna bring him up with a different song tonight." So I got the band together and went over "It's Your Move." And we hit that just like the record was. I think it's a great song. So Freddie came up and played it, and boy, you would have thought it was the best song of all time, the way he played it. When he ended it, he walked backwards, all the way back to where I was, and whispered in my ear, "Big Leg Woman!" I just laughed. I couldn't talk him into changing it.

Eric Clapton was also on RSO and that gave Freddie a chance to record and tour with him. They became close friends. We went and played in London, and Eric came out and sat in. He just stood in the back. He wasn't trying to be Eric Clapton or anything. He just came in and stood there, played a few songs, and then he left. He was crazy about Freddie.

Deacon remembers that he and I wrote two songs together that were supposed to be on Freddie's next album for RSO. One of them was called "Together," and Freddie even tried it out onstage one night, looking over at Deacon with a big grin on his face as if to tell him that he was already rehearsing it in preparation for the studio. Jack Calmes had told Deacon and I to get our things ready to produce Freddie's next record. Unfortunately, Freddie would never get around to recording our songs.

We played a show at the Starwood in Los Angeles that was one of my most memorable gigs with Freddie (mind you, I said one of them--there were many). It was so amazing that Deacon and I called it the Super Jam. There on one stage were Eric Clapton on guitar, Joe Cocker, Noel Redding from Jimi Hendrix's band and I on bass (he and I played out of the same amp) and Buddy Miles on drums. Cocker was great as usual, but for me the high point was when Eric and Freddie played "Hide Away" together. Eric knew Freddie's notes so well that you couldn't tell it was two guitars playing at once. Freddie gave Deacon permission to tape that night's show, but after Freddie died, the tape came up missing.

We played another gig south of Los Angeles at an auditorium, and as we were getting ready to walk in the door, two marshals that served warrants walked up to Freddie. He didn't know who they were, but he knew something wasn't right.

"How do you do, sir," they began.

"All right. How you doing?" said Freddie.

"Are you Buddy Miles?"

Freddie said, "Yeah!" He was sharp. He had this street sense.

The marshals said, "We're serving you a warrant for child support."

Freddie said, "Okay." They gave him the warrant. So Freddie put it in his glove compartment. I don't know if Buddy ever knew that Freddie stood in for him like that. That was funny. I took a lot of that stuff out after he passed away.

On April 11, 1976, Freddie and I played duets for a captive audience when we were in Austin to play at the Armadillo: the inmates of Travis County Jail. He had to twist my arm to get me to do that. He said, "Man, come on! I want you to go down here with me, man. I don't want to go by myself." I said, "Where are you going?" He said, "Well, I'm going down here to play some music at this jail for my friend." Richard Halpin from the Jail Arts & Education Project had talked him into it.

I said, "Man, I don't want to go do that!" He said, "I just want you to go with me. I ain't making no money, but they've got to give me something, so they're giving me $100. I'll give you $50." I laughed, "Man!" He said, "Man, come on!" So I said, "Okay, okay." So we went down. They gave us two acoustic guitars. Freddie got one and I got the other. They took us up on the elevator and let us out. I said, "I don't have a pick." Someone handed me a coin to use. It could have been one of the prisoners, because I looked down at it and it said, "One Day At A Time." I think he played for the women first. A film crew was on hand to capture our duet versions of "Sweet Home Chicago" and "Let the Good Times Roll," which we performed for some very appreciative prisoners while strolling corridors from one cell to the next.

I'm so glad I decided to go that day, because it was the last time he and I played together, just the two of us, like we did way back when we were kids. Only eight-and-a-half months later, on December 28, 1976, Freddie passed away.

L to R: Charlie Robinson, John Hopkins (road mgr), me, Robert Griffin

1973

145

Poker with Freddie

Calep Emphrey, me and Edd Lively

Freddie and Edd Lively

L to R: Edd Lively, Calep Emphrey, Gary Carnes (road mgr) and me

In Paris with Freddie, July 1973. Photo © Jean-Pierre Arniac

On stage at The Armadillo with Freddie. Photo © Gary Dair Jones

Freddie, me, Edd Lively

7

THE DEATH OF FREDDIE AND JOINING MIGHTY JOE YOUNG

Death was an inevitable part of the blues scene. Little Walter left us in early 1968, and Magic Sam followed him out in late '69. Sam's death was a big surprise to everybody, because he was a young guy. We knew he was having problems though. He went into the service, and when he came out, he never was quite the same. Even so, we were really surprised when Sam died.

The mid-'70s were particularly rough. Cancer claimed Hound Dog Taylor in December of 1975, and the following month we lost the mighty Howlin' Wolf, who was so good to Freddie when he was just getting established on the Chicago circuit. I just loved Wolf's harmonica playing. I'll never forget that funeral. It wasn't all fire and brimstone, it was much more a celebration of his life. They had his music playing and everything. The preacher even quoted one of Wolf's lyrics, "He asked her for water and she gave him gasoline!"

One of my favorite memories of Wolf was when I was with Freddie on tour. We were on a show just across the line in Canada with Wolf and Big Mama Thornton, and we got snowed in. We were in the basement of the venue, and Freddie and Wolf were cracking on each other and talking. It was really a good night because nobody could go anywhere, so we all just had fun hanging out together. Big Mama was in rare form, just being herself. Eddie Shaw and I still laugh about it today. If I ever decide to follow this biography with a tell-all book, I'll be sure to write all about it. She was something!

We lost our dad around Christmas of '75. The injury he'd suffered when he was hit by that car years earlier eventually claimed him. We were up in Toronto performing at the El Mocambo when he took a turn for the worse, so I went to Chicago to see him. As we stood around talking, he told us that we should all look after my brother Carl, so he knew his days were short. I had to go back to Toronto to do the gig. When he passed away, me and Freddie went to Chicago for the funeral.

It was a Jehovah's Witness funeral, probably because of my Aunt Corinne's influence on my mother. I'm sure my dad wouldn't have enjoyed it, because he was like me—he didn't appreciate Aunt Corinne's strong influence on my mother. I was sitting at the service like everybody else. Freddie was behind me, and my close friends and my kids were all sitting with me. And they had the casket open. They started singing this song. You could hear my Aunt Corinne singing over everybody. Just about the time the song got ready to end, she would pick it up again. This went on and on and on. I'm sitting there, looking at my dad in the casket, and I said to myself, "Boy, if he could sit up, he'd tell my Aunt Corrine to shut her mouth!" And when I said that, it really hit me that he was gone and I started bawling. "Shut your goddamn mouth," that's exactly what he would have said to her. Then I lost it.

I took it hard at the funeral, and Freddie took it hard at the gravesite. He cried at Restvale Cemetery in south suburban Alsip, where our dad was buried that day. It's ironic that my dad had no musical ability at all--he couldn't even whistle or pat his feet--yet he's buried at the same cemetery as our old pals Muddy Waters, Earl Hooker, Magic Sam, Johnny Jones, and Hound Dog Taylor. He's in great company. At the gravesite afterwards, Freddie was sitting in the car and told me, "Yeah, you look like your homeboy." I asked him what he meant, and he said, "Johnny Mathis. That's your cousin." I don't know what made him say that, but I really wasn't surprised, because I knew my dad was half white, but never knew anything else about it. After my dad was gone, my mother wasn't able to care for my brother Carl, who suffered from severe cerebral palsy and required constant care which my mother couldn't provide. She had to put him in a home, which was a tough thing for all of us.

What I didn't realize was that Freddie's time on earth was growing short too. Looking back, several things happened that should have given me clues something was wrong, but I didn't read them. The first was when we were on the West Coast. Deacon and I got out of Freddie's black Cadillac, which he had just gotten. Deacon accidentally dropped his money and went on inside, and I picked it up. I looked at Freddie and said, "Deacon done dropped his money." He said, "Let him sweat awhile. Let him sweat. Get inside. I want to talk to you." So I got back in the car and sat down.

Freddie said, "I want you to know that anything I've got, you're welcome to. And I want you to know that you'll be taken care of. I want you to know that."

I said, "What are you talking about?"

He said, "Listen to me!"

"Man, I don't want to hear that stuff!"

"No, listen to me. Listen to me! You want my car, you come and get my car. Anything. My boat."

I said, "Boat?"

He said, "Yeah, I've got a boat." I didn't even know he had a boat.

He was telling me all of this stuff, and how I'm going to be taken care of. I said, "No, I don't understand that."

He raised his voice and said, "*Listen*! Just listen."

I said, "Alright, alright, alright," like I was paying him some attention. I was going on inside, and I said okay.

He said, "Are you hearing me?"

I said, "Yeah, I can hear you." Then I went on inside to give Deacon his money and didn't give our conversation another thought.

After that gig, we came back through Dallas, and he went to see my mother. She had moved back down to Gilmer because her Uncle Casero was kind of ailing and getting old, and he had things that needed looking after that he couldn't do. Chicago had been a hard life for my mother. She wasn't working or anything, and we couldn't support her. Early on, Freddie was going to provide for the family, but he had his own family to provide for, so he couldn't. So my mother decided to go and live with my

Mother's Uncle Casero Criddle

uncle, and that's where she lived out her days, right there. That's where Freddie went to talk to her when he was scared about something.

She called me Junior. She said, "Junior, I'm worried about Fred." I said, "What do you mean?" She said, "I'm worried about him. He came to see me." That was at 512 Miller Street, where she lived in Gilmer. She said, "We sat in the car and talked. We didn't even go in the house. We sat in the car and talked, and he cried and he cried." I think she said he was worried about his stomach. What do you do when you really get scared? You go home to Mama, you know? But at the time, I still didn't put two and two together. I said, "Okay, okay," because Freddie didn't ever say anything to me about his stomach.

On the way back South, we stopped in New Orleans for a gig. It was a normal night. We were playing "Hide Away," and Freddie keeled over. He passed out while he was playing guitar on the stage. He fell off the stage onto his back on the floor. The stage was about two feet off the floor. Deacon jumped off the organ to see what was wrong, but Freddie immediately came to, got up and finished the song. After he finished the song, we came down on a break. He went in the back by the cigarette machine, and I followed him. I said, "Man, how are you doing? Are you okay?" "I'm alright," he told me. "I kind of hurt my tailbone."

So we went on to Sarasota. We stopped at our rhythm guitarist Greg Poulos' house and he showed us around, then we played a big gig. On the way back to Dallas, we were on the bus playing poker like we normally did. "Okay, y'all. Everybody listen up. I want y'all to know that I'm giving everybody a Christmas bonus this year!" We looked at each other and said, "What's wrong with Freddie? He doesn't give anybody a bonus!" And we laughed it off. That was the final clue he gave that something was wrong.

In Sarasota, FL with our last rhythm guitar player, Greg Poulos

Then we got back to Dallas, and we played at the New York Ballroom on Christmas night of 1976. I walked in the dressing room, and Freddie had a bottle of gin sitting on the table. He was sitting there by himself.

I asked him, "Are you alright?"

"Yeah, I'm okay," he said. "I'm okay."

"Okay, it's about time to start the show."

So we got up and we did the show, and everything went fine. I got ready to leave, and did something that I never do. I got the poster from the show, folded it and put it on the bus. To this day I don't know what made me do that, because I never collected our posters, but that night I did.

Then I walked over to Freddie's Cadillac to say goodbye. He was having a meeting, but he rolled the passenger window down so we could talk. I looked at him and I said, "Take it easy now! No arguing or fighting

On stage at the New York Ballroom for Freddie's last gig

Poster from Freddie's last gig. I was with him when he played his first note, and I was with him when he played his last note

about nothing." He said, "Okay!" He gave me the thumbs up and laughed. And he went on to hang out at Mother Blues. A couple days later, I called the house to speak to Freddie. His wife said, "He's in the hospital. You'd better get on down there and see about him."

I got to the hospital and found him in intensive care. He was in the emergency room, and the lady there told me, "You can't go in." I said, "Bullshit!" I kicked the door in and I went in. I'm glad they didn't have security at that time. They had him wired up, tubes running out of him. I said, "Damn, what happened?" He said, "Man, I like to have been gone." I said, "Gone? What do you mean?" And he said, "I don't think I'm going to be able to get out of here in time. You take the band and do the gig

157

at Cain's Ballroom. And be sure to take Deacon. I said, "Okay." And he told me that he had a big check in one of his dresser drawers back home, and to make sure his wife cashed that check.

Then the nurse came in, and Freddie asked her what his blood pressure was. It was a low number, and when she did that he just kind of shook his head, like, "Damn!" Then the lady pushed me back out of the room. As it turned out, that was the last time we talked and the last time I saw him alive.

His wife called me the next day and said, "You better go down and see if you can snap him out of it." When I got there, John Henry Branch, Freddie's long-time friend and promoter of his last gig, was in the waiting room, and he started talking about the old blues people that had alcohol problems, that went into the D.T.'s. He was connecting whatever Freddie was having with the D.T.'s. He named off a couple of the old musicians and said, "Don't worry about it. He's going to be alright, because a lot of people had this here." He named off some more names and said, "Everybody came back, and they were alright. You just have to go through it."

Just about the time he said that, the doctors started running into Freddie's room. Then they came back out and went straight to his wife and said, "Mrs. King, he had a rough night, and we lost him."

Goddamn.

"What? Oh, man!"

It took a while for me to come down off of that. They let us go in, and I touched my brother on the face. He was gone. He'd had a blood clot, but Jack Calmes put out a story that claimed Freddie had hepatitis. I didn't know anything about that.

That was the second time in my life that I decided to smoke marijuana. I was staying with a friend, and I told my friend to roll me a joint when I walked through the door. I just wanted to get fucked up and escape. It took me a couple of days for it to register that Freddie was really gone. Then my mind went back, starting from California to Florida, and I realized, "He was trying to tell me! Yeah, he was trying to tell me, and I didn't listen." I wish I had. There were a lot of things I would have liked to have said.

Freddie died December 28, 1976. He was buried in Sparkman Hillcrest Memorial Park in Dallas. It was a closed casket ceremony. I served as a pallbearer.

A King of the blues passes from the scene

By SEAN MITCHELL
Staff Writer

Freddie King led the way for more electric guitarists than we'll ever be able to count. He was a blues virtuoso, a musician's musician, a riveting performer, a sight to behold. The London Times once described him as "a huge, stooping man like a nonconformist preacher frosted with black ice." Sometimes referred to as "The Texas Cannonball," he was even more popular in Europe than in his homeland. Eric Clapton once said that Freddie King was the reason he took up the guitar.

When he died Tuesday in a Dallas hospital, Freddie King was considered the chief Texas exponent of the famous electric blues style molded in Chicago in the early 1950s. It was a style that produced such artists as Muddy Waters, Buddy Guy and B. B. King, and influenced a whole generation of rock guitarists, among them Steve Miller, Jimmy Page and Jeff Beck.

Born in Gilmer, King moved to Chicago when he was 18, and had made Dallas his home since 1962. At his death he was 42.

Funeral services were scheduled for 1 p.m. today at the Munger Avenue Baptist Church. Burial was to follow at Hillcrest Memorial Park. Pallbearers included King's manager, Jack Calmes, brother Benny Turner, his old booking agent, John Henry Branch, and guitarist Bugs

Henderson. Honorary pallbearers were listed as musicians B. B. King, Albert King, Muddy Waters, Tyrone Davis, Carl Radle and Johnnie Taylor.

It is still not clear exactly how King died, though Jack Calmes explained, "We think he died from heart failure." According to Calmes, King became ill late Sunday night and went to Presbyterian Hospital at 2 a.m. to get some medication. He then returned to his residence at 7703 Morton in the Love Field area. At 6 a.m. he went back to the hospital and was admitted. He remained at Presbyterian and died at 5 p.m. Tuesday.

Heart failure was believed to have been caused by internal bleeding and a blood clot detected in his leg. No autopsy was performed.

King had a history of ulcer problems, Calmes said, but was otherwise thought to have been in good health. A large man, he had lost weight in the past year and was observed to be in good shape by several people who saw him play at the New York Ballroom on Hall Street Christmas night. It turned out to be his last performance.

Although he was well known in musical circles, King never achieved the fame of fellow blues men B. B. King and Albert King (both older and no relation). His biggest hit, "Hideaway," recorded for King Federal Records in Cincinnati, came early in his career. The

See A KING on Page 13

Freddie King as he appeared on stage in a recent concert

Fellow musicians serve as pallbearers at simple rites for blues guitarist Freddie King

King eulogy links blues, religion

By SEAN MITCHELL
Staff Writer

Several hundred mourners, both black and white, filled the Munger Avenue Baptist Church Friday afternoon to hear a funeral service for blues guitarist Freddie King. A resident of Dallas since 1962, King died Tuesday in a Dallas

were simple. The only music was provided by a small section of the church's regular choir, which sang two hymns before the Rev. Rowe delivered the eulogy.

At the height of his sermon the Rev. Rowe remarked that the blues and the gospel had a lot in common. "There's a

ling Ready," was borrowed appropriately enough from the title of one of King's last record albums.

Many local musicians who had played with King through the years were in attendance, including Bugs Henderson, Lee Pickens and Showco president Jack Calmes. Also present was a representa-

Republic." The funeral procession, led by King's wife, Jessie, and their seven children, then proceeded to the graveside, where the performer was laid to rest. Among the pallbearers were Calmes, Henderson, Pickens, and King's brother Benny Turner.

who has been King's man-

People from all over the world sent flowers, but what really caught my eye during the service was an arrangement sent by James Cotton, in the shape of a wagon wheel. It was really appropriate for Freddie being a "Country Boy." When we got to the gravesite, my mother pulled me aside and spoke up. She said, "Junior, I didn't get to see him. I want to see him." So I went over to Freddie's wife and asked her, and she agreed to it. When they opened the casket, people started going over to view him, and my brother Jerry kissed him goodbye. It broke my heart when my mother saw him and said, "Fred, I didn't want to see you like this."

J.T. Christian, Freddie's birth father, attended the funeral. Freddie didn't really hold a grudge, and he respected the Christians. They lived around Candlestick Park in San Francisco. We would go out there, and

Freddie would meet his father, talk and have dinner, and hang out with him. He was getting back together with his dad. So when Freddie died, I knew he would want me to bring his father down to Dallas. I think that was the first time J.T. saw my mother since he deserted her when Freddie was a baby. I checked them out, and they didn't have that much to say to each other. Getting through the services was difficult enough, but the hardest was to come once all that was over.

During that time, Johnnie Taylor came by Freddie's house to pay his respects. It was the first time I had seen him since we sat together at Sam Cooke's funeral. Johnnie, Freddie and Tyrone Davis were best friends. Not only that, but Johnnie and I had both sung with The Soul Stirrers, so we were connected in more ways than one. He reached out and invited me to play with him. After everything was over, I went to Johnnie's office to have a chat, and when I got there he was sitting behind the desk smoking a cigarette. I never saw him in that role before and said, "Well, look at you!" and he and I both started laughing. It was funny to see him like that. He turned me over to his right-hand man, Fisher, to get all of the details about me playing in his band. Fisher arranged a rehearsal, and everybody showed up except Johnnie. As nice as he was to offer me a place in the band, my heart really wasn't in it anyway, so that was all I needed for a way out. I was packed up and out the door in a New York second!

The next person to reach out to me was Renata Coe, a relative of the original Rhinestone Cowboy, country singer David Allan Coe. She was a huge fan of Freddie and his band, and also his friend. Renata was with Channel 13 in Dallas. When Freddie passed away, she called me and said, "You know, your brother would want you to take the band and go on with the band." I said, "Yeah, I know that." I was going along with it just to carry on a conversation, not because I really wanted to. She said, "Come on and go with me. I'm going to take you over to where David Allan's publicist is."

She took me over, and while I was standing there, the publicist came up to us. He had David Allan's stuff all laid out, posters and things all laid out on the tables. He said, "I tell you what we can do—I've got it right here. You've got Freddie King stepping out of his shoes, and you can put your foot right in his shoes." The cat was quick, and he was good. And I said yeah, and Renata said, "We'll let you use one of David's Double Eagle buses, and you can travel in that." And I'm saying "Yeah," but it's going in one ear and out the other. I wasn't taking it seriously. Although it was really a wonderful gesture, my heart just wasn't in it. She took me back to the hotel, and I just headed on back to Chicago. I was so heartbroken that I couldn't even think about nothing else.

Reality kind of set in slowly. I realized we weren't going to any more gigs, and we weren't going to get on the bus and play cards ever again. I had lost my brother, my best friend and my bandmate all at once. The things that we used to do, whether they were happy days or not, we weren't going to be doing those anymore. Slowly but surely, I went into a deep depression that lasted for two years. I lost weight and my energy level sank.

Out of habit, I would get in my old white Toronado that I won in the poker game and I'd drive to Dallas to see some of my old friends. I'd always go see my friend Hop and hang out with him at the junkyard, where Freddie used to spend some of his happiest times. Johnnie Taylor always used to say, "I don't know why Freddie likes to hang out at the junkyard." But I knew. When Freddie was at the junkyard, he felt like a king. When his Cadillac would come around the corner, everybody would start heading for the junkyard to see Freddie, even people from the bottom. When he was with Johnnie and Tyrone, he was just one of the guys. Hop and I spent many nights talking about old times on the road.

Then I'd drive back to Chicago. I'd drive back to Dallas, and back to Chicago again. I was just going back and forth. I didn't really have any aim or purpose. I just was not getting over the death of my brother. Once when I was in Dallas, I went to a movie with some friends of mine, and I was sitting in the theater and all of a sudden something hit me in the stomach and I had to leave. My friends asked what happened to me, and I said, "I just got sick or something." I couldn't sit there. So I said, "I'd better jump in the car and head on back to Chicago."

I started back to Chicago, and I got around the St. Louis area and I had to stop again. I went to the hospital. They put me in a room and they said, "One thing we know--you're upset about something. Something is bothering you." So they put me in a room, and they put the lights out. They said, "Just lay there." So I laid there, and I finally settled down. They said, "There's nothing we can do." So I said okay and I jumped back in the car and headed up to Chicago. Then I started having the same problems there, so they put me in Cook County Hospital for about five days. They said it was a nervous breakdown.

Finally they let me out, but I was losing weight and I couldn't even drink water. I mean, water would literally burn when I drank it. That's how bad I was. So I read a book that said if you've got any kind of problems with your gastrointestinal tract, eat cayenne pepper. I said, "You've got to be crazy! I can't drink water, and now you want me to eat cayenne pepper? Crazy as it sounds, I'm going to try it!" I was desperate. The book said, "It's going to hurt, but you keep on eating it

and you'll be fine." I wasn't eating anything but salads. I'd sprinkle cayenne pepper on those salads, and I started eating more and more and more. And it worked. Do you know to this day I can eat anything? There isn't anything I can't eat, and it started with that cayenne pepper. But it was a trip eating it for the first time. Then finally I started kind of coming back.

My brother Jerry bumped into Mighty Joe Young on the street one day.

Mighty Joe asked, "How's Benny doing?"

Jerry said, "He ain't doing so good."

"What do you mean?"

"He's just sitting at home."

Joe said, "What? Give me his phone number!"

Joe called me up and said, "Hey, man, you're too good to be sitting around like that. You've got to get out and do things."

I said, "I just don't feel like it, Joe."

"Hey, man! Look, why don't you come and play with me?"

"Joe, I ain't got the spirit, and I'm just not feeling well. I don't have no step or anything." "Come on, just try it for one night."

He sat there and talked to me and talked to me. I finally said, "Alright, Joe. Okay, Joe."

And my family in the background was clapping real quietly, saying, "Yeah, hope you do it! Hope you do it!"

The day of his show, Joe came all the way out to my home in Markham in Chicago's southern suburbs. He picked me up and drove us all the way to Biddy Mulligan's, a club on Chicago's far North Side. My kin was standing in the window when I left, giving me the salute like when you're going off to war. I got to Biddy's and played my first set, and I was so weak when it was over that I got down and sat on the stage. Then I leaned back and laid on the stage until Joe got ready for his next set, but I made the night. Joe said, "You can do it! You can do it!" He got me back home, and my family was still waiting on me. They said, "You made it! You made it!" Then Joe called me again. I made another gig and another gig. Mighty Joe was the one that brought me back. He was a good guy and a really great friend. I said, "Yeah, cool! It looks like I'm going to be alright!" I was with Joe for eight years.

Mighty Joe was easy-going. Nobody was ever upset with Mighty Joe. He went out there to have fun. He and I were a little bit different, because Joe could be not feeling good, and yet he would go out and play his guitar and always have a smile on his face. He could relate to the people, for some reason. You can't miss when you do that. You make people feel good. Joe didn't just stick to regular 12-bar blues, either. He liked to do some funky things too.

Joe treated the musicians okay. He did have problems with the bass player that he fired before he hired me. He was a good bass player until he'd take that drink. One of our best lineups we was me, Joe, Willie Hayes on drums, and pianist Ken Saydak. That was a great band. Willie could solo well, and he could sing too. He had a deep bass voice. His featured number was Tyrone Davis' "Turning Point." That's when he would go down and sing in that heavy voice. Ken was a good blues keyboardist, and he wasn't one of those guys that acted like he knew everything. If he had something that he was interested in learning, he would sit down and listen. I introduced him to a tape I made of New Orleans piano great James Booker, and he flipped. He would sit down and try to play some of that stuff that Booker was playing, which was not an easy job because Booker was one of the greatest.

I'd had the pleasure of meeting James Booker on a gig in New Orleans that I played with Freddie at a place called Rosy's Jazz Hall. After the gig, we were all packed up and sitting on the bus ready to go, but Freddie was nowhere to be found. I told everyone to stay put and I would look for him. When I got inside, Freddie was sitting on the stool beside James Booker. James was playing and Freddie was singing. My mind went back to the early days when we used to listen to Charles Brown, and we both loved the piano. I looked at Freddie's face and could see how much he was enjoying it, so I knew we weren't going anywhere. Next thing I know, Freddie invited me to join in and sing, too, and we all sang "Danger Zone" together. I still have it on that tape somewhere. The poor guys on the bus ended up waiting for not just Freddie, but for Freddie and me, too!

Mighty Joe had a really good band, and people took notice. Once when we opened a show for Albert King, we caught his attention. He was impressed with our band more than his, and he wanted to play with us. Albert was from the old school of blues, and it wasn't easy to find good blues players to work with. Everyone thinks that blues is an easy I-IV-V, but it's how you go to the IV and the V that separates real blues players from all the rest. So we played a set with him, and don't you know he gives me a solo in the key of G, which is my worst key! I made it work and I think he was satisfied, but man, I could have done so much more in another key. It was a fun night. We discovered that Albert and I had diamond rings that look almost exactly the same, and there's a picture of us with our fists together, showing off those rings. I wish I could find it!

"Trouble In Mind," my favorite song to sing when I was in Joe's band, actually came later, when we had Darryl Mahon on drums and Jesse on keyboards. I remember Freddie had done the song, a blues standard, on one of his Shelter albums with the O'Neal Twins singing behind him, and with my gospel background, I loved their harmonizing. Freddie liked it too. That's one of the reasons the O'Neals were on there. We would do some harmonizing before I started to sing the song with Joe. He said, "Man, I just sit back there and listen to you and Darryl and Jesse. You all sound great!"

After Ken left the band, we hired Leo Davis, who was also one hell of a keyboard player. But he came with baggage we weren't aware of: a drinking problem. He liked Old Grand Dad and Heineken beer. He'd get drunk, and Joe would get pissed off. Leo would come to our gigs drunk. He'd say, "I'm just a little tired! I'm just a little tired!" And Joe would say, "You're drunk!"

Leo decided he wanted to quit drinking at one point, because Joe and I didn't drink at all. Willie Dixon had a place on the South Side of Chicago that we used for rehearsals. So the first thing Leo said when he walked through the door was, "Man, I stopped drinking!"

I said, "What do you mean, you stopped drinking?"

He said, "I quit cold turkey!"

I said, "That's not good, Leo. I think you're supposed to stop gradually."

"No, I quit!"

So we were playing and Leo got up on the piano—they had a little stage there—and all of a sudden he fell backwards off that piano stool and hit the floor. He looked just like Jimmy Reed did that time—he was kicking and going on, a full-blown seizure, although we didn't know it at the time. Me and Joe said, "What's wrong with him?" I said, "I don't know, Joe! Maybe he's having a heart attack!" Joe said, "What should I do?" I said, "Hit him in the chest, Joe!" Joe had big hands, bigger than mine. Joe said, "Hit him in the chest?" I said, "Yeah, hit him in the chest!" Bam! Joe hit him. You know how they shock you with a defibrillator when you're having a heart attack? That's how he reacted. Leo bounced on the floor. Joe hit him again. Bam! After Joe hit him a few times, he started to get worried. He was feeling bad, like Leo was going to die. Then someone called the paramedics, and finally Leo came out of it.

He sat up, and Joe said, "How you feel, Leo?" Leo said, "Man, I feel alright--except my chest is a little sore!" Joe looked at me, and I looked at him, and we kept that little secret between us. Two of Willie Dixon's sons, Butch and Bobby, also did some gigs on piano with us.

Willie Hayes was our drummer for the first few years that I was in the band. After Willie split, we tried a few drummers including Jimmy Tillman. We gave a shot to a jazz drummer who came in and was the worst drummer in the whole world until he figured out that playing blues is a simple beat. Then he turned into a great drummer. We ultimately settled on Darryl Mahon. He's still around Chicago.

Our local stronghold was Wise Fools Pub on North Lincoln Avenue. Its owner, Dave Ungerleider, was crazy about Joe's band. We could get anything we wanted at Wise Fools. Mighty Joe played New Year's Eve there for 12 years straight. Film director Michael Mann walked in one evening while we were starring there. I had just written a song for Joe to bring him up on the stage, and Michael was sitting right there by the bandstand. I didn't know who he was, but I saw him pick up a napkin and write stuff on it. Next thing I know, I get a call from Mighty Joe's manager. "They want you to be in a movie called *Thief*, and they want to use your song in the movie!"

On the set of *Thief*. L to R: me, James Caan, Willie Hayes, Mighty Joe, Conrad Black, Michael Mann, Tommy Giblin

I said, "What song?"

"The song you bring Joe up on. I already told them what it was." But the problem was that our manager didn't realize that I had played a different song the night Michael was there, and so he was pushing the wrong song and didn't know it. The song I'd usually bring Joe up on was called "Cruisin' Down Highway 99." LeRoy Crume came up with

Wise Fools Pub, 2014

that title. He liked that highway, which was somewhere in California. But the song that Michael heard was a brand-new one that I wrote, and he loved it. So when we got "Cruisin'" together to play it for Michael, he didn't recognize it. I forgot that I had played a new song that night. Michael wanted to use it for chase scenes all the way through it. He's really a smart guy.

He said, "This is not the song. I'll put it in the movie, but this is not the song."

I told him, "Well, that's 'Cruisin'!" That's the one we bring him up on." It wasn't until later that I figured out what happened.

We ended up filming the actual scene for ***Thief*** at a bar called Katzenjammer's that was right next door to Wise Fools.

We were down there two or three days, just to film that little bit. It was fun to see how they filmed it. I left out of there with great respect for Michael how he put that stuff together. I said, "Man, this is really cool!" He left us in the movie, but he cut out Willie Dixon, who was supposed to be in it too.

Joe's manager came to me and asked, "Well, Benny, who's got your publishing?" I said, "I don't have any publishing." He said, "You want to put that song in my publishing? We'll split 50/50." I said, "Yeah, cool!" So all the years went by, and I never got anything from the publishing. We finally dug the contract up, and looked at it. And in big words there, it was listed that the publishing was to be split 50/50. But little bitty words beside it said, "50/50 percent of five percent." This kind of deception was too common with the old blues musicians in those days who didn't know anything about the record business, and got screwed out of a lot of money because of it. I guess I'm lucky this only happened with one of my songs.

When we played at Wise Fools, Joe would bring in rhythm guitarist Conrad Black to expand the band. Conrad played a lot with us. He was even in the movie with us. Conrad is a really good guy to get along with, a really nice guy. But we never took a rhythm guitar player with us on the road. We made a live album at Wise Fools too.

Another of our main haunts was Biddy Mulligan's, way up north on Sheridan Road. It was one of the places that would always call us back. A lot of Joe's local gigs were now on the North Side, rather than the South and West Side joints that we'd played for so many years. I liked it. It was safer, and when we played up there, we were sure to get paid and we made more money. We got to mingle with a mixed crowd, and we learned that whites respected blues by then more than the blacks did, because blacks liked other styles of music. Later on when I was with Marva Wright in New Orleans, we went and played a black gig, and they didn't pay us any attention, as good as she was. But then they put on Al Green on the turntable, and man, they went crazy!

Kingston Mines was located just north of Wise Fools on Lincoln Avenue at the time, and one night my old friend Monk Higgins stopped by when we were gigging there. He and Otis Clay were hanging out and they decided to come over and see me. I hadn't seen Monk since the One-derful! days, and he was so happy to see me. I got up and sang a song, and he was sitting there enjoying it, and Otis enjoyed it too. Then Joe started playing. I looked over, and Monk was asleep. I think he must have had some kind of sleep disorder.

We toured the Midwest quite a bit, playing the bar circuit in the college towns of Southern Illinois and Iowa. We were either on our way to play a club in Iowa or had just performed in one, and there happened to be a snowstorm that night. We pulled up, and I think we must have sat for seven or eight hours in one spot. Fortunately, our van had two gas tanks on it. It was running and the snow was falling and the temperature was way down there, and traffic was at a standstill. I swear those two tanks saved our lives. Greyhound buses were in the ditch and 18-wheelers were too. We finally moved maybe a half-mile in 12 hours, and we pulled off and got a hotel. That was a bad night.

We did a lot of work there in Iowa. We played a festival, and after it was over, we got everything loaded up. Joe was the last one to get in the van. I was in the driver's seat. And Joe said, "Goddog it!" I heard him curse. I said, "What's wrong, Joe?" I've got the window down. "Oh, I done stepped in some dogshit!" I said, "Joe, dogshit is forever. Just like a bad relative that comes to visit and won't leave!" He said, "Well, I just bought these shoes!" I said, "Well, you know what, Joe?" I hit the automatic lock button, and all the doors clicked locked. And I raised up the window, and I left a little crack in the glass, and I said, "Joe, you ain't getting in the van!"

He said, "Hey, man, this is my van!" I said, "I don't care. Possession is nine-tenths of the law. You ain't getting in this van until you get rid of them shoes!"

"These are brand-new shoes!"

I said, "You ain't getting in here!" So he started laughing, and walked around and circled around the van. He picked up the shoes, put them in a plastic bag, and put them way in the back of the van at the back door. He refused to throw those shoes away at first, but he finally did. Yeah, he threw them away because they couldn't ride with us. Man, we laughed about that for years and years.

Further from home, we loved to play Albert's Hall in Toronto. Ben Powers, the actor who played Thelma's husband Keith on the sit-com Good Times, used to like to sit in and sing with us when we were there. Kenny Neal sat in on rhythm guitar once or twice there, too. Unfortunately, it was never easy for black people to cross the border in and out of Canada. Like so many other situations, we always had to have our guard up because we were automatically targets just because of the color of our skin. I never will forget one time when we were coming home from Canada, and "Professor" Eddie Lusk stayed behind but sent his luggage home with us. As luck would have it, they pulled us over at the border and decided to check every square inch of our van. We were all escorted inside to a waiting room while they were doing the inspection. Next thing we know, one of the customs officers comes in and says, "What are we going to do about the marijuana?"

"What?" Joe asked, in shock.

"The marijuana. What are we going to do about it?"

"We don't have no marijuana!"

The customs officer said, "Well then what's this?" and held up a bag full. Man, you could have bought Joe for a nickel! He was very, very strict about not having drugs in his van, and this totally caught him off-guard. His jaw dropped to the floor and he said, "Where did you get that?" The officer proceeded to show us the Professor's bag. Goddamn! I think we ended up paying a $500 fine and they let us through, but man, Joe was rattled. I know Joe got his money back from the Professor when he got home, you can be sure of that!

We were going to play at Tramps in New York, and we stopped first to get our hotel rooms. Joe went inside, and I didn't go in for some reason. I told Joe, "Just go in and get my room, and I'll sit in the van," because I was tired. I had been doing some work on his van, and I had a hatchet in there. I was sitting in the very back, and this guy was walking around the van, and I'm looking at him. Then it dawned on me--he was going to pull the passenger door open and see what he could steal. When he got to the passenger door and got ready to step up to the van, I had that hatchet lined up with the blade facing his face. He opened the door and went to step up, and he saw that hatchet right in his face. He squealed like a pig and jumped off the van, and he didn't stop until he got to Broadway. This was in the middle of the block. Then he stopped and thought about it and got pissed off, and he came back. He was on the other side of the street, and boy, he was just cursing me out. I said, "Well, just come on back. I've got a treat in store!" Finally, he gave up and left.

Joe would always get his seat in the front of the van, and everybody knew that was his seat. I never heard him say nobody could sit there. It was just taken for granted. Either I was driving and Joe was sitting by the door, or he was driving and I was sitting by the door. Sometimes Willie Hayes would drive. But mostly I would drive, just me and Joe talking all night long.

We played with B.B. King in Europe in a bullring. It may have been in France. B.B. came up to me, because it was the first time he'd seen me after Freddie passed. He said, "You're doing okay! You're back playing and you're doing your thing and you're looking good! Congratulations!" Then we went on down to the Riviera, and we played a gig. Back at that time, the beaches were nude and my room was overlooking the showers, which were right out my window. You win some and you lose some. And I was a winner!

Joe loved his iced tea. He would sit there and tip one of those glass sugar containers into his tall glass of iced tea so a long stream of sugar came out. His glass would be filled 50/50—half iced tea and half sugar, with all the sugar sitting on the bottom. He'd say, "I can't get it sweet, man! I can't get it sweet!" I said, "Joe, look at the glass! All you got is sugar!" And he started laughing. When it came time to order dinner, he would ask, "What you gonna have?" Whatever I would eat, Joe would eat. It didn't matter what it was. He would have his iced tea with dinner, and then he'd order a Diet Coke. Then he would look at me and laugh and say, "Well, man, I gotta do something right!"

We were coming down through California one time, and I was driving. Me and Joe, we were always talking fast. I said, "Joe!" He said, "Yeah, man." I said, "You know, I got a feeling." He said, "What?" I said, "I've got a feeling somebody we know is going to hit that lottery!" He said, "You think so, man?" "Yeah!" We talked about it and then kind of forgot it. We went and checked into a hotel, and Joe called me. He said, "Man! You know what? Ann's numbers came out in the lottery, and she didn't play." And Joe was pissed. "She didn't play the numbers!" I said, "Joe, don't worry about it. They're going to come back again." He said, "You think so?" I said, "Yeah, they're going to come back again!"

That next week he called me. "Hey, man, you sittin' down?"

I said, "Yeah."

"She hit it!"

"Hit what?"

"She hit that Lotto! $2.5 million!" And those millions came in handy later on after Joe got sick.

I was Joe's right-hand man. I remember him saying one time, "Man, I wish I had three more just like him!" I looked out after him, and I had his back if anything would go wrong or if he wasn't feeling good--whatever it was that he needed. Joe appreciated that over the years. That's why he never did break that bond with me. Except in the really early days of my career, I would hire on with one bandleader and stay with them if I liked the person. But that didn't stop me from going into the studio at one point with my old friend Otis Clay.

Otis was playing mainly in black clubs on the South Side back then—the Bonanza and the High Chaparral. Me and Joe were up at Biddy Mulligan's. I can't remember who I was talking to at Biddy's, but whoever it was was as close to Otis as I was. I told him, "If you're going to see Otis tonight, give him a message. Tell him we should make a gospel song together!" Because he and I sang gospel. I gave the guy my number, and Otis called me. He said, "Man, yeah, let's do that! Let's do that!" So we talked about it for several months. You know how musicians are—today it's a good idea, tomorrow you done forgot it.

But we kept it on the front burner, and Otis finally said, "All right man, let's do it!" So he got trombonist Bill McFarland, and his piano player that was in demand. Otis called Paul Serrano and said he wanted to record. So we went in, and Otis came up with the song "When The Gates Swing Open." He knew I played with the Soul Stirrers, so he came up with a song from the Soul Stirrers. We put it down at practices, and everybody looked at each other like, "This is it!" But it wasn't clicking. Then he went home and came back the next day and made it slow. That clicked. When we recorded the song, I played bass, overdubbed guitar, and I sang the tenor and bass backing vocals too. So I did four parts on it. But when we got ready to mix the thing, the bass and drums weren't matching. I said, "I tell you what, leave the drums out." Then, after a few bars, "Now bring the drums in." When we hit the IV it was killer. It set the song up perfect for Otis. We found out it was the drums that wasn't matching us. Otis released it on his own Echo label (I shared production credit with Otis and McFarland, it got on the radio, and that record hit locally overnight.)

Otis was very, very proud of that song. It was one of his biggest songs, and he made money off it for I don't know how long, 30 years? He sang it at personal gigs and funerals. Anytime I came around, he'd say, "You sang the bass, you sang the tenor, you played the guitar, and you played the bass!" He gave me my propers. He gave me my respect.

At some point, Mighty Joe started to have problems with his right arm. He went and had a checkup, and they found out that he had a pinched nerve in his neck. So he went and had surgery to fix it in 1986, and when he came out of surgery he had no sense of anything with that arm. He'd shake your hand and almost break it because Joe was strong and he didn't have any idea of how hard he was squeezing your hand. His days of playing guitar the way he had for so long were over. His wife Ann had all that Lotto money when Joe had the first operation, and she gave him a recreation area in the basement, complete with treadmill and big screen TV where he could watch boxing. He loved boxing because he once was a boxer himself. His wife took care of him and treated him like a king.

Joe and I remained close friends long after I left his band. Ann said that when I moved to New Orleans, not a day went by that Mighty Joe didn't call my name. He and Ann would drive down to New Orleans on my birthday every year. We'd just sit and talk. He'd stay about four or five days, and then he'd get in his car and drive back to Chicago. Me and Joe got along really, really well.

Even though he couldn't play anymore, Joe tried to make a comeback in 1997. After all, he could still sing. He did a gig in Rock Island, sharing a bill with Koko Taylor. He wanted me to come back and play

Mighty Joe talking to Bruce Iglauer while I show off my bass

that gig. I was on my way to Hawaii, and I stopped in Chicago and drove up to the Quad Cities to do that show with him.

Alligator Records owner Bruce Iglauer was the emcee. Joe had his cousin playing the guitar, who later passed away in a hotel where he was getting ready to play. He went in and laid down and never got up. He was from Milwaukee. Me, Darryl Mahon on drums, and our old keyboard player Jesse played that gig. I really enjoyed seeing Joe make a comeback.

Later on, Joe called me in New Orleans. He said, "I've got to see you. I've got to talk to you." And I said okay. So I went to Chicago. My **Blue and Not So Blue** album had just come out. My two daughters and Ann went in one car, and me and Joe went in the other because he wanted to talk. He said, "Man, I'm thinking about going back in the hospital and having some corrective surgery so maybe if they fix it up, go back in and try to straighten some things out, I might be able to play the guitar again. What do you think?" I said, "Joe, you know what happened on the last one. I can't say, but if it was me, I wouldn't do it." And he said, "But my kids are pushing me to go, and I know they want to see me up there playing the guitar again. I think I'm leaning toward doing it. I just wanted to hear what you thought." And I said, "Well, that's what I think. I don't think so."

But he went in and had the surgery, and I went on a cruise, playing with Marva Wright. When I got back, I think it was on a Sunday, I called him, and he was in the hospital. I said, "Joe?" He said, "Hey, you ought to come see about me." I said, "What's wrong?" I found out he had pneumonia. That Monday, I called back and he was brain dead. I said, "What?" His wife was crying. She said, "Benny, his kids want to pull the plug. I don't want to do it." I said, "Yeah, you're right, because people come back even when the doctors say they're not going to come back. People have come back after years!"

Ann rushed down to the hospital, and when she walked through the door she saw Joe take his last breath. They pulled the plug before she got there. She didn't have a chance to do anything, but she saw him take his last breath. She took it hard, and so did I. It was like, give the guy a chance, you know? Give him a chance. You don't know what will happen in this day and age, the way medicine is going.

But Mighty Joe was gone. He died March 24, 1999.

Ken Sadak, me, Willie Hayes

Top Left: Munich Jazz Fest, 1980. Photo © Jan Scheffner; Top Right: Photo © Jan Scheffner; Bottom Left: Clockwise from top L: Eugene Carrier, Eddie Lusk, BB King and Mighty Joe in Canada; Bottom Right: On stage at Nightstage in Cambridge, MA. Photo © Peter Jordan;

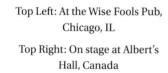

Top Left: At the Wise Fools Pub,
Chicago, IL

Top Right: On stage at Albert's
Hall, Canada

Bottom: Lone Star Cafe in NYC. Photo
courtesy of Stephen Nicholas

MARVA WRIGHT

When Mighty Joe had his first operation, it left him disabled. After he came out of surgery and went into his rehab, we knew that he wasn't going to be able to play anymore. That's when I decided to make my move. I headed for New Orleans because musicians down there could make a good living without going anywhere. I could make as much money locally as I did when I was touring. I was tired of traveling anyway.

Me and Mighty Joe had played at Tipitina's down there with Buddy Guy and Junior Wells before he had to quit playing. Joe put on a much better show than they did. He got up there, and he was serious. Joe got out there and played his guitar and sang his blues, and they liked him. The man there at the bar said he didn't ever want to see Junior and Buddy anymore because they clowned more than they played. Junior Wells was a great blues musician, though, and he proved that when he went solo.

I had an old white van that I used to drive Joe around in when his van wasn't working. We'd load in there, and I'd take him to the gigs. When I got ready to leave town, I loaded my jukebox in my van along with my amp, my guitar, and one suitcase and headed south. When I drove across that long bridge spanning Lake Pontchartrain heading into New Orleans, I didn't have any money.

My mother inadvertently inspired my lifelong love for jukeboxes. We were living on Madison Street, and I couldn't have been any older than 13 or 14. We went to a second-hand store that had a Wurlitzer 1015 jukebox for sale. They only wanted 50 bucks for it. They sell for $8-9000 now. The 1015 has the bubble tubes. I loved that. It was the prettiest thing I ever saw, and it was in top condition, sitting right there on the floor for $50. I put my hands on it. I rubbed that jukebox, and I told my mother, "I want this!" She said, "We can't afford it, son." It started from that. From then on, I always wanted a jukebox. I finally got into collecting them when I was playing with Joe.

Several decades later, I made contact with the ex-mayor of a small town somewhere outside of Rock Island, Illinois. He was a collector and he had this big barn. He was getting rid of all kinds of stuff, because the barn had started to leak and rot so he had to get his stuff out of there. He had an old 1936 Wurlitzer. I went there, and he said, "I don't know, it's got to be worth $4-500." One of the guys said, "No it ain't, because it's starting to rust here." So he let me have that jukebox for about 50 bucks. I shined that boy up with a pretty veneer. It was a pretty box. It didn't have any plastic on it. It was all wood. And I brought it back. That's what got me hooked on collecting jukeboxes, right there.

I started to acquire more jukeboxes, and I wound up with maybe 20. I eventually sold them all, except for a 1428 Rock-Ola Magic Glow from 1948 that plays 78s. I got it from a Rock-Ola technician up in Grand Forks, North Dakota. That's the one I've always kept with me. And I recently acquired a Seeburg Happy Days model that plays 45s. It's a real work of art. The mechanism looks like a big loaf of bread moving up and down a rail. To look at the workmanship that went into this thing, you wouldn't believe how intricate it is. Everything has a function. There's got to be a million parts in it. Over the years, I've collected hundreds of

45s and 78s to play on my jukeboxes too. I'm especially proud of my autographed collections of Charles Brown and Hank Ballard 78's which they personally signed for me.

Anyway, I found a steady five-nights-a-week gig as a sideman at the Old Absinthe Bar on Bourbon Street in the French Quarter that I held onto for about five years. It was nothing to see world-famous musicians come through the door. Some of them would sit in, such as Cindi Lauper, David Clayton Thomas and Jimmy Page. The guy that owned the bar, he liked to fight. We used to play and watch him fight. He would go up and down Bourbon Street fighting. He was a nice guy, but he was a street guy. The place was very near the Old Absinthe House at Bourbon and Bienville, where the pirate Jean Lafitte and Major General Andrew Jackson allegedly mapped out the Battle of New Orleans in 1814.

Top: With Jimmy Page at the Old Absinthe Bar. Photo by Marc Adams

Bottom: With Jimmy Page, Marc Adams (keyboard) and Allyn Robinson (drums)

New Orleans was very different from Chicago. But once I got to know the French Quarter, I loved it. I didn't get out of the Quarter that much. The Absinthe Bar was in the 400 block of Bourbon, and in the 300 block I met a guy that was renovating a building. His name was Ron Murray. I walked in, and said, "I'm looking for a place." He said, "I've got two!"

I said, "What?"

"Right here on Bourbon Street!"

I said, "Let me see!"

I walked up to the second floor at 325 Bourbon and I was out of breath, not being in shape. He said, "I've got another one on the third floor." So I went up on the third floor, and I'm huffing and puffing. I said, "I'm a young man. I ain't got no business doing this!" So I took the apartment on the third floor. I stayed there almost 20 years, going up and down those stairs, and I think that has a lot to do with the reason I get around so well now. Up and down those stairs every day, going for food and hauling it up to the third floor. It got to a point there where I could run up and down the stairs all day. Ron's wife got to be a good friend of mine too. He used to come down to the club with me. Ron liked to party, and he would overdo it. His wife would call, and I'd say, "Ron is lying on the couch." She'd tell me, "Oh, he's with you. That's okay then!"

Hank Ballard, who sang lead with the Midnighters on the '50s R&B classics "Work With Me Annie," "Annie Had A Baby," and the original "The Twist," was playing at the nearby Fairmont Hotel. He came by the Old Absinthe Bar and sat in. We got to talking about music, and he and I kind of hit it off. When I walked over to Hank's hotel room, he had a hot plate there, and he was making butterbeans. He liked butterbeans. Then I told him, "Look, I've got a surprise for you!" We went over to my place and started looking through my old 78s and played them on my jukebox. He enjoyed that. You can play those same records on a record player, but when you play them on a jukebox, it's just different. I guess standing there looking at it as the records spin around makes it a different experience. That's when he signed all of his records that are in my collection.

There was a strip club directly underneath my apartment. It was called the Show Bar by then, but it was previously known as the Gunga Din, a joint Jack Ruby used to frequent. Some of the strippers stayed next door to me, so I got to know a lot of them. If you ever want to have fun, try to get a spot like that. The guy that owned the Show Bar had this parrot. It was green with a little yellow on the back of its neck. He could talk his ass off. I ended up with that bird.

The club owner was in love with this one stripper. He stopped her from stripping, and took her for his old lady. But she still had some of those old habits, and the bird knew all about it. I could be sitting eating my dinner or something, and he would go back and reminisce. He'd start repeating what he'd heard: "I didn't fuck him! I didn't fuck him! I did not fuck him!" Then the bird would go through a thing like he was getting strangled. I'd sit there and listen. He's going through this whole thing where the club owner beats the girl up and chokes her. That bird would tell everything.

The Royal Sonesta hotel was across the street from my place, so my balcony looked directly down on it. The Royal Sonesta's balcony came up to the second floor, and my balcony was on the third floor. Let's put it this way: there's nothing that goes on in life that I didn't see at that hotel. Yeah, I saw it all.

A bird's eye view from my Bourbon Street apartment balcony

The guy that owned the Old Absinthe Bar eventually sold it. Before he left, he found money stacked on the wall of the place an inch deep--and I mean old money. Some of the old customers had put it there. It started in the old days with the pirates. Sometimes they didn't have money, so when they did they would leave it on the wall with their name on it. That way when they came back, they would have money to drink on. It became a tradition, and people started leaving dollars stuck on the walls. It was quite a place. Sadly, the new owners turned it into a daiquiri shop, and that was the end of an era.

Bourbon Street was great in those days. There was a lot of blues, although the sound was different than it was back in Chicago. There it was definitely all about bass, guitar, and drums, with maybe some keyboards thrown in. But when you got to New Orleans, you had trumpet, saxophone, trombone, even tuba. And then you had the second-line rhythms. You had all that stuff put together.

Back then, Mardi Gras was about wearing festive costumes. Today it's about showing your tits. It was a fun crowd that worked on Bourbon Street, and the people that worked at the bars, everybody knew everybody. We'd get off work at night, and we had two bars that we'd hang out at where everybody would unwind. We'd talk about stuff and drink shots. Some of them moved away, but every once in a while they come back and they'll want to hook up with whoever's available and hang out again.

Valerie McCreary, the designer and seamstress who made some amazing suits for Freddie during the '70s with likenesses of naked ladies decorating them, moved down to New Orleans from Boulder, Colorado.

Freddie met her through Leon Russell, who owned some of her hand-sewn suits too—maybe 20 in all. I recently learned that Valerie was also a designer for Bob Dylan, Brad Whitford (Aerosmith) and The Commodores Tour with The Emotions. She let me know that she wanted to come down and live in New Orleans, and I told her I had a vacant apartment in my building. By that time, the landlord had given me the run of 325

Top: Freddie and Valerie McCreary; Middle: Valerie wearing Freddie's boots; Bottom: Freddie modeling his new outfit by Valerie

Bourbon. So I rented her the apartment next to mine. She moved in and stayed there long after I left, in the apartment right next door. She's very professional at what she does. Now she works with miniature oyster shells. She can paint miniature scenes on those oyster shells. I mean, you talk about photographic qual-ity—she's that good at it.

Out of the blue, my brother Bobby came down to New Orleans. He didn't announce that he was coming. Matter of fact, he didn't know where I was. Bobby decided to come down and find me because I had come down to New Orleans and just kind of dropped a curtain. So Bobby came down and he rang the bell one day, and I go down and there's Bobby, standing at the door there, saying "Hey, man!" And we talked and talked and talked. He said, "Man, I want to start playing again." There was nothing I could do, because I was down here and he was up there. So we never got it together. I gave him a guitar. But I never saw him again. He went back to Chicago and passed away a few years ago.

I've always preferred to work steady with one bandleader, rather than jobbing with several. I like to learn what that person is about and stick with them. It makes the gig easy and you get along with the person you're working with better. They get to know you, and if you like each other, it works out great. That strategy has proven lucky for me with Freddie, with Mighty Joe and with Marva Wright, who came to be known as the Blues Queen of New Orleans.

Marva came to the blues relatively late in her life after getting her start singing in church. She lived in the projects. I don't know how many kids she had. At least five, and they all stayed in the projects. She wasn't working, but she was trying to support those kids. They couldn't have had no more than two or three rooms in all, and no money. Marva went down on Bourbon Street and sat in somewhere, and some guy heard her. He brought her down to sit in at the Old Absinthe Bar.

She was a church-going girl, a serious churchgoer. She thought about singing blues and thought about it, and she said, "Well, let me try this here. If it goes good, I don't have to work on Bourbon Street. There are other places I can sing." So she went down there and sat in. And they gave her a job singing at the

Marva with our dear friends Ann and DP Hughes

Old Absinthe Bar. She only knew four songs and she packed that place. That's how good she was, and she was tearing it up at that place. Her voice would resonate all up and down the street. The church people heard about her going down on Bourbon Street to sing the blues and got on her. And Marva said, "I've got to feed my kids. So what am I gonna do?" And that's what she did, and she did it well.

The band she was playing with there, they played blues. But then she started to put together her own band. And the guys in her band leaned more towards jazz. She was talking one day with my friend Eugene Carrier, who I met up in Canada when I was playing with Mighty Joe. Eugene spent most of the '80s playing keyboards for B.B. King. Marva was bitching at Eugene telling him, "I just hate jazz! I can't stand jazz!" She wanted to sing blues, not jazz. So Eugene said, "I've got somebody that don't play nothing but blues!" Marva said, "Who?" He said, "Benny Turner." She said, "Benny?" And she called me up. "Benny, you want to play with me?" I said, "Yeah, I'll play with you, Marva!" She caught me just right. I was getting ready to leave town.

The first gig I had with Marva was at the Hilton Hotel on the river at nine o'clock in the morning for a brunch set. When they got ready to kick off, I was in bed asleep. Her husband, Tony Plessy, called me up. He said, "Hey!" I said, "Hey!"

"How you doing?"

"I'm doing fine."

"What are you doing?"

"Man, I'm still in bed. I had a long night last night."

He said, "You know where I am?"

"No."

"I'm at the Hilton."

I said, "Oh, yeah? The Hilton? Shit! I'm supposed to be working this morning!"

He said, "Yeah, man. We're going to hit in about 15 minutes!"

Believe it or not, I hit with them right on time. I couldn't take a shower, but I jumped in my clothes, got my guitar and my amp and jumped in a taxi, and I was there. That was my first gig with Marva.

Top: On tour in France with Marva. Seated L to R: Anthony Brown, Greg Dawson, Tony Plessy, Gwen, Sam Berfect; Bottom: On board the Commodores Enchanted Isle, 1999. L to R: Lauren Welch, Merline Kimble, Les Getrex, me, Tony's sister, Tony Plessy, Sam Berfect's sister, Marva

Marva's band didn't play any one place exclusively. We were all over the place, and we traveled to Europe fairly often. After I played that brunch with her, I think our next gig was at the Le Meridien Hotel in Paris. It was right by the Champs-Elysees. The band was sort of loose because the keyboard player that usually fronted the band wasn't with us and we were kind of winging it. Even with that, Marva was spectacular. Then we toured the rest of France. We made a big loop around the bottom and came back around to Paris. At one concert, they presented me with a bottle of Ray Charles Wine that I still have.

One night a lady got my attention while we were on break between sets. She asked me, "Do you know 'Since I Met You Baby?'" I said, "Sure I do!" I got up and sang the song. Then she reminded me of a similar number by the same artist, Ivory Joe Hunter, "I Almost Lost My Mind." It was a surprise to me that an older white lady would know them both. So Mary Cox and I got to be friends, and she gave me $100 for singing the song. She had two people with her, a husband and wife.

Mary said, "I'm down in New Orleans having fun, and we're gonna drive back to Bakersfield." I said, "You're gonna drive all the way?" She said, "Yeah, I kind of want to see the country." She owned a trucking company in Bakersfield. I didn't know she was terminally ill and that was part of her bucket list, to drive back across the country. She sent me a nice little package after she got home—some original "Old Black Joe" sheet music that I still have.

One day I was playing at Storyville again and a man walked up to the stage and gave me $100. He said, "You don't remember me, do you?" I said no. He said, "I was with Mary Cox. She told me to give you $100 every time I see you!" He told me that she had passed away, but made him promise to bring me that $100. Those are some of the most meaningful times as a musician, to know that you touched somebody's life like that with your music.

We did some gospel on each show. Marva was just as spectacular with that as she was with the blues. We were in the south of France, and Sam "The Bishop" Berfect, the organ player that played with me on my first solo record **Blue and Not So Blue**, who I consider to be the best organ player I ever heard, was accompanying Marva as she sang

"Walk Around Heaven." The two together were untouchable. I saw this lady stand up in the back of the room. Marva was walking and singing, like she might have done in church when they get happy.

The lady started walking towards the front slowly. She got within five feet of Marva, just looking at her, and keeled over. They picked the lady up, thinking she had just fainted, and they laid her on a stretcher and gave her CPR. Naturally, we went on break. I walked over by Marva. She had a paper up to her face, because she was only a few feet from where they were pumping on the lady's chest. Just kidding her, I said, "Marva you done killed that lady!" She said, "Hush, boy!" Just about that time, they pulled the cover over the lady's head, and her hand fell out. The lady really was dead. That was the vocal power of Marva Wright.

Samuel "The Bishop" Berfect

The only thing more powerful than Marva's vocals was Marva singing with Sam Berfect on the organ. One special memory I have is when they were asked to perform the National Anthem at a party during the Democratic Convention. You always hear people adding their own personal touches when they're in the spotlight like that, but not Marva. She sang it straight up, the way it's supposed to be. Nothing fancy and no little tricks. And she killed it! I have never heard it sung that way before, and I know I never will again. Never. Sam had that B-3 going behind her. Lord have mercy. I had tears in my eyes. After they finished, Al Gore came up and kissed Marva on the cheek, so I know I'm not the only one who felt the magic. It was one for the books, that's for sure.

I'll never forget one flight back from Switzerland that we endured. As soon as the pilot took off, maybe 15 minutes into the flight, he came on the p.a. system and said, "My flippers are not working, and we don't know what's wrong. But we need them to land." He said he was going to give us an update later. Next time we heard from him, he said, "We still can't get the flippers to work, so we're going to go to England and land in London, because they've got a longer runway." That was about an hour away. The stewardesses started running to the back of the plane, preparing us for a crash landing. They told us, "Take off your shoes!" I was sitting in an exit row, and we were supposed to help people. A lady came and asked me, "Are you willing to help?" I said, "Lady, get away from me!" A woman across the aisle from me was passing out little strips of paper with prayers on them. I said, "Oh, man!" The organ player, Marc Adams, was in the back asleep, because he had three or four seats together to lay across.

Marva was sitting way back from me, tears running down everywhere. Tony came up to me. He said, "Marva's freaking. Can you go back there and talk to her?" Tony wanted me to go back and tell Marva everything was okay, because they thought I was psychic. A lot of things I would tell them would come true. I had told her daughter when she was going to have a baby, and I told her it was going to be a girl, and it was. I went back there, and I was shaking too but I wasn't going to show it. I said, "Marva, everything's going to be alright. Don't worry about it. They're going to land, and the flippers are going to start to working, and everything's going to be fine." She said, "You sure?" I said, "I'm sure. Everything's going to be alright." So she quieted down and wiped her tears away, and she stopped crying. So I went back and sat down, scared as shit, not knowing that that's just what would happen.

We got ready to land, and we all put our heads down and had our shoes off and everything, ready for the big one. Then the pilot came on the loudspeaker and said, "Ladies and gentlemen, I don't know what happened, but the flippers are working now!" (Just like I said they would). This was just when we were getting ready to touch down. We landed without a hitch. Nothing went wrong. Fire trucks were lined up on each side of the plane, waiting for us to hit the tarmac. So that was it. Marc in the back slept through the whole thing. He said, "What's going on?"

We pulled up to the gate, and this little guy with a little handle-bar mustache and a red coat--I guess he was a supervisor--got on the plane and said, "Well, ladies and gentlemen, we're going to go ahead and repair what we have to repair right here and get you right back in the air again." I said, "You may go in the air, but I ain't going back up in this plane!" He said, "What do you mean?" I said, "I'm not going to ride your plane." Pretty soon, everybody was getting ready to follow me out, because everybody was pissed off. They said, "Y'all done scared the shit out of us, and you think we're going to get back up there?"

He said, "Well, do you know what we have to go through to get your luggage off here?"

I said, "I don't give a damn! I'm not going to ride this plane!"

Everybody had been scared to death, man. We were thinking we were going to die, and now we were going to go back up in the same plane? Slowly but surely, everybody else came to life, yelling, "I don't want to ride it either!" Then someone came on the loudspeaker and said, "Ladies and gentlemen, this flight has been canceled." They canceled it because nobody was going to ride it. The next morning, here comes the same guy in the red coat with the little handlebar mustache. "How are you feeling today?" he asked. I think it was our drummer that said, "Y'all pissed him off yesterday." And the supervisor said, "Well, hopefully everything's alright today." And he started to walk away.

I said, "Hey!" He turned and looked at me. I said, "Listen to me! The summer breeze may kiss the sky. The bumblebee may kiss the butterfly. Her ruby red lips may kiss the glass. But you, my friend..." Everybody in the area where we were busted out laughing. It was real funny—I told this guy to kiss my ass in a nice way. But I had been scared to death. My blood pressure was way up, and I don't have high blood pressure. They had to bring a physician in to calm me down.

I didn't know much jazz at all, so I had kind of a hard time with a lot of the tunes Marva and her band played, like "The Girl From Ipanema." I had a tough time playing it, because it was just not my thing and I didn't like it. I'd stumble through it, but my heart wasn't in it. Marva announced one day that she was going to pick a bandleader, and I didn't think that I would be chosen. I thought it would be one of the guys that was really, really good at what they were doing, with

191

the jazz and the horns. Everyone was sitting around waiting for the news. When she said "Benny Turner is going to be my bandleader" my mouth dropped to the floor. I told her I didn't know anything but blues. She said, "But that's what I want!" I never played "The Girl From Ipanema" again. But I did play on Marva's 1993 album ***Born with the Blues*** and its followup ***Bluesiana Mama***.

The band changed personnel a lot. I was the only one that really stuck. Brian "Breeze" Cayolle was in and out on saxophone. Jeffery "Jellybean" Alexander came into the group. Then Earl Smith played drums until Jellybean came back again. He lasted the longest and he's still with me now. I consider him to be one of the best drummers in the country, and I was proud of his recent playing on Bobby Rush's Grammy Award-winning CD, ***Porcupine Meat***. He gave me some of the credit and respect in his interview in ***DRUM!*** magazine, which made me feel good. "Benny developed my shuffle to a T," Jellybean said. "Bobby hired me because I was able to play the shuffle groove."

At the start, our guitarist Anthony Brown was more on the jazz side. That's what was making Marva go in that direction. After he left, we just picked up whatever guitar player was available, but Anthony played a lot with us. Herman Ernest III, Dr. John's longtime drummer, was not just my friend, he was my biggest fan.

Herman Ernest

He would come to our gigs and watch me direct the band. He just loved it. Herman never was an official member of Marva's band, but whenever we needed a drummer, I'd get him to play with us. He would often go to Dallas to play with Jack Calmes and his band, the Forever Fabulous Chickenhawks. It felt real good to still have that connection with Jack after so long.

And of course, Sam Berfect was one of my favorite organists. He died in 1999 at the age of 56, when we were away touring in Paris. Sam was really, really unhappy he couldn't make that trip with us. He had kidney problems and had undergone a kidney transplant. Marva decided not to let Sam go on that Paris tour because she didn't want him to get sick on the road. His death was the end of an era for Marva and me personally, but also for the band. He was a real musical genius.

On the Steamboat Natchez with Eugene Carrier. We were on a gig with the band, Cinderella.

My sixth sense that helped save Dee Clark's life kicked in again, this time about my friend Eugene Carrier.

At seven o'clock one morning, something kicked me and woke me up and said, "Call Eugene!" You just don't call a musician at seven a.m., especially one like Eugene who didn't usually get in until five a.m. I'm sitting there twiddling my thumbs, saying, "Why do I have to call Gene at seven in the morning? Finally I said, "What the hell." I picked up the phone and dialed him, and he picked up the phone. He was mumbling incoherently.

I said, "Gene this is Benny!"

More incoherent mumbling on the other end of the line.

Then I started laughing, and I said, "Gene, I tell you what—just call me later on."

More mumbling in response.

I said, "Okay, I'll see you."

He hung up the phone. He was having a stroke, and the phone woke him up. He got in his car and he drove himself to the hospital. That's what saved his life. Why did I call him at seven in the morning? Something told me. I thought he had just woke up and he couldn't get himself together, but he was having a stroke. Eugene eventually moved back to his hometown of Houston and died there in 1997.

I had a joyous reunion with Tyrone Davis when he headlined a bill at New Orleans' Saenger Theater that Marva opened. Not only was he happy to see me, he couldn't believe it because I didn't tell him I was there or anything. I just opened the door, and he just stood and looked like he couldn't believe it. He said, "Junior!" They all called me Junior. And he grabbed me and hugged me. He wasn't going to be satisfied unless I watched his whole show. So we went around with a bottle and sat by the side of the stage. I watched Tyrone sing his smash "Turning Point." He had a great band with him, the same guys Otis Clay used.

Something similar happened when I renewed acquaintances with Chicago blues harp great James Cotton, although our reunion took place a little further from home--in Sao Paolo, Brazil. We had finished our gig with Marva and it wasn't time to go home yet, so I came out to the show Cotton was playing. He was at a really nice place called the Bourbon Street Bar. It was kind of upper class, for Brazil. And I went to his dressing room. Just like Tyrone, I knocked on the door and Cotton opened it. He looked at me, and he had this funny look on his face and he reached and grabbed me. Boy, James almost broke my back, he was so glad to see me, even though I wasn't really that close to him back in the old days. I just saw him with Muddy. But all of us old Chicago blues guys have a special bond.

Then there was Jimmie Lee Robinson. He never stopped being a tireless advocate for the West Side and its brand of blues. He was one of the coolest guys I ever met. I never saw him get mad, or wanting to beat up anybody. He was just a genuinely good guy. I hadn't seen him for decades when he crossed my mind one day. I was in touch with Mighty Joe's lady Ann, "You know, Jimmie Lee's on my mind. Think we can find him?" She found him. Then she said, "We can all meet over at T.J.'s place over on Lake Street."

So myself, T.J., and Johnny Dollar all met up and sat around a table in a little circle and talked to Jimmie Lee, and he gave me a bunch of his CDs. He was the same guy. He looked the same. It was such a high for me to see Jimmie Lee because I hadn't seen him in years and years and years. That was the last time that I saw him. Jimmie Lee died in 2002.

Marva and Tony

I was in Sao Paolo when my daughter got word that my brother Michael had gotten killed. He was on his way to the store, and an 18-wheeler hit him while he was walking. I don't think I made it back in time for the services, but I got there the night after. Michael had been a roadie for Freddie for awhile. He was a really cool guy, real easy to get along with and liked to have fun. He was more like Freddie than any of my brothers were, and they got along good. He moved back to Texas, and he traveled with Freddie quite a while.

I got very tight with Marva and Tony.

He would come to me a lot of times when he had questions, because he thought maybe I could help out. Marva was kind of special. Sometimes nothing satisfied her. She was a temperamental genius. He would come to me, and I would help him out a lot of times to calm her down. Marva reminded me a lot of Freddie. If she needed money or something like that, she'd come to me and I'd give her money. And she loved to gamble.

We were maybe 30 miles outside of Chicago, and we stopped at a casino. Tony and I were hanging out in the food area, because he didn't gamble. We were sitting there, and Marva came up and said, "Benny, let me borrow a thousand dollars!" Tony kind of looked at me. I gave her a thousand dollars, and Tony said, "Uh-oh!" Then she came back and said, "Benny, let me borrow another thousand dollars!" I gave her another thousand, and she went away. Tony said, "I'm getting nervous now!" She came on back. "Benny, let me borrow $500." I gave her $500. And she came back with all that money and gave me back every dime. Sure did. If she needed money for other things, she knew she could always come to me. And it was the same with her. If I needed money, Marva would give it to me.

Eventually I bought a house on New Orleans' West Bank. I got tired of Bourbon Street, and I had this cool white Rolls-Royce that I was having problems parking in the Quarter. I decided to buy a house and have a garage and a driveway. I had a housewarming party, and one of my musician friends brought me a little bag of weed as a gift. Since I don't smoke pot, I tucked it away and lost all sight of it. That bag is still here somewhere. I'll come across it one day.

Although playing with Marva was my main gig, I also did some shows with the Wild Magnolias, one of the funkiest Mardi Gras Indian groups in all of New Orleans. Glenn Gaines, who was the manager of the Wild Magnolias, was also managing Marva Wright, and he would book them together on tours. Sometimes he wouldn't have a bass player, and he would ask me to play. It was strange to play with the Wild Magnolias. I'm a blues bass player. That's what I am. A lot of the bass lines I played with the Magnolias weren't quite like the lines that were in the original tunes. I played my own thing, and their Big Chief, Bo Dollis, liked it. He pretty much gave me my head. I picked up how they played it later on, and I got into it. They had one guy in there whose name was Norwood "Geechie" Johnson. That was his thing to play that, and Geechie knew how to keep that beat going. I could follow Geechie and stay on the one with him. That was his thing to play that, and Geechie and stay on the one with him. And they had another drummer, Raymond Weber. With us three,  man, we could hammer out a beat. Bo even had a special shirt made up for me with my name on it. I've still got it.

I really don't remember much about where I was when Hurricane  Katrina hit New Orleans with all of its fury in late August of 2005, but I do remember I got out of town—first to Newport Beach, California, then to Chicago. Marva went to Florida, and from there she traveled to Baltimore and stayed there for awhile. I didn't lose my home or any of my

In Washington DC at my first gig after Katrina Washington DC

possessions because the destruction was relatively light in the area of town where I live, but I did have some roof damage that I didn't know about at the time. As it turned out, I would have been in better shape if the house would have blown away. Katrina took both my job and my savings.

We were away from New Orleans for at least a month or two. Even after we returned, the city was still broken. It took a year or two before it got back to close to being normal. Businesses had to open back up, and new bar owners came in that didn't know a damned thing about the blues. We were basically starting over again.

I used up my savings trying to survive those years when nothing was happening musically in New Orleans. To pay a house mortgage with no job is quite a feat. I thought we'd been given a break from paying our mortgages by the federal government, but it turned out that my payments were still due. I think President Bush had suggested that the mortgage companies let us tack our past due payment balances onto the end of our loans, but I guess mine didn't believe in that. Those guys were like piranhas. They wanted their money now. So not only did I have to catch up on what I didn't pay, I had to cover the current payment that was due too. Man, I had a hard time. A NARAS-operated organization called MusiCares in New York helped me out a lot, but aside from that, I still had to live. I'd find a gig here and there, but there wasn't that steady gigging thing that kept us going prior to Katrina. I've had a hard time, and I'm still struggling. I haven't recovered from Katrina yet.

Marva finally came back to New Orleans. She came down first for a visit, and she was at Tipitina's one night. They were doing a fundraiser because the Katrina recovery effort was still underway. We were sitting up in the balcony. Marva said, "I'm going to come back, Benny." I said, "Marva, what are you coming back to? Ain't nothing here." She said, "I just miss it." The last thing she said before she left was, "I want you to send me some Blue Runner Red Beans! Blue Runners!" I never will forget that.

I thought she was kidding, but Marva did come back down here. We started gigging at the Ritz Carlton. It was a good gig, but Marva was used to doing bigtime stuff, big festivals. A little room like that didn't excite her, so she didn't want to sing half the time. They gave her a big birthday party, and fired us the next night.

Our 2008 journey to Harlem's Apollo Theatre for a MusiCares charity show remains a much happier memory. We brought saxist Gary Brown along with us, and Danny Glover and Chevy Chase were among the celebrities on hand. MusiCares raised a lot of money that night.

I walked through that Apollo stage door again, and I took Marva by the hand and I told her, "Look up!" She looked up towards the catwalk, and I said, "That's where me and Eddie Kendricks used to sit and watch Roy Hamilton, because we loved to hear him sing 'You'll Never Walk Alone!'" They didn't give us the opportunity to visit any of the dressing rooms, but they did have us hang out in the green room in the basement, the same room where we used to rehearse before the shows with Reuben Phillips' orchestra. Being in that room again was a big thrill. That was another walk back in time. The basketball courts where I used to shoot hoops with the Temptations were still there too.

My younger sister Gracie had passed away in 2009. She was living in Kansas City along with our brother Donald. She was either lying or sitting on the couch, and when Donald got up the next morning, he went in and saw she wasn't moving and had passed away. Boy, did he take it bad. When I called, he was just out of control. It hurt him bad. So now there are just three of us Turner siblings left—me, my sister Nella, and Donald, who currently lives in Dallas. Me and Donald, we're the bookends. I'm the oldest Turner, and he's the youngest.

Marva got a new regular gig at the CoCo Club, at Bourbon and Bienville in the Quarter. That's where we were playing in 2009 when Marva had the stroke that ended her career and ultimately took her life on March 23, 2010. Actually, she'd suffered a previous stroke when we were playing that brunch at the Hilton during my very first gig with her. She was onstage singing, like she'd normally do. Marva made a spin where she'd turn around and sing, then she got down and sat down. She was just sitting there, and she said, "Y'all, if I didn't know better, I'd think I'm having a stroke!"

She'd just gotten married to Tony, and she told her husband, "I don't want to go to the doctor." He responded, "You're going to the doctor! I'm your husband!" That was his first order as her spouse. So they called an ambulance, and sure enough, Marva had suffered a stroke. But she fought back real fast from that one. She wasn't bothered with anything health-wise for almost 20 years after that until she suffered the strokes that killed her less than a year later.

Marva's funeral was the last one I'll ever attend, except for my own. I said then I'd never go to another one, and I meant it.

L to R: Scott Thomas, me, Brian "Breeze" Cayolle, Tracy Griffin

At the Mid-City Lanes Rock 'N Bowl, New Orleans. Photo by Caesar Elloie

Sam Berfect, my daughter Yvette and me at the studio

Top Left: On stage with Jeffery "Jellybean" Alexander at New Orleans Jazz and Heritage Festival; Middle Left: Annie Hughes at my Blue and Not So Blue recording session; Middle Right: © Jean-Pierre Arniac; Botto Left: Davell Crawford on keyboard; Bottom Right: At a session with Marva Wright in Paris, 1992. Photo © Jean-Pierre Arniac

Top Left: Marva and I ran into BB King in an airport overseas; Top Right: With Jimmie Vaughan at Byron Bay Blue Festival in Australia; Middle Left: Talking with Michael Douglas about the impact of Hurricane Katrina. At the Economic Summit in Switzerland; Bottom: Earl Smith, Walter "Wolfman" Washington and me, celebrating my birthday while on tour in Switzerland

Top Left: On stage with Marva and June Yamagishi; Top Right: My daughters can sing! They did backup vocals on *Blue and Not So Blue*; Middle Left: Junkyard Dog and me on the tour bus in Switzerland; Bottom Right: Tor E. Bekken (keyboard), me and Marva in Chedigny, France, 2006. Photo courtesy of Tor E. Bekken

ON MY OWN

After Marva passed away, I took the band over. Even though it was never my goal to be a front man, it seemed like it was time, ready or not. The owners of the CoCo Club liked us and wanted to keep us on, so we stuck with that gig until they lost their license and had to close. Joey Alonzo, a friend who was managing a few clubs on Bourbon Street, opened the door for us by suggesting that we go down to Storyville on Bourbon Street, and that's where we played next.

Jobs where you played the same club night after night were hard to find in New Orleans by then. We had about four or five nights a week at Storyville, and we were doing good. We would pull people in from the street who wanted to hear the blues and liked what they were hearing as they walked by. It was hard to find too much blues on Bourbon Street by that time, so we'd end up with nice big crowds. They were older people, and they'd like to sit and drink and listen. The room wasn't that big, but we would fill it, and our crowds would stay all night. The club owners made good money on us and it felt like we had found our new home.

In April of 2012, I attended the Rock and Roll Hall of Fame's induction ceremony for Freddie with my niece Wanda. I got back on a Sunday. I went in to the club to set up as usual, and the manager told us, "Hey, guys, this is your last night." I said, "What?" He repeated,

"Your last night." Man, we were so upset. My mind wasn't working after that as I kept asking myself, "What are we gonna do? What are we gonna do?" I was so distracted that I lost my camera that I had taken to the Rock and Roll Hall of Fame, which contained a lot of pictures with Wanda and a couple more with me and one of the Rolling Stones. That camera got away from me and I hate that because I got to see some of the older guys that I knew from the old days while we were in Cleveland. Storyville closed after that, and the site became a Hard Rock Café. It was the most recent in a long line of other New Orleans blues clubs that were either replaced by daiquiri bars or other tourist spots along Bourbon Street, just another casualty of the *new* New Orleans that emerged after Hurricane Katrina.

So we moved over to another bar on Decatur Street, just trying to stay alive. It wasn't a real gig, because we played for a percentage of the bar and you never knew what the percentage was, because we didn't see it. They'd just come out and give you a few dollars and say, "That's what we made." The first time we played there, my percentage was fair. They gave me $500 or $600 because the place was packed, and we did a great job. But the last Saturday that I played there, it was even more packed and they only gave me $160. And that was for my whole band! So I said, "Fuck this!" I didn't go back. Sadly, this is typical of many bars in New Orleans to take advantage of the musicians and not give them fair pay for the work they do.

We paid musical tribute to Marva at the 2010 New Orleans Jazz & Heritage Festival, and that same spring we celebrated her life at Bayou Boogaloo in Mid-City New Orleans. Marva's younger daughter Betty sang with us at the Boogaloo and blew us away. At the funeral, she'd gotten up and sang "Walk Around Heaven." If you'd closed your eyes, you'd have thought it was Marva singing. It surprised everybody because we didn't know she could sing. So Betty came up and sang with us at Bayou Boogaloo, and that was kind of emotional for me.

For a concert performance in France that had been booked prior to Marva's passing, we brought Charmaine Neville along as our vocalist. She sings a different style of music than I play. I'm a blues guy, and she's not a total blues lady. It was a little tricky, but we got through it, and she did a great job. We went over there just for that one gig.

Through MusiCares, I played a fundraiser at Harlem's legendary Lenox Lounge in 2011 along with keyboardist Davell Crawford and drummer Jeffery 'Jellybean' Alexander. They invited some of the artists from New Orleans to play, and Davell invited me there. He and I have a close friendship and I was one of his mentors as he grew up as a performer. He calls me Uncle Benny, and I'm really proud of him and everything he has accomplished. For this gig, he just sat down at the piano and backed me up. He wasn't Davell Crawford the star then. He was Davell Crawford, the sideman. We had fun. I said, "Man, I'm in the place on the stage where Billie Holiday played! This is an honor!"

At just about the same time that I released my *A Tribute To My Brother Freddie King* album near the end of 2011 (it was another local release), the Rock and Roll Hall of Fame announced Freddie's induction as an "early influence." To be honest, I never thought it would get that far, or that his induction would ever happen. That never entered into my mind because we usually don't get that recognition, so I have to put a feather in my niece Wanda's cap. She went to bat for that, and she stayed on it until they did it. When I went there, I said I wished he was alive to have seen that he got this award.

I traveled to Cleveland with Wanda for the awards ceremony in April of 2012. They wouldn't let me walk on the stage with her to receive it, so I took her to the stage and then she walked up on the stage. Then they had ZZ Top and some other big musicians get up onstage and play a Freddie King tribute. I was standing off to the side, and nobody invited his brother, who was pretty much his lifetime companion, to do anything. My name wasn't even mentioned, other than when my niece mentioned me when she talked about the Regal Theater during her acceptance speech. But I was there. I felt like somebody should have said, "You're his brother. You're his bass player." But they didn't do it. I felt kind of bad, but I understood.

Marva's husband, Tony Plessy, died in July of 2013. He took care of her right until the very end. When I first met Tony, he was real nice looking and dressed really nice. I didn't know how to take him when I first met him, but after the first night, we sat down and talked. I walked away feeling real good about him, because I could tell that he really loved Marva. Over the years, I learned just how much. Tony took care of her and gave her whatever she needed. If she wanted to throw a tantrum, he'd sit there and let her throw one. I had a great friendship with Tony. He would even joke with me sometimes when he wasn't sure about things with Marva. He'd say, "What do you think? You know my wife better than I do!" That's how close we all were. Like family. After Marva passed away, we'd get together and just drink beer and reminisce about the old times and all the things we did. It really left a void for me when he died.

That same year, Marc Stone, a local guitarist and WWOZ deejay, invited me to participate in a Freddie King tribute show at Little Gem Saloon, which is at Poydras and Rampart, outside the French Quarter. They called me to speak, and I did. The club owner said, "Come back and I'll give you a couple of days, like a Friday and a Saturday." I ended up playing quite a few gigs there. It's a great club. The food is really good, and the atmosphere is nice. I still do private parties there; anytime they'd have a party, they'd call me to play the party. One of the owners got married recently. Nick's wife-to-be said, "Get Benny Turner to play our wedding!" So I went and played the wedding.

I don't play many clubs in the Quarter anymore. It's too dangerous, with people getting shot and all. Also, a lot of the bars don't treat the musicians fairly salary-wise. For the amount of hours you put in, you're not compensated enough for your time. I knew one musician, Humphrey Davis, who worked there for years before I got there. He got off his gig one night and dropped dead. It will kill you playing all night long and making shit money. Marva and I played a club where Humphrey played when we couldn't find any gigs. They would only give each band member $60 to play a full night's gig. Although normal wages would be $100 or $125, you would equal that in tips. The bar owners figured out that since we were making good tips, they decided to use those tips as part of our salary. So they only paid us $60, and assumed our tips would make up the rest. That was how they treated those musicians, and some still do. Still, the guys have got to work and feed their families.

What with all the crime and violence and sky-high homeowners' insurance in the wake of Katrina. I was seriously thinking of leaving New Orleans. Then an old friend, Sallie Bengtson, came back on the scene, and things started turning around. Sallie was in town for New Year's Eve 2013. We first met around 2000 through our mutual friend Debra Clark. She had just closed a business and was looking for a new venture.

With LeRoy Crume, 2014

I told Sallie "If you like the music business, let's do it!" It all made sense. So she and I got together and she drew up the papers, and the rest is history. My name wouldn't be out there as far as it is now without her, because nobody else was knocking the door down to do it. I certainly wasn't going to do it. So she came along at the right time, and she's doing a great job. She's good at what she does. She doesn't do anything half-assed. She's in it every day, every minute.

I went down to Florida in April of 2014 to visit my old friend LeRoy Crume, and I'm so glad I did. He had called me, and we hadn't talked in a while. He said, "I've had congestive heart failure." I said, "Man, you alright?" He said, "You know, it's like one day I'm okay and one day I'm not." So I said, "I'm gonna drive down and see you." I got in my little white car and I drove down to Ocala. I saw that he wasn't looking too well. I stayed down there maybe two or three days. It was so great to reminisce with him and of course we played dominoes, just like the old days. He said, "I'm thinking about maybe going to Chicago, to my people. I'm not using these guitars. Why don't you take 'em?" He had one old Gibson guitar that he gave me, and another one that he played that's really pretty. I opened up the guitar case, and there was a set list with all of Sam Cooke's songs on it and the way they were played. He gave me a keyboard too. I opened it up, and it had written on it, "Soul Stirrers."

They were going to have LeRoy cremated after he died that October. I guess nobody had any money. Then Otis Clay said, 'Man, do y'all know who you've got here? Do you know who this is?" Me and Otis and LeRoy we were like the Three Musketeers. We always hung together because we were all gospel singers. So Otis stepped in and stopped it, and they took LeRoy to Indiana and had a funeral for him. After Otis did that for LeRoy, I said, "Well, I'll give the guitar to Otis, because I know he'd appreciate it." Then Otis passed away unexpectedly, and I said, "Damn, I'm just gonna go on and keep it."

In 2015, Otis and I and Bobby Rush had been in Memphis together. We were sitting around, talking about old times. One of us said, "We've got to do some things together!" Then Otis said, "Well, I'll tell you what, man. Whatever we're gonna do, we'd better do it now!" Now when I look back, I realize he was telling us then that he was having some health problems, the same as Freddie did. But in the moment, you don't always pick up on those things. He told me,

With Otis Clay and Bobby Rush, Memphis, 2015

"Whatever you do, we've got to do it now because people are dropping. We've got to do it now." Otis passed the following January. Me and Bobby Rush met more recently in Memphis, and it was just the two of us. This time we said, "We'd better make a record now!"

I went over to Germany in May of 2014 to perform with pianist Thomas Stelzer during his birthday celebration. I had known him a long time because he was a big fan of Marva's. He came over here, and he wanted me to play a little bit of bass on one of his albums. I learned that

Photo courtesy of Thomas Stelzer

he had recorded "Homesick Blues" from **Blue and Not So Blue**, and it became a hit over there. He played it just like Dr. John. When we went over there and I heard him play "Homesick Blues" he had three or four thousand people sitting in the bleachers. There was nothing in back of us. Everything was in the front, like a stadium, and the bleachers were outside. They did a singalong on "Homesick Blues"--4000 people in all--and it made me feel great! I didn't know the tune was that popular. The way he performed it was really, really good. I know it's a great memory for him too.

Photo courtesy of Thomas Stelzer

I traveled to Thusis, Switzerland that September to appear as part of the Louisiana Blues Throwdown on Blues & Rock Night, sharing the stage with Marc Stone, Vasti Jackson, Bruce "Sunpie" Barnes, Kirk Joseph and Walter "Wolfman" Washington. That was one of the few times I got to work with Walter and really see what kind of guy he was. He was great to hang out with, a great guy and a really good artist, and he's good with a band. He doesn't give the band shit. He gets up there and plays to have a good time.

Just in time for my 75th birthday that same year, we released my next album, *Journey*, on Sallie's new Nola Blue label. All original material, including "Breakin' News," which was named a finalist in the 2015 International Songwriting Competition in the blues category. I wrote that song for a country and western singer, but I didn't know any. I had written it back when I was with Freddie's band and kept it that long in my head, and when I came to New Orleans I still had it in my head. I had Maggie Kitson sing a version for me in a country and western style, but I eventually decided, "I'm not going to ever meet a country and western singer." So I changed it to a blues song and came up with a beat, and I had Marc Stone play the beginning and the lead, the head part, and then we jumped right on into an old Chicago blues shuffle.

Journey was the brainchild of George and DeVona Haight, who are from Laramie, Wyoming. They helped me out during Katrina, and they came up with the idea to do *Journey*. They put up most of the money to do it, and DeVona was really helping me with a lot of promotional stuff. Then she got sick, and Sallie happened to be in the right place at the right time to help me finish it, which was very important to me. I didn't want all of their great support to go unfinished.

Two songs on *Journey* were especially close to my heart. I played guitar on "My Mother's Blues" and "My Uncle's Blues" to pay tribute to my earliest musical influences. I learned other styles by playing with Dee Clark and folks like that, but the stuff my mother and my uncles taught me will remain forever. When I pick up a guitar and start playing, I automatically go right to the old E and the old A blues, because that's what they played. I can still do it. I could do it when I was a kid.

Me and Freddie, that's all we knew, and that's what we did. So I decided to try and figure out a way to make this legacy known, because nobody knew that my mom played guitar. And my uncles, if it wasn't for them, there wouldn't be any us. So I came up with "My Mother's Blues" and "My Uncle's Blues." *Journey* made some real noise in the blues world, climbing the *Living Blues* charts and earning nice reviews.

Just before the end of the year, the Freddie King Tribute Band made its debut at an 80th birthday celebration for my brother at the Texas Theatre in Dallas. That was my brainchild. This was when Sallie had just started to take on my manage-

Hanging with Deacon, just like old times

ment, and she had been talking to me about other tribute bands and concerts, wondering why nothing was ever done for Freddie King. So I got on the telephone and I called Deacon and then I mentioned to one of the guys that I was thinking of doing it. So finally it all came together. The main rhythm section was going to be me, David Maxwell, Deacon and Charles "Sugar Boy" Myers on drums, who played a lot of gigs with Freddie's band, including the Montreux show where we backed Memphis Slim.

Then the King family got involved, and we did the first show. Maxwell was sick, and he never did get to participate (he died in February of 2015). He wanted to do it, though. He was excited about the idea, and I know he even contacted a booking agent about it. Wanda had asked me, "Who do you want?" I said, "Well, I want David Maxwell on piano. Yeah, man, can't do it without David!" Other alumni of Freddie's band also participated, including keyboardist Lewis Stephens, and Andrew "Jr. Boy" Jones on rhythm guitar. I really wanted

2015 Blast Furnace Blues Festival with Freddie King Reunion Band. Photo by Martin Goettsch

Charlie Robinson to play with us because he was part of our driving force, but I've tried to find him and have never been successful. Other former band members not previously mentioned are Mike Kennedy (drums), Butch Bonner (rhythm guitar), Alvin Hemphill (keyboards), Edd Lively (rhythm guitar), and Tao (keyboards). My nephew Larry King played drums with us around Dallas a few times, too. If I missed anyone else, it isn't intentional, but my mind is full from more than sixty years of memories and sometimes I forget things. I played a separate gig with another alumnus of Freddie's band, drummer Calep Emphrey, Jr. We hadn't seen each other in years, and he had a booking at a barbeque place in Mississippi called the Shed. I brought along Keiko Komaki because I love her keyboard style and skills. We got out of our car, and Calep got out of his, and we were like two gunslingers looking at each other. First thing out of Calep's mouth was, "You still ugly!" I looked at Calep and said, "You uglier than me!" We were throwing good-natured insults back and forth. Keiko was on the ground laughing. It was great to play with him again, and of course to have such good fun too.

I was in Florida on business in March of 2015 with Sallie, and she read that Muddy's former guitarist Bob Margolin was playing in DeLand. I said, "Man, I have a hard time connecting with older guys from back then," and I decided to go to the show. Sallie jumped in the car and drove me down there. While Bob was on the stage, he kept looking at me, and he told me later he was saying to himself, "I know that guy!" After he finished

With Bob Margolin

the song, I walked up and he said, "Oh, man! You ain't changed, but I've changed!" That was the start of a nice reconnection between the two of us. Bob and the Nighthawks were scheduled to play a Muddy Waters 100th birthday tribute show in Washington, D.C. at the Hamilton club the following month, and he invited me to sit in for a song or two.

It was great to see the Nighthawks' Mark Wenner again, and so cool to hear his band. Man, do I love their four-part harmonies!

I had been thinking about writing my book for many years and Sallie was just the push I needed to make it a reality. In preparation for this book, I decided to start my research where it all began. They say you can't go back home again, but in February of 2014,

With Mark Wenner

Sallie and I began to do just that, revisiting the places where I grew up and capturing the entire journey on video. We started out in Gilmer, and the feeling of being there again is hard to describe. We went to where my school used to stand, and it wasn't there anymore. We got together with my teacher from back then; she taught me and her husband taught Freddie and vice versa. We went back to where we used to watch my uncles and my mother play guitar, when Freddie used to sneak into their beer supply and get drunk. We saw where my Uncle Leon got killed in a car accident. And we visited my mother's unmarked grave. That July, we came back to Gilmer to install her grave marker. I had wanted to have that done for a long time. It's really nice. She's buried right by my Uncle Leon. During that second trip to Gilmer, we also explored some Turner family landmarks.

At the cemetery visiting my two earliest musical influences, Mother and Uncle Leon

Our next stop in August of 2014 was Chicago. The very first address we stopped by was 1659 W. Adams, where we all lived when we first came to the city. That building was almost like a New York slum back then. The building had been torn down, so we headed over to Bishop Street. That little block had been like a city in itself, and I saw everything there. It's all different now. Except for 25

My Mother

N. Bishop, all the buildings that were on the block and across the street have been torn down. Madison Street had changed a lot too. I didn't look to see if the Century Theater was still there. We went by Crane High School, but we didn't go inside.

There were happy reunions during my Chicago visit. I called Eddie Shaw, Howlin' Wolf's longtime saxophonist. Freddie would always call Eddie when he'd come into Chicago, and they would hang out together. Eddie would bring his car over, and Freddie would use it while he was in town. They would go down and play poker when Eddie had the 1815 Club on the West Side. I called Eddie and he told me, "Hey, Junior! I'm just getting in off the road, man.

With Eddie Shaw, 2014

I'm gonna go home and clean up a little bit, and then I'm gonna come out and I'll meet you at Kingston Mines." So he did, and we sat there and talked. I hadn't seen him in a long time. It's always great to see the old guys. I can't relate to a lot of people because they don't go back to that time.

With Otis Clay

Otis Clay and I got into a limousine and covered every spot we could think of from the old days. The main thing I wanted to see was where the Squeeze Club was. That's where everything started for me, when Freddie was at the Squeeze Club.

We also went to where Walton's Corner used to be. Otis knew where everything was. Of course, all those places are gone now. The last stop we made was Rev. Amos Waller's old Mercy Seat Baptist Church, where me and Otis had gone to debut "When The Gates Swing Open." When we got there, they were in the process of demolishing that house of worship with a wrecking ball.

Demolition of Mercy Seat Missionary Baptist Church

I had been trying to get in touch with Ann, Mighty Joe's wife, for months with no success and I knew something was wrong. While in Chicago, I went to her house to track her down in person. I knocked on the door at her house and didn't get an answer, but luckily as I was walking back to the car one of her neighbors appeared. I talked to him and he gave me her daughter's phone number. I wasted no time in

calling her and finding out that once again my sixth sense was right. Ann was in a nursing home. I headed over there immediately, and when I walked in the door and she called me Joe, I knew something was very wrong. It turned out she was suffering from Alzheimer's Disease, and man, that was hard to see. She still had her sense of humor though, which was great. Even though she might

219

not have remembered my visit, I was so thankful that I had that time with her.

When she passed away, my mother still had two things in her possession that Freddie had given her. One was a picture that he'd had taken at the Apollo Theatre. When you played the Apollo, they gave you a collage of onstage action photos. Each time you were there, the photographer took those shots right at the beginning of your show, and they gave them to us later on. Freddie got his, signed it, and gave it to my mother.

The other thing of Freddie's she had was a white suit of his that he gave her. I got that suit after she passed away, and it was just hanging in my home. I thought

Freddie King's suit on loan, courtesy of Benny Turner.

Freddie King inducted in 1982

about giving it to Freddie's son Larry, and I probably will some-day. But the people at the Blues Foundation in Memphis were cel-ebrating the grand opening of their Blues Hall of Fame in May of 2015, and I decided to trust them with Freddie's suit. We handed it to the Blues Foundation and they took that suit and cleaned it up, pol-ished all the little rhinestones and things. It made me feel very, very good just to see it after they got through cleaning it up with the lights hitting it in the display case. It made me really proud.

People were now asking me for interviews. In May 2015, my video interview as part of the NAMM Oral History series was published. The guy came in and he rented a hotel here. He brought in his cameras and he wanted to know a little about my history, as well as a lot of things me and Freddie did together growing up. He actually interviewed a lot of friends of mine too.

Not long before the holidays, I released a single, "I Want Some Christmas Cheer." That was Sallie's idea. I said, "I'll think about it." I was going into the studio to do something, and then the idea came. It wasn't difficult to write at all. The idea had to come to me, and then the music line, and they matched. They have to fit together. We cut it at Fudge Studio in New Orleans with Jack Miele engineering. Anytime I 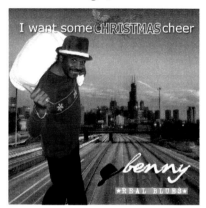 think about recording, I always think about Marc Hewitt, because he's got so much patience and I'm so comfortable with him. But Marc moved his studios maybe 50 or 60 miles from New Orleans, so I started to do a lot of things with Jack at Fudge. He actually played rhythm guitar on it, and he's a great musician! He's a perfectionist and a true professional, which shows in his award-winning work.

I get a lot of respect whenever I visit Austin, Texas because we spent a lot of time there when I was with Freddie. Some of the people on the scene now were around during that time, and then you've got younger guys coming up, and everybody talks to each other. Whenever I come around there, people just want to talk to me. It's respect and it feels good, because when I leave Texas and I go somewhere else, I don't always get the same thing. Here in New Orleans, we weren't that big of a deal. But I can go to Texas and sit down with the guys and talk about blues. You can't do that in New Orleans.

Freddie's famous shows at the Armadillo are a big part of the reason. The Armadillo looked like a big airplane hangar. It held 1500 people, and it didn't have chairs. People would come in, bring blankets, and it would be just like an outdoor concert on the inside. Every time we'd go down to play there, that place would fill up, and we would be there no less than two or three days at a time. Sometimes we had guests come in to join us. Whenever we'd play there, there would be people everywhere.

Jim Franklin was one of the founders of the Armadillo. Jim is a man of many talents, but he's best known for his artwork. He created all of the posters advertising the acts playing the Armadillo, including several terrific ones for Freddie. Jim's masterpiece was the one he painted that showed Freddie playing guitar with an armadillo jumping out of his chest. That painting hung right there in the Armadillo. Jim also did the striking cover illustrations for the covers of Freddie's Shelter albums *Texas Cannonball* and *Woman Across the River*.

Jim emceed Freddie's shows at the Armadillo back then, and he definitely had his own style. He'd wrap himself up in a flag (I can't remember if it was an American flag or the Texas state one), and he had a hat made out of an armadillo. He'd do a little speech, kind of like a beatnik. He would fire the crowd up and get them ready for Freddie. Jim had a ladies' leg from a mannequin that had a whistle in it, and he would blow that leg! Then he would introduce Freddie. Jim even traveled with us to Europe to emcee some shows for Freddie.

Reconnecting with Jim after 40 years was one of the coolest things that happened when I did several gigs at Antone's in 2016.

Although Clifford Antone opened his club back in 1974, Freddie didn't play there because we mainly

With Jim Franklin at Antone's in Austin, TX

played the Armadillo when we were in Austin, I did do Antone's later on with Mighty Joe Young. That was good. And Hubert Sumlin used to stay down there a lot.

I got the Antone's gigs through playing a South by Southwest (SXSW) showcase the year before. It was a pretty quick appearance. It didn't look like the people that were putting on South by Southwest were really into the bands that much--hustle 'em on and hustle 'em off. I wasn't really too impressed with SXSW because we didn't get a proper sound check, and they were just rushing. Luckily, Zach Ernst, the booking agent from Antone's, was in the crowd, although I didn't know it. We got up and did our thing, and I guess we did enough to get his attention. We've been there at Antone's a few times now, and we've gotten great respect from the other bands.

In March of '16, we had a CD release party at Antone's for my album **When She's Gone**, and that's when Jim and I had our reunion. He even emceed our show. He wasn't up there onstage as long as he used to be. He's kind of quick with his introduction now. And he didn't have the mannequin leg with the whistle in it anymore, either. I think he said he lost it, or somebody stole it from him. But we had a great reunion.

2016 got off to a difficult start for me personally, but turned into an exciting year for my career. In early January, I got a call that Mighty Joe's wife, Ann, was declining quickly, so I made a quick trip to Chicago to say my final goodbyes. She had been pretty unresponsive but when I got there and spoke to her she opened her eyes and looked right at me, so I have to hope that somehow she knew I was there with her and for her until the very end. Joe would have wanted that, and it was very important to me too. As I struggled with that reality, I never could have expected to get the news that Otis Clay passed away unexpectedly on January 8 while I was in Chicago saying goodbye to Ann. Had I known, I would have never headed home, but as it turned out, I was back in New Orleans by the time I got the news. Two weeks later, Ann passed away, too. She was my last connection to Joe, and it was the end of another era in my lifetime of friendships.

Six of the songs on **When She's Gone** were originally issued on **Blue and Not So Blue**. It was Sallie's idea to re-release them on her Nola Blue label for a worldwide audience. But I didn't want to put a few of the older songs on the new album, so I added four others. That made it a really good CD. Debra Clark, who originally introduced Sallie to that CD, did the graphics and layout for the booklet, and my friend Valerie McCreary took the cover photo.

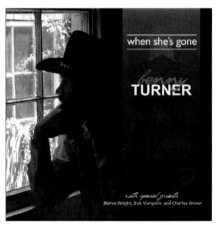

We added another song with Charles Brown on piano from our session together a couple of decades earlier to the album. I just wished Freddie was alive to participate on that, because we both loved Charles Brown and he never got the pleasure of playing on a record with Charles. I got to have the pleasure of not only playing with him, but to record one of his biggest hits, which was "Black Night." We cut that tune in Oakland. We sat down, and Charles wanted to talk about this, talk about that. He was a sweet guy. I tried to get the guy in the control room to let the tape roll so we could get some of that history he was talking about, but he didn't get the hint.

The first time I met Charles Brown, at an in-store event in New Orleans

We were storing the tapes at Marc Hewitt's New Orleans studio. Then Katrina hit, and the studio was underwater. All the machines were floating, so we thought the tape was lost. But Marc went in and saved it, and took it to Florida for safekeeping. The tape was actually damaged. When we were going to put it on **When She's Gone**, Jack Miele from Fudge Recording Studio here in New Orleans put the tape on and hit the play button. Luckily he hit the record button to record the first run because we wouldn't get a second chance. The tape started disintegrating, and pieces were flying everywhere. But we managed to save that one take, and it was real good. You can still hear a little wobble in it, but we did a lot of stuff with the technology today and managed to come out of there with a pretty good cut.

The other new tracks on the CD were covers that I did in New

Top: Blues Blast Award Nomination plaque, Bottom: Independent Music Award for Best Blues Song

Orleans with my band, featuring Keiko Komaki on keyboards and drummer Jeffery "Jellybean" Alexander. We were honored to have Bob Margolin contribute his guitar work to my remake of Bill Withers' "Ain't No Sunshine." He came up with a lick that I think was a Muddy Waters lick or something. He played it with a slide, and man, did it fit! I did my part here in New Orleans, and we shipped the tracks off to where Bob was.

One of the reviewers said that when they saw "Ain't No Sunshine" was on **When She's Gone**, he thought, "Just what we need—another version of 'Ain't No Sunshine.'" Then he put it on and said, "Oh, my God--great!" Bob was also on my revival of Lowell Fulson's "Reconsider Baby" for the album. I heard it so many times with my brother. That was one of his favorite songs, and I still do that one. I played lead guitar and bass on my remake of Jimmy Rogers' "That's All Right"--another favorite of

Freddie's—which I paired with my own song "I'll Get Over You." I figured they matched up pretty good.

The response to **When She's Gone** was fantastic. Betsie Brown of Blind Raccoon did a great job promoting that album worldwide. We officially released it on February 14, 2016 to honor my mother's birthday, and the night before we held a release party in Richmond, Virginia with Margolin and the Nighthawks. The album debuted at #5 on **Living Blues'** radio chart, stayed at #1 for three weeks on the Soul Blues Chart of **Roots Music Report**, and in July of 2016, **When She's Gone** was nominated for a **Blues Blast** Music Award as soul blues album of the year.

L to R: Henry Gray, Mighty Joe Young, Koko Taylor and me

That September, I was on the cover of **Back to the Roots** magazine, which had a 12- page feature article inside.

Then in November, the album's lead track, "I Can't Leave," won an Independent Music Award as the year's best blues song. I didn't think I was going to win anything, to tell you the truth. I was invited to go to the award ceremony in New York, and I said, "We won't win nothing anyway, because we never win anything." Those other guys from the big companies always walk away with it. When the guy said, "Benny Turner," I couldn't believe that. I fell on the floor.

I returned to Austin to perform on Antone's Chicago Blues Weekend as part of their 41st anniversary celebration. That gave me a chance to reconnect with pianist Henry Gray, who spent many years backing Howlin' Wolf during Henry's Chicago years (he lives in Louisiana now). We got a chance to really sit down and talk. After he finished his set, Henry sat down and watched my whole set. He's a great keyboard player, and he's not hard to play with. He'll let you know what he's going to play. He didn't even have to call the key out.

Henry and I really didn't know one another when we both lived in Chicago. I've got a picture with me and Mighty Joe and Koko Taylor, and Henry's standing to the side. He was in the picture by accident. He wasn't posing for the picture. He was lighting a cigarette. I always wondered who that old guy was. I never knew who he was. Later on, it hit me—it's Henry Gray. I said, "Lord, have mercy--he's an icon!"

At Antone's 2016 Christmas party, I shared a bill with Miss Lavelle White, whose recordings for the Duke label made her a Gulf Coast star during the late '50s and early '60s. That was a great time too. I sang a gospel song for her that night, "Lord, Lord, You've Sure Been Good To Me." When she heard that, she jumped up out of her chair, came up to the front, and started to sing it with me.

With Miss Lavelle White

I had received an early Christmas present from my nieces and nephews: a brand-new red Gibson ES-345, a Freddie King signature model. My nieces and nephews decided I deserved one. We went out to dinner and they presented me with that guitar. Man, was I surprised. They all came out. When I picked up the guitar, my fingers magically started to play "Sweet Home Chicago" which happened to be the way my mother would have played it, and they all joined in singing. It was really, really nice. And there was more reason for holiday celebration: *When She's Gone* won the Blues411 Jimi Award for Best Traditional Release.

I've been playing quite a bit lately at B.B. King's Blues Club on Decatur Street, directly across from New Orleans' famous French

Market. It's a great gig. The place has been remodeled since the days when it was known as Jimmy Buffett's Margaritaville, and Storyville before that. It's got good food too. I have to applaud the owner, Tommy Peters, for having blues music in his blues club, which doesn't happen very often at House of Blues. Also, like Little Gem Saloon, he treats the musicians fairly, which is why I'm happy to play there.

I still have a lot more that I want to say and share musically. My next big project is the completion of **My Brother's Blues**, a CD honoring my brother. Like **Blue and Not So Blue**, my first Freddie King tribute CD wasn't properly released, and this will be a chance to give it the attention it deserves. I see myself doing just what I'm doing now in the years to come. I have fun when I play. I think the hardest part about it now is traveling, because it kind of loses its glimmer the older you get. You get tired of it. In fact, I was tired of it when I moved here to New Orleans. It's a little better now, but I can't get in the car and drive a thousand miles like I used to. When I was with the Soul Stirrers, we'd drive all over the country in that Cadillac with six people in the car. That's not easy. I did that with Freddie King too. Then they started making vans that were kind of comfortable, and we started using vans.

I'm hearing more and more people playing blues. I don't hear enough young people that come out and play the traditional blues anymore, but they still hit it. Look at Brandon "Taz" Niederauer, who's just entering his teens but already plays some mean blues guitar. I first met Brandon at the Little Gem Saloon. A photographer that lives here walked up and introduced

With Brandon Niederauer at Little Gem Saloon
Photo © Sidney Smith

himself. He had this little kid that wanted to sit in. I don't normally do it, but something said, "Don't blow this off. Don't blow the kid off!"

I called Brandon up onstage, and man, he could play that guitar. I met him at a couple of parties later. Then I was going to play in Bethlehem, Pennsylvania with the Freddie King Tribute Band, and I invited him to come down and play with us there. I got a message back that he would come down, but then I got another one that said he couldn't make it because he had a previous engagement on Broadway in *School of Rock The Musical*. The kid's killer.

I believe that the blues will survive in years to come, although we don't have many bigger-than-life blues heroes on the scale of Howlin' Wolf or Freddie King anymore. But it will survive.

Take it from this blues survivor.

INDEX